Adopting Grace

ANNA JINJA

ISBN: 979-8-9917897-1-4

Cover design by: eBook Cover Designs

Published by Midwestern Books

801 W Washington Ave, Polk City, IA 50226

Contact: Info@midwesternbooks.com

Acknowledgements

Adopting Grace came to life through the people, places, and experiences tied to my own adoption journey. I wrote from what I knew, weaving and twisting those threads into Grace's story.

My deepest gratitude goes to everyone who walked alongside me during this creative process, whether I was in England or Iowa. A special thank you to Anne Fleck for her unwavering encouragement, giving me those gentle pushes when I was ready to give up on this writing project. To all of you, thank you for helping me quiet the doubts and fears. You hold a special place in my heart!

Chapter 1

My husband Marc hates our annual "A&W-keep-depression-afloat event," as he calls it. My siblings and I see this, and every other tradition we have around Dad's life and death, as a way to keep Dad with us a little longer. Marc says we are extending the post funeral pity party. Since he's officially moved out, I arrive fifteen minutes late—thirty minutes earlier than usual—because I got to skip the part where Marc and I argue about whether we should go.

Mom decorated our section of the restaurant with hundreds of orange tissue-paper marigolds she made and strung together with green ribbon, visible even from the parking lot. I wave off the hostess as I enter, in no need of help finding the technicolor altar to Erik R. Solberg. Bananas (Dad's favorite fruit), tropical-punch-flavored gel chews (he insisted that ingesting these shaved seconds off his run time), a first edition copy of *The Stranger* (his most-read book), and his lucky keychain, iPod, and remote control are arranged around two metal-framed photographs, one with his family and the other on his own after completing his first marathon. With his widow's adaptation of Día de los Muertos, Dad's spirit is most definitely present at the Indianola A&W.

Amaya, one of my younger sisters, turns a sugar skull so it's facing the window and not her plate. Her blue eyes are exactly the same shade as Dad's. Mathew, our baby brother, leans on an elbow next to her. He not only shares Dad's blue eyes, but Dad's everything—except confidence. Christina sits across from both of them, arms crossed, dark eyed and black haired—both artificial. She is as naturally corn-fed Iowan as my other siblings, under the hair dye, make-up, colored contact lenses, and plastic surgery. She's started drawing her eye makeup to make her eyes look exotically slanted. She looks like the cartoon version of a hot Asian girl. Next to her I look like the potato version of a Korean mom. There must be something to Korean skin care, because I can tell you, it is not genetics that keeps those women looking perpetually twenty.

Our Mom is the only one of our group not in evidence.

Mathew gets up to give me a hug, saying my name "Grace" and nothing else before patting my hand and gently guiding me to the opposite side of the booth, where I slide in next to Christina.

Amaya puts a hand on Mathew's shoulder.

"Are you doing all right?" Her sandy brown ponytail swings in time with her worry.

It's been a couple of weeks since I checked in with Mathew. I've been tied up with work. And being legally separated. That too.

"More or less." Mathew scrubs his face with his hands, but his tiredness is as much a part of his round face as his freckles.

"I saw Nadia and Jacob yesterday," Christina says, referring to Mathew's wife and son. She taps perfectly manicured nails on the table.

"Oh ya? where?" Mathew asked.

"At McDonalds. The nasty thing didn't see me, but Jacob did, and I gave him a little wave. He looked all right. Will he be with us for Thanksgiving?"

"Think so. She's flying to Germany next Thursday for a couple months to visit her family. Last I heard, Jacob's staying with me, but she could always change her mind last minute. Ya never know with Nadia."

"How long are you going to stay married to that ugly slut?" Christina shakes her head, stark black bob not moving an inch out of place. "She'll never change her cheating ways. It's time to rid yourself of that skank and go for full custody."

"Let's leave it alone, ya?" Mathew snaps.

"I wish you'd listened to us from the start. We all warned you she'd be a damn nightmare," Christina continues as if Mathew had never spoken.

"Cut it out. I told you to leave it alone," he mumbles.

"Hey, you're not the only one in our family who's a

loser in the relationship department." Christina cuts him off to sweep me into her line of fire. "She doesn't give a flying fuck that her husband's pretty much a bigamist."

"You can be such a mean little bitch," I glare at Christina.

Mathew nods and adds, "Not to mention a hypocrite with her own screwed-up morality issues . . . let's see, starting with a sorry-ass man who doesn't . . ."

"My darling utterly lazy linguists." Mom's shawl, vest, flowing skirt, and the scarf with which she's tied back her red hair all flutter as she moves towards us, shaking one long slender finger. "I cannot for the life of me understand how my offspring have come to rely on the vilest of words to express how they feel about most everything. One would think since their parents never expressed disgust and condemnation by swearing, their children would have learned to use language in a way that doesn't make them sound like vulgar fools."

We stop turning against each other and turn our attention to wait for the right moment to begin our countdown:

3 . . .

2 . . .

1 . . .

We recite the Alexander Pope quote:

"To swear is neither brave, polite, nor wise" in

unison, followed by laughing at and with our matronly lexicologist.

We order and laugh over Dad stories, told so many times they shouldn't be funny anymore. Mom tears up a little. Eventually we move on to chit chat about our own lives.

"—didn't show up," Christina complains to Amaya, who is almost succeeding at looking like she cares. "—didn't call to let me know or anything, so I just hung around at five in the fucking morning, not getting paid. By the end of it I was so pissed I didn't want to work with Mindy ever again."

I make eye contact with Mathew and roll my eyes. If I refused to work with one of my dressmaking clients because they forgot to show up to a fitting, I wouldn't have a business left. Word of mouth made me my living, and if word of mouth was that I was rude and unforgiving, goodbye clients, new and old.

Christina is professionally skinny and as bitchy as she is profane, but nothing seems to affect people's desire to hire her as their trainer. Most of her clients are men, hoping for something Christina will never give them. I suspect she dangles the possibility in front of them just often enough to keep them paying her hundreds of dollars to tell them they're ugly old men while they run on the elliptical.

"Anyway, it had been, like, four days," Christina says,

"and she started leaving messages and texting. I deleted them all. But then she showed up at the gym," I drop out of the conversation.

Christina angles herself so she addresses the whole table. She makes purposeful eye contact with me, which doesn't make me feel great.

"Mindy's birth mom found her on Facebook and contacted her. She asked Mindy to come out to see her in California. Said she'd paid for the plane ticket and everything. So Mindy just dropped everything and went."

Next to me, Mom stills.

"Anyway, I figured I could forgive her for missing the run. Now she's paying me an arm and a leg to train her." Christina looks smug. "She wants to do three marathons on three continents, and she's paying to have me go with her for the one in London. Max had to re-schedule our getaway to Cozumel, but it'll work out better anyway. The week it's on now, his wife's going on a girls' trip to Manhattan, and his mother-in-law is going to watch the kids anyway."

Mom slams down her fork. "You understand that's not the real mom."

Chapter 2

"**W**ho?" Christina asks.

Mom makes a noise in her throat somewhere between a derisive grunt and choking. "And that girl should be ashamed of herself!"

"Who are you talking about?" Christina and I ask simultaneously.

"That Mandy who turned her back on her family to fly last minute all across the country."

"Mindy," Christina says.

"Mindy, Mandy, who cares?" Mom flails her arms, and I get a face-full of shawl.

"Who rocked her to sleep at night? Who took her to doctor's appointments? Who taught her to say please and thank you? Who was it that dealt with poopy diapers, projectile vomit, fibbing, broken curfews, lying, bad attitudes, snotty noses, messy rooms, scraped knees, hurt feelings, temper tantrums, and the monsters hiding under the bed and in the closet? Not that woman. Just because she was the one to experience labor pains doesn't mean she is automatically entitled to being called mom. Only the woman who accepts the responsibility for raising a child earns and deserves this noble title of motherhood. It isn't fair to do all that hard work for another woman to think she has the right to breeze in one day and steal credit for what she wouldn't, couldn't, and didn't do. And it's even worse when her child thinks it's acceptable to do so. My heart breaks for every mother who has to deal with this kind of betrayal."

"Betrayal?" Amaya repeats with a frown and a worried look at me.

"That irresponsible and thoughtless woman relinquished all of her rights when she handed that baby over at the hospital. She had no right to reach out like she did all those years later. If anything, she should have contacted the real mother first to request permission to send that message. Marci is to blame, as well, for making her real parents feel second best."

"Mindy," Christina blurts out.

"I don't care what her name is. Let's call her Miss Insensitive Selfish Tactless Arrogant Knavish Embarrassment."

Mathew pats Mom's hand, which has a death grip on her fork. "That's pretty harsh. You know this isn't about you?"

Amaya puts her head in her hands.

"I know," she hisses, accompanied by the finger wag of rage. "It's the principle of the matter. I'm expressing what we really feel when we hear these horrible reunion stories. We're supposed to be gracious and open-minded. Well, let me be the first to tell you the honest truth—we are not."

She stands and sweeps out of the restaurant.

"I'll go," Amaya sighs. Mathew stands to let her slide out. I watch Amaya catch up with Mom in the parking lot and give her a hug.

"Good night." Christina sits back in the booth. "What a fucking drama queen."

My phone rings, and I fish it out of the depths of my purse to silence it. But the caller ID says, "Marc."

"Hey," I answer, getting up and waving at Christina and Mathew to continue or leave or whatever.

"Grace." Marc sounds a little too stiff and formal for someone who had fathered two children with me.

Christina crosses her arms. "It's Marc isn't it?"

I shake my head at her.

"It totally is. Tell him he can—"

I hustle to the ladies' bathroom, praying Marc has heard none of that. He's never liked Christina.

"Are you busy? Should I call back?"

"No, no. Now's fine. I'm not doing anything."

Somebody flushes a toilet, entirely drowning out whatever he says next. I jam a finger in my free ear.

"I'm sorry honey, I didn't quite catch that."

He clears his throat again. "I said, could we get together sometime soon? This week?"

My heart catches in my throat. We haven't been on a date since he moved out. And it's hard to fix a marriage when you only see each other at parent-teacher conferences, birthdays, and debate club competitions.

"Um, sure." I glance in the mirror. My eyebrows are . . . not great. And crap—what am I going to wear?

"Tomorrow?" An urgency is in his voice that makes my heart gallop.

"Sure. We could do Latin King." The Latin King is our usual date-night pick. There is silence for a moment.

"How about Perkins?"

Perkins is, well, Perkins. But I'm not going to turn down a maybe-date just because he wants fast casual with the elderly. "Sure."

"So tomorrow at noon? Or would eleven o'clock work better?" My heart falls. Lunch at Perkins is about as platonic as it gets.

"Noon is good," I say, my voice exuding positivity and easy-going good will and not a desire to go home and cry in the bed that used to be ours.

* * *

As I pull into our cul-de-sac, I grimace, as I have done every day since my new neighbor moved in a month ago. His yard might as well be a neon sign that reads "I'M ASIAN." Tibetan prayer flags are strewn across the internal roof line of the front porch. A nearly life-size Buddha statue sits on a marble slab facing the house. Bright red waterproof Chinese lanterns dangle in tree branches and in a line of eight or nine over his deck. A four-piece stone pagoda has overtaken the flower garden, and an assortment of rocks with Kanji symbols are tucked in random places along the perimeter of the fence.

If he were white, I'd roll my eyes, but he is, in fact, some kind of Asian. I object to his commitment to stereotype. Since I am, genetically if not culturally Korean, I feel that I have the right. I don't know his name because I have not found a single reason to be polite and bring him a plate of brownies and a welcome.

Once I am safely inside, eyes safe from whatever kitsch Mr. "I'M ASIAN" may have added to the medley, I dive into my closet. I dismiss five outfits for being too clingy. One dress, the backless one with an asymmetrical hem, brings back memories of our vacation two years ago in Hawaii, and is too painful to look at, let alone wear. Slamming one hanger against the next across the wooden bar until all my clothes are on the left side of the closet, I realize everything I own is a wardrobe set for Act I of the Marc and Grace story. Act II has yet to be written, but very well may call for considerable set and wardrobe changes.

Chapter 3

Saturday, the day of the non-date, I wake up before the alarm clock shakes me out of dreaming. The divide between the night and morning is blurry, and as there is not enough light in my—our—bedroom to make me feel like I need to get up, I am lying in bed with disconnected thoughts darting around the margins of a lengthy "to-do" list to include ideas for my co-worker's birthday present, pinpointing possible locations for my daughter Kelsey's missing and overdue library books, ingredients for weekend meals, and a list of current and upcoming jobs. I try not to think about the empty space next to me. I make a snow angel in the sheet, spread my left arm and leg to Marc's side, and leave them there.

The side of my hand nudges the oversized diamond-tufted headboard behind me. I selected it because of an article authored by a relationship expert stressing the importance of setting the mood for intimacy in the bedroom, especially if you have children. Taking the advice to heart, I channeled what I considered the powerhouses of romantic kindred spirits, Jane Austen and Jane Seymour, into the décor. There are visual cues to encourage honeymoon activity no matter where you look—groupings of votive candleholders wrapped in lace, a crystal and cut-glass chandelier, a series of photographs of fluttery and fragile purple tulips displayed in distressed wooden frames, and any amorous trinkets I could find and purchase. Marc said he felt like he was growing a pair of tits from sleeping with so much lace and satin. I thought he said it to save face in front of his male friends, to cover for really liking and appreciating my effort to create an everyday private retreat for the two of us in our home. Maybe this is why he left. Maybe he hated the overdose of romance. Honestly, it's too frilly for me.

* * *

My daughter, Bailey, comes back from a walk with Moby, our border collie, around ten, full of news about Our Neighbors of the Bad Taste. Moby pulled her up their driveway chasing after a squirrel.

"The dad is called Ian, and the kid is Caleb. They live with their Grandma Tomoko. She's from, like, actual Japan." I forgive them a tiny bit for the terrible decor. But not much. It's the son I've seen out inspecting his prayer flags with satisfaction. Plus, Tibet is in China. Japan is, you know, Japan.

Bailey and Moby sit on the bed together and watch me dab concealer on a blemish above my right eyebrow.

Bailey sees I'm wearing something new, rolls her blue eyes—inherited from Marc; I can't pass on my father's genes—and says, "I didn't think we had money to spend on anything frivolous."

I remind myself she is the child and I am the adult. I shouldn't feel guilty or obligated to explain to a fifteen-year-old why spending thirty-five dollars on a vintage designer dress on sale at a consignment store gives me the confidence to spend time with her father. How, when I tried it on, the silk fabric draping elegantly into a full skirt and floating angel sleeves transmitted prettiness. How when I looked in the mirror, the image reflected back didn't look like an exhausted woman scared to death at the thought of a fortieth birthday only a year away, but a woman who was flirty and fun. It didn't matter what was marked on the price tag.

"You only need to keep an eye on Kelsey for a couple hours," I say, ignoring the start of her scowling. "I'll be back in time to take you to work."

"She's not a baby, you know. Since the great state of Iowa currently doesn't have a law that defines the appropriate age for a child to be left at home on their own, you have to decide based on individual circumstances," she says with the maturity of a first-year law student. Then she continues with a big-sister opinion, "And dorky dipwad Kelsey, the walking definition of a geek, is def-o responsible enough to take care of herself."

"Where is she anyway?"

"In her room reading those insanely stupid comic books. Oops, sorry. I mean anime. Don't want to get it wrong, or she'll go all ballistic."

"Manga—" I cut myself off. "Don't go anywhere while I'm gone. Don't you have homework to do anyway?" Asking this is gross manipulation on my part.

"Oh my God, I can't believe Mr. Boddy assigned an additional hundred pages of reading because that imbecile kid, Simon, thought he could get away cheating on that pop quiz. Do you know that because that jerk wouldn't shut up and accept the fact that he got caught, now all of us are being punished with a five-page response paper due on Monday? I haven't even started. Maybe I should call Ellen and ask if she has."

"I think you should." The dress gets a final adjustment, the front sections of hair are tucked behind ears, and I check for lipstick or mascara lingering in the wrong places.

"How do I look?"

"Fine," she says in a flat, noncommittal tone. "Tell Dad he promised to pay for driving lessons. He'd better not forget."

* * *

It annoys me that I'm the first to arrive. Marc won't see me enter and walk toward him in my new dress, giving him a dramatic invitation to fall in love with me again and realize he has made a big, big mistake moving out.

I'm scanning through the hunter green and orange sections of the laminated menu, but I already know what I will order. Butterball turkey and dressing, a timeless favorite. When I order, I'll request the "Every day is Thanksgiving" meal (Kelsey still thinks this is funny even though Bailey says it's definitely getting old) and a bottomless pot of coffee. And as I always do, hoping it makes Marc smile, I'll order and eat my dessert first—a slice of the chocolate French silk pie.

"Hey, sorry I'm late." Marc slides into his side without giving me the chance to stand up and greet him with a hug or kiss. We are separated by the table and uncertainty. "Did you order yet?"

"No, of course not." I work up the courage to look at him. I can tell he recently visited the barber and has taken up smoking again. He was an occasional-to-heavy smoker, depending on the situation, before Bailey was born. As far as I knew, he hadn't put a single cigarette to his lips for the past fifteen years. My nose twitches, taking in the aroma of Marlboros, peppermint Altoids, and an unfamiliar cologne.

"Should we do our usual?" He throws out a suggestion, pitching longing for everything we are together into the back of my throat. "Make it easy?"

My first attempt to say yes gets stuck in a choke of emotion, but eventually comes out as, "Why not? Why change now?"

He doesn't hear—or chooses to ignore—the subtext of what I said, and nods at the waitress who has come over to take our order. We tell her what we want, then wait to see who will make the first move.

He does.

"You look nice. Is that new?"

Vanity takes a bow, and I thank him for the compliment. My heart is pitter-pattering as a greyhound's would racing around a track chasing a rabbit decoy. Words are sticking to the roof of my mouth, and unable to peel them away, I know I'm letting the chance to plead my case for why I'm the better woman slip away.

"Are the girls doing okay?" Marc's voice wiggles away from steadiness. He flicks open the ketchup bottle's lid even though there is no need to do so—his burger won't arrive for at least another fifteen minutes.

This kick-starts me into a familiar and comfortable topic of conversation. Prattling on about homework, dentist appointments, removal and reinstatement of various privileges, and their overall well-being goes on and on, but I forget to remind Marc about the promised driving lessons for Bailey.

"How is the Meredith project going?" I ask about his first client, the one that made it possible to start his own IT and project management company last year, another neutral subject to inquire about. He can't stop himself from diving into the details of implementing his business plan, no matter the audience or circumstances. His update today is strung together with a series of acronyms and LinkedIn searches for an unfilled position. I listen and even ask questions leading to more hurriedly run together capitalized letters—DMI, FIPS, SMTP, and RIP (Routing Information Protocol, not Rest In Peace). Fear stands between me and asking about his new apartment, how he's doing on his own, if he misses me, or anything that might bring her name into our conversation.

Our food comes, and between the innocuous chatter and eating, our rhythm together comes back too. When Marc finishes his last fry, he sits back in the booth.

"Grace," he says in a "big news" voice. I smile at him. He's moving back in? He wants to go out again, a real date?

"Emily is moving to Iowa."

Chapter 4

The adult version of me will not allow myself to cover my ears and scream, "LA, la, la, LA, LA, LAAAAA, la, la," to drown out his latest news, so I'm forced to listen to their most recent decision.

She is moving from freaking Florida to freaking Iowa with her freaking son to live with my freaking husband in his freaking two-bedroom apartment which is freaking supposed to be his freaking bachelor's pad to get his freaking priorities straight and not their freaking place to freaking start a freaking life together and I am so freaking pissed off I want to freaking scream. . . .

The rage comes out as pathetic pitter-pat whimpers. The tears are welling up, and I'm forced to look out the window to give myself a focal point to prevent a full meltdown. There's a rusty pickup truck with its hood being held up by a tall, skinny kid. An elderly man, likely her father or grandfather, appears to be fiddling with something near the vehicle's engine. I wonder if they need help, but I don't know anything about fixing cars.

"I didn't want you to find out from anyone else but me," Marc says.

He thinks he's being noble and kind. How he can think this is so beyond me. I know he doesn't want to be thought of as the bad guy, but why do I have to make him feel better about having an affair? Where does it say the victim should take responsibility for the perpetrator's self-esteem? I feel guilty for my inability to grant him a pardon for ruining my life.

"We'll figure out how to make it work so there won't be unnecessary pain and suffering for all of us during this transition," Marc tells me in a calm, matter-of-fact tone.

I wonder who the "we" is. Is it Marc and me? Or is it Emily and Marc? Is it all of us including all of our children? He looks over at me while sipping Mellow Yellow through a straw.

I can see pity stomping out love for me. And this makes me cry—what Oprah Winfrey has identified as the ugly cry. I am slobbering, blubbering, hiccupping, sniffling, and sobbing on my side of the booth. All eyes dart towards us to get a peek, and then quickly turn away to give us privacy.

"Grace, please stop," he pleads. "You're embarrassing me. Please stop crying and pull yourself together."

"How . . . how did this happen Marc? What did I do so wrong you would do this?"

"Oh Grace . . ."

"I'll do better," I interrupt and swipe the underside of

my nose with a crumpled tissue. "Did I nag you too much about moving to a bigger house and better neighborhood? Or about expanding both our businesses to earn more money for the girls' college fund? Was it too much pressure?"

He slumps back into his seat as if a thug has just shot him in the chest and stolen his wallet. I take this as a sign he still loves me, that he has only been moving forward with Emily thinking it might be too late for us because he's embarking on the ultimate relationship deal breaker.

"Don't be silly," he murmurs.

"Please don't do this," I beg. "Don't do this to me. Don't do this to our girls."

"I've just been so unhappy for so long." His voice is barely above a whisper. "Your dad dying. The funeral. Everything after that. Starting my business in the middle of all that craziness . . . everything changed . . . you changed . . . and I don't know why, but this feels like the right thing to do . . . for all of us. We all deserve to be happy, don't you think, Grace?"

"We can be happy if you give me a chance. I know I've been in a terrible funk, but I promise I was—I am— working my way out of it."

"It's more complicated than that."

"It's that damn Emily."

He doesn't respond.

"Why didn't you marry her in the first place? Why did you marry me if you knew all along she was the love of your life?" A vile bitterness cuts its way through the thorns choking my questions.

"There was no one I could talk to about everything and nothing at the same time. You had this way of making me feel like I was a better person than I really was, and I loved you for it."

"Loved?" It comes out with a squeak.

"Love," he corrects himself.

"I still love you. Our girls love you. Don't throw everything away because of a couple bad years. Can you just think about it a little before you move her here and not rush into anything that can't be undone?"

"I'll try."

"Promise?"

"Promise."

I stop crying. There are just the minor aftershocks left, slight tremors of hiccups that won't go away. We finish our meals, pay the bill, and leave the restaurant. He didn't start by giving me a physical acknowledgement of affection, nor does he leave me with a hug or even a peck on the cheek. But I see him crying in his car as he drives away, and this gives me hope.

* * *

Tuesday afternoon, I sit in the car in front of our house while Kelsey pelts down the driveway, *Piano Adventures* lesson book in hand.

"Where have you been?" I demand as she dives in and slams the door.

"I was at the neighbors'. I know you have a lot on your mind and funds are short, so I thought I'd help out and take something next door before they aren't new anymore."

And there you go, my own kid—my younger kid—is the better person. I should have set a better example to my children by being the first to greet the new neighbors, but that is what happens when you don't take the time to get to know a person before judging him for having an over-the-top spectacle of Asian kitsch in his front yard.

"Oh. Thank you. What did you take them?"

"I got a movie-themed gift basket. I figured everybody likes movies."

I pull out and drive too fast because we are late for the lesson—again. I do not ask with what money, because the only option is with her own allowance. I squirm internally.

In the back seat, Kelsey bounces with enthusiasm. "They're so awesome. Caleb—that's the kid—and his dad went this summer to the San Diego Comic-Con, and he showed me the loads of free stuff they got. Look—he gave me his *The Pet Girl of Sakurasou* poster. I told him he could borrow any of my *Assassination Classroom* books. He knew all about the series because they lived in Japan for a couple of years, and he wants to be a manga artist, but his mom wanted him to be a doctor, and now that's what he'll probably do, which is so sad—but I get it, you know, because his mom died a couple years ago, and they moved here 'cause his Dad couldn't handle it."

I jerk the car to a stop in front of Mrs. Hazel's house.

"Out, out. You're late. Go, go, go!" She sprints up the walk. Mrs. Hazel opens the door, waving one gnarled old hand at me and smiling at Kelsey, who charges into her house with the same energy as Moby chasing a frisbee.

I lean my head back and sit in the car for a minute. I have been thoroughly shamed by my daughter. Because of a Buddha statue, I've been avoiding doing my neighborly duty, and the family is still raw from grief. I drive to Marc's apartment to pick up Bailey, who went over to have him drill her on her affidavit for mock trial.

She hops into the van and announces, "Emily is coming up here next weekend."

I say, "Oh ya?" in a mild tone that does not fool Bailey one bit. Bailey announces, "It wasn't really planned. Just kind of a last-minute deal to check out Dad's place. To, you know, bring a carload to the apartment, but he didn't expect her to make the trip this soon. But you know—well you don't know—but she's interviewing for a job, and it makes sense for her to drive up so it will be less stuff they'll have to move later, I guess. Anyway, Kelsey and I haven't met Emily—or her son either, so maybe it'll be better if we all get it out of the way together. I mean, it'll no doubt be crazy awkward, but it'll only be for an hour or two out of our lives. And Kelsey and I've agreed one of us will stick by you, so you won't ever have to be alone with her or the two of them together. We won't let you feel outnumbered is what I mean. Can I tell Dad you're all right meeting at their—at his—apartment? He said he'd treat us to pizza and as much Häagen-Dazs as we can handle."

It takes me a minute to process that this is an invitation to dinner. With my husband, his mistress, her son, and our children. It would have been more appropriate and courageous of Marc to ask me directly rather than sending his daughter to do his dirty work. What has Marc said to our children about the Emily situation? It must be a good story, as neither Bailey nor Kelsey appears to be devastated by the news. I had counted on the two to be the *Parent Trap* duo and come up with over-the-top schemes to get us back together. Or at least for one of them to act like Karen Newman in Judy Blume's *It's Not the End of the World* and express outrage about her parents' split. But they are modern children, accepting and understanding about separations and divorces. Stupid modernity. What happened to good old-fashioned values?

I have a choice about how to deal with this. The pre-baby me wants to pull on a pair of adult diapers and drive nonstop to Florida and do in the home-wrecking bitch. The mom who is responsible for raising law-abiding daughters knows what has to be done. I go back and forth about how I want to respond, but this schizophrenic episode plays out a little too long.

"Mom? Are you okay?" Bailey asks.

Bailey and Kelsey are more important than anything I have in this world. It is not because I am mature, accepting, or a class act, but rather that childbirth has rewired the network of nerve cells in my brain and blocked the transmission of my needs and desires. And this is why I offer: "Why don't you tell your father I'd rather host a dinner here. I'll make lasagna and all the fixings if they bring dessert. Have them check their schedules, but I'd prefer Sunday if that's okay with them."

"Really?"

"I think it's best to do it this way."

"That's really cool, Mom." Bailey praises me as if I'm an inferior subordinate. "I know it sucks to be you right now, but it'll get better."

It was a very odd confirmation that I made the right decision to set aside the rejected woman in favor of the benevolent parent. She pulls out her phone and texts my invitation to dinner to Marc. As the implications of what I have suggested fall into place, I feel nauseous.

Chapter 5

Wednesday, when I greet Mary Anne, a prospective client, at the front door, I realize she will not fit into either of the reception chairs in the basement workshop, and I worry she might even have a difficult time descending the rather narrow staircase leading to the basement. I quickly improvise and scoop Kelsey's sweatshirt and comic books off the sofa and into the wicker laundry basket on the floor. I apologize for the mess and invite her to sit down. Mary Anne's hollow gasps of air are noticeable as she walks the short distance from the entrance area into the living room. She accepts my offer of a glass of water and empties it in two enormous swallows, but a refill is politely declined.

"Thank you so much for meeting me." I hear and feel a slight tremor roving through her vowels. "I know you said it's only in rare cases you'll take on a wedding dress, so I hope now that you've seen me, you can understand why I need you."

If I had remembered this was an appointment for a

wedding dress yesterday, I would have cancelled. I am definitely not in the mood to listen to plans for forthcoming nuptials. I'd rather go swimming with agitated and famished alligators, but it is too late. It is my punishment for waiting until the last minute to prepare for an appointment, and now I will be forced to ask questions about her happily ever after.

She shyly looks up at me, and I see she is absolutely stunning. Not just the "if you only lost weight, you'd look fantastic because you have such a pretty face" sort of stunning, but genuinely picture-perfect beautiful. I'm confused by her appearance. It appears her outer shell is hanging on the wrong internal framework; her natural bone structure seems too delicate to be crushing the plush sofa seats to the same size as a slice of white Wonder Bread.

"Wedding dresses are complicated and extremely time consuming—"

Mary Anne interrupts. "I totally, totally get it. I've watched enough episodes of *Bridezillas* to know there is also the added stress of dealing with a shrieking crazy woman, but I promise there will be none of that from me. If you say yes, that is. I'd be too grateful to think of uttering even the tiniest of complaints. It won't be my attitude, but the alterations I'm hoping you'll need to make as I fight to lose a significant number of pounds before my wedding day that will be the most frustrating part of having me as a client. You'd be a witness to the shedding of the burden I've carried with me for a long time, and I recognize this is a lot to ask of a stranger."

She rapidly blinks, her long eyelashes catching her tears. I get up to find tissues, and while my back is turned, she continues.

"I've never talked about this with anyone except my therapist . . ."

"Don't worry. I've got one of those myself," I call out casually, letting her know we have this in common, while searching through the clutter in the bathroom shelves. As I return with an unopened box of ultra-strong and soft store-brand tissues, I lightheartedly add, "She's yet to hear the worst about me, but I've got an appointment today, so think this might be her lucky day."

Mary Anne smiles, and I'm glad this sets her at ease. Lack of self-discipline and bad habits have turned her into a food addict, I assume. She will tell me how cognitive behavioral therapy sessions are modifying her eating patterns, so I don't need to be concerned about dealing with a yo-yo dieter throughout the dressmaking process.

"I had a crush on an older neighbor boy who always ignored me. One day, he asked me to be one of the first to visit a treehouse he and his two friends built. I hesitated, but he said it would be my one and only chance to be initiated into their secret club. I felt like I shouldn't go. But I wanted to be a part of his secret club so badly . . .

"They—he and some of his friends—assaulted me, you know . . ." She looks up at me, and I nod so she doesn't have to say the word out loud. "And then my crush said, 'Don't worry. You're still pretty.'

"Those words hurt. It wasn't until recently that I started working with a therapist. I realized that those words are why I eat so much. I'd rather be fat than be seen like that. Like if I keep from being pretty, I will be safe.

"I'm not telling you all this to guilt you into saying yes. I just thought if you understood how I got this way, you'd take a chance with me. When Patty told me about how you didn't once make her feel fat or ugly—and she never in her life felt as drop-dead gorgeous as she did wearing the party dress you made for her—well, that's how I knew you were the right person to help me with the most important dress I'll ever own. I'm pretty confident I can lose the weight, now that I understand it's a symptom, not the problem. But if I fail, I still want to feel beautiful on my wedding day. It doesn't help that I own two Dairy Queens, but this was how I made my living before I met Dr. Reed, my therapist, and Herbie, my boyfriend."

I wish I would've spoken up sooner, but I hug Mary Anne and announce, "I'm incredibly honored you want me to create the dream dress for your special day. There is absolutely no way I wouldn't be part of it."

She hands me a picture of Bette Davis in the film *Dark Victory.* "Do you think you could make a bit fancier version of this dress for me? I'm mad for Bette Davis and all her movies, but this one is very special to Herbie and me.

He wrote 'She's everything a woman can dare to be' in the first card he gave me. It's a line from the movie trailer, and he wrote a sweet message to go with it all about me being everything he wanted and more, so I want to surprise him by walking down the aisle wearing a wedding dress he'll hopefully recognize. What do you think?"

"I think it's perfect," I say, and I really do think so in spite of being worried whether I can pull it off or not.

* * *

After the appointment with Mary Anne McDonald, I take Moby for a walk before my therapy appointment. Dad told us all that when you assume, you make an "ass" out of "u" and "me." Christina once had a client named Chris Turner who was grossly overweight. He never missed a workout session, but consistently cheated on his diet. At Christina's recommendation, he contacted me to tailor all his newly purchased business suits for a job with an international accounting firm. He was the nicest guy, but it didn't stop the two of us from mercilessly chastising him for eating one too many Twinkies. Our insults were many and mean. Behind his back, we called him Chinny-Chin-Chin, poor old four-chinned Chris.

I made all sorts of unkind assumptions about Mary Anne's physical appearance before having all the facts. By the time I get back home I have realized that I am not, in fact, a good person. I chastise myself as I let Moby off his leash just inside the door. Moby takes advantage of my distraction and the half-open door, barreling straight through the screen—again. He thinks of a screen door as nothing but a doggy door waiting to happen.

"Moby!" I chase after him. He does not come when I call. Marc and I disagreed on the best training method. Marc was, in my opinion, overly strict, and I felt bad for the dog, giving him love and treats immediately after Marc gave him a scolding. The result was that he learned absolutely nothing. You get just as good results shouting "Banana" at him as his own name.

He has a goal though—the neighbor. Moby sails over the chain-link fence between our properties and attacks his unsuspecting prey with enthusiasm, butt wiggling, and drool. Ian gets a firm hold on his collar.

"Is your pooch named after Moby Dick?" Ian asks.

"No, for the musician."

"That's cool," he says, clearly surprised. "Your dog's named after a multi-talented guy. I checked out the exhibit of his photographs in New York a couple years ago and was so impressed I bought a signed book."

"Cool," I reply and mentally scold myself for sounding like a pubescent imbecile. I clear my throat to regain my composure. "Thank you so much for your help. If it weren't for you, it would've been a mile-long chase, and I definitely don't have the right shoes or the time to do it. Speaking of which, I'm so sorry I have to chat and dash, but I have an appointment, and if I don't leave now, I won't make it."

"Chat and dash?" Ian laughs. "That's a new one. I have to get going myself, but glad my day started with a dog rescue—creating good karma and all that, I hope. And he's great, your dog. Caleb and I'd love a lab or retriever, but it's not possible right now with my mom living with us. She pretends to be allergic because she doesn't want to admit she hates dogs, so we are hoping you'll let us borrow yours once in a while for a walk or two."

"Moby is yours anytime you'd like," I agree but feel myself blushing, worrying it comes across as weirdly overeager to share our family pet. I walk towards Ian, and it is the first time I get a good look at the mutual fan of Moby, the dog and the musician.

From what Kelsey told me, he must be at least five years younger than I, but he looks older by at least a decade. I'm guessing unresolved pain is to blame for the accelerated aging process creased into the corners of his mouth and eyes. I recognize it so well—the physical evidence of an ongoing battle to drive away sorrow and regret. His facial features and expressions are reminiscent of those of medieval warriors. He looks like a samurai wearing a suit and tie. I stiffen and lead Moby over to my side of the fence.

"Thanks, we'll take you up on that offer . . . Grace, right?"

"Yes . . . Ian, isn't it? I'm sorry. I should've stopped by

earlier to introduce myself. I'm just so busy these days." My voice and words trail off to a dead end. I am stopped in my tracks with his amused and all-knowing look, like he is calling me out for waiting for his car to pull out of the driveway before I make my exit or the many times I pretended to be engaged in a cell phone conversation too serious in nature to stop and say hello when he was working in the yard.

"You're welcome to come over any time, and I'll make you a cup of green tea and bring out the Moby book. Think you'll be impressed." He extends the open invitation with a whiff of boldfaced arrogance.

Irritating, I decide. Just like his oversized ornamental dragon statue nestled in his flower box.

Chapter 6

Dr. Bennett-Hill has asked me to call her by her first name, Beth, but I just can't do it. Acknowledging her by level of education gives me confidence in her ability to help me with what I have identified as the main issues blocking happiness in my life.

However, her first question is not about my failing marriage, but about my parents. Therefore, most of this session has been sharing their story and how they came to the decision to adopt a child—me. I regret picking a therapist that I first heard about while standing in line at the Iowa Department of Motor Vehicles.

Taking a deep breath, I dive in. "Homecoming Day is a special occasion fabricated by adoption agencies to commemorate when an orphan is officially adopted by a family," I find myself explaining. "Mom will use any excuse to throw a party, even Johnny Appleseed Day, so she took the idea and ran with it.

"In a photo album she made, our first Homecoming Day pictures take up almost all the pages," I explain.

"The rest include a copy of the restaurant menu (all items ordered, including drinks, were circled in blue ink), the front page of that day's edition of the *Des Moines Register*, a couple of congratulatory cards from friends and family, and a thank you note from the Wong family for hosting the first party in their new restaurant."

"New restaurant?" Dr. Bennett-Hill prompts to move me past a moment of silent reverie.

"I have a picture of my father lovingly looking at Mom holding me in her arms," I continue, "and Kenneth Wong standing and grinning in the middle". I smile, thinking of the joyful affection captured in that Polaroid.

"Mom decided to create a Solberg family tradition out of this one-time made-up holiday." I sigh. "We went to Wong's every year. When I was thirteen, she made all seven of us wait in the CRAP Monster while she set everything up."

Dr. Bennett-Hill interrupts. "Crap Monster?"

"Cranberry Rolling Awful Paneled Monstrosity," I explain, "our Dodge Caravan. Anyway, it felt like forever before she popped out and waved us all in. Dad and I would always whine about it. Dad, because he was always ravenously hungry. Me, because I detested eye-witness accounts of being part of a family who owned a CRAP mobile."

I stop and look around. The rest of this story is pretty embarrassing. I'm not sure I want to tell it.

Dr. Bennett-Hill seems to sense my discomfort. "Just relax and let the story unfold as you remember it."

I nod settling into my chair as the story starts to spill out. Suddenly, I am back there again.

Mom insisted on standing up and welcoming us before giving us permission to order. She said what she said every year: "We are here on this joyous occasion to mark the day when Grace Miju Solberg officially became our daughter." She dramatically opened a folder and took out the note that came with my adoption records and passed it around the table for us to see.

Written on an aged yellowing index card were two lines of Hangul block letters hand printed with what looked like an ink brush. Although I'd seen this artifact many times, I had only recently learned that the Koreans called their alphabet Hangul.

We took turns pretending to see the note for the first time. When the note returned to her, she held it up and continued with her annual speech. Mom likes being in the spotlight.

"Take care of my little girl as I cannot." Mom interpreted. "I imagine this anonymous woman with a generous and beautiful spirit placing our swaddled Grace into a cardboard box and tucking this very note in the folds before leaving her to be found and delivered safely to the social services in Seoul, Korea. We honor this brave

mother and thank her for making it possible for her little girl to be taken care of by us."

Mom ended the story in her traditional way. "Your father and I were told we would be a childless family, but boy were they wrong! We beat the odds as, lo and behold, the day we signed the adoption papers, I didn't know my excessive craving for fried wontons was Amaya letting me know she was to be born seven months later. And then, of course, we later added Christina and Mathew to our clan. We are blessed indeed."

It may have been the millionth telling of the tale. The words had completely lost their luster. I'd heard it all before. The only new thing she added to her speech this time was that my dad had something he wanted to share. I knew this would add on at least another ten minutes before we could order, eat, and go.

At that age, I was either annoyed, angry, or offended by almost everything—a sullen teenage tyrant with a big chip on my shoulder who didn't think eating egg rolls with my family was a good time and certainly not cool. I saw Cody Lockheart and his girlfriend, Heather Watson, with other members of the popular crowd sitting three tables away. I could hear giggling and chattering. I was convinced they were talking about and laughing at me.

Dad had written a poem a couple months after I arrived from Korea. Dad was a numbers guy, the shy and reserved CFO at a nursing home. He hated being the center of attention. This was his first and only attempt to be creative. I couldn't help but feel impressed and honored, but also prayed he would change his mind and keep quiet.

To my embarrassment, shock, and horror, he recited the entire poem as if he were performing to a sold-out one-man show at Carnegie Hall.

I think the unfortunate timing of the sniggering from the cool girl is to blame for my response to my dad's reading. I told him, "That isn't even a real poem." I was loud enough to be overheard at least three tables away in each direction. "It only rhymes for the sake of rhyming and doesn't make any sense at all."

Mom leapt up, and wagging her finger at me, said in a stage whisper, "Stop talking, young lady!"

To which I said at full voice, "I wish we didn't do this silly Homecoming Day thing. If it wasn't for me this stupid tradition would never happen. If it's all about me, then I want it to stop. No more cheap-shit presents. No more shit Chinese food. No more of these shitty, stupid, horrible poems!"

Mom and Dad sat there dumbfounded.

Christina, of all people, called me out for cussing in public. I snapped at her to shut up, and she actually did. Mom considered it a personal insult if any of us used what she deemed verbal filth. I was the first of the four of us to swear in a public place.

Amaya said she liked the poem, but everyone ignored her.

After a long ugly silence, Mom said, "Dad worked on the poem for hours and hours the night they brought you home. You will be gracious, and you will not act like a spoiled little brat." She look over at Dad. "This is the first time he's shared it with anyone, including me. You don't know how brave he is being"

Dad put his hand on her shoulder. "Now calm down, darling. I don't care if Grace likes the poem." Then looking around the restaurant he turned to me. "Can we just not make such a scene in our friends' restaurant."

I took his discomfort as an opportunity to press my advantage. I flailed my arms and screamed, "It probably took you about five minutes to scribble that pile of gibberish down. You knew all along that it was trash, and that's why you didn't share it with anyone until now." I will never forget the stricken look on my dad's face, but in my fit of rage I couldn't stop twisting the knife. "If it did take you hours and hours, then it was a complete waste of time, just like I am wasting my time being here now!"

Of course I didn't mean any of it. I lashed out because I wanted out of there and, ironically, so my peers wouldn't have any material for gossip about me or my family.

As I shot up and slammed my chair under the table, I caught a glimpse of my dad slipping his pages of poetry under the paper Chinese zodiac placemat. He looked like a child holding a deflated balloon in the middle of a lion's den, humiliated by his daughter's response and scared to death of feeling stared at by fascinated strangers.

I was just getting ready to meekly return to my seat and apologize, but Mom barked out, "Sit down! Where do you think you're going, young lady?"

So instead, I shouted, "Anywhere but here," and gave the chair one more shove before I stormed out of the restaurant. I was very aware of Cody's table watching me leave my family behind.

Dr. Bennett-Hill looks down as she scribbled notes on her pad of paper. "Do you think your mother made you feel like an outsider in your family?"

"Uh, no," I realize that she had completely missed the point of my story, "No, never."

I take a moment to frame an explanation. "I don't regret being adopted. I regret being a self-involved brat. I hate myself for the temper tantrum that made my dad think his homage to my adoption belonged in the trash. I thought he left the only copy of his poem under the weight of generous portions of vegetable fried rice, knowing it would be thrown away with everything else when the waitress cleared the table."

Dr. Bennet-Hill looks thoughtful. "So you always felt like you were fully accepted into your family?"

I stare at her for a moment trying to comprehend what she is driving at. I decide that telling her the rest of the story might help. "A couple of weeks after Dad's funeral, Mom handed me an envelope containing his poem, the pages stained with egg foo yung grease. She had saved it from being incinerated, but never told me, wanting to wait for a time when she felt it was appropriate to do so. While grateful, I couldn't help thinking that sometimes punishment for an earthly wrongdoing is not a deferred sentence waiting at hell's gates. It can be swiftly and severely carried out during one's lifetime."

Dr. Bennett-Hill chuckles.

"I'm still kicking myself for messing up my chance to set things right," I go on, as if she has asked the right questions. "Near the end of my teenage years, my dad and I were eating Chinese leftovers. It was past midnight, and instead of saying I was sorry for hurting him, I revised my review of his poem, spewing only disingenuous adjectives: *really good, moving, special, lyrical, touching, poetic, and articulate.* . . . There was this horrible pause while I struggled to come up with another affirming descriptor. Dad assured me he knew it was the raging hormones, not the real me who threw that temper tantrum."

I start to choke up as I always do over this part of the story. Dr. Bennett-Hill hands me a tissue. I blow my nose before going on. "He said he knew all along the poem didn't rank with the likes of one penned by Walt Whitman. It wasn't really a poem per se—more of a random jotting down of notes from the day they brought me home. And the only reason he shared it on that specific occasion was he always felt Homecoming Day came with an expiration date. Like adulthood. Or the teenage years."

"Why don't you feel your apology was good enough?"

"I don't think I ever actually apologized. Still, Dad understood, and what he said was meant to be comforting. But it only made me feel worse. My bad behavior had transformed what could have been a happy memory of the last Homecoming Day into a shameful and humiliating one for both of us."

I look to see if she is understanding me now. Our eyes meet and I see my pain reflected there.

Going on I say, "That's what I regret. It has everything to do with a dreadful memory inserting itself into my dad's short life because I was embarrassed to be seen in public with my family. It has nothing to do with the context of the celebration itself. The real difficulty is that I can't stand it that my Dad died, and now I just don't see how the future can hold anything good."

Dr. Bennett-Hill is quiet for a moment as she scratches at her notepad. "Well, Grace, we've come to the end of our session for today. For next time, I'd like to have you think about how being adopted impacts you as a mother yourself."

I wonder if I should find a new therapist — or maybe just start calling her Beth.

Chapter 7

"**A**re you fucking crazy?" Christina yelps. I hold the phone away from my ear. I can still hear her barking. "In what world did you think it was a good idea to invite that slut to your home, the house that has you and your deadbeat husband's name on the mortgage as a married couple? Really, Grace, what were you thinking?"

"I wasn't. I just panicked at the thought of going to Marc's apartment, and before I knew it, the invitation was extended and accepted. I'd look like a petty jerk if I changed my mind."

"Well, now you look like a chicken-hearted, milquetoast weakling."

"Nice. Real nice, Christina. That's what I need to hear now."

"I think you do, 'cause what ya got planned is way messed up."

"Well, it's done. Nothing I can do about it now."

"You can tell those two to fuck off, and that you've changed your mind about the whole thing. All you need to do is grow a pair and swing that stank around like you mean it. They need to know they can't treat you like a stinking doormat."

"I've gotta go."

The next thing I know, Amaya is calling to inform me not to plan anything for Saturday afternoon. Because of a last-minute bachelorette party cancellation, her salon was able to schedule appointments for the three of us at the same time for cuts and styles, pedicures, and an eyebrow-waxing treatment. "You're going to be pampered and prepped like you deserve for going above and beyond what's expected from any normal human being."

It's the same thing Christina said, just softer and kinder. She doesn't give me a chance to object and continues with strict directions to not bother bringing money—it is their treat.

"That poor bride-to-be discovered her fiancé's repeated indiscretions at his Vegas bachelor's party, and she postponed the wedding, possibly forever." Amaya relays the circumstances an octave lower than her normal range, as if by disguising her voice, she isn't the one spreading gossip. "But lucky for us, or we'd never get in with Fiona and her team." Fiona has been Amaya's stylist for over a decade and has seen our sister through a couple of bad perms, a pixie cut, the Jennifer Aniston, and the repeated use of hair dye to transform her into different versions of a blonde or redhead. Amaya trusts Fiona completely.

I, however, am suspicious of anyone who looks like the cartoon version of Æon Flux, a gaunt, scantily clad secret agent with inexplicable and morally neutral motives. For this reason, when she asks how I wear my part Saturday, nothing registers, as I'm fixated on Fiona's sharp V-shaped chin and cheekbones. She looks bored and annoyed when I finally provide a response that my hair kind of flops wherever it wants to go. She exhales slowly before her consultation: "You have coarse hair typical for Asian women, so let's give you a blunt, medium-length bob to help you conceal some of those features you don't want to accentuate."

Which features is she speaking of? I am so nervous and flustered, I agree to whatever she thinks is best.

Amaya applauds my new look as she takes her turn in Fiona's chair. "You've turned my sister into a sleek and sophisticated woman. She should've come to you a long time ago."

"So are you like, *real* sisters?" Fiona asks while pulling Amaya's hair back in a clip. "Or are you just very close best friends?"

"Our mom is a fake, but we're real sisters." I give her my standard reply to people who use "real" as a Snuffle-upagus adjective, suggesting my familial relationships are a product of my imagination. Fiona doesn't know how to respond. Amaya shoots me a disapproving look and shoos me away to join Christina at the pedicure station.

Christina shows me the bottle of dark purple polish

she selected from twenty rows of color on display. I settle into my chair and punch a series of buttons to customize settings for the perfect back massage. "It's called 'Skating-on-Thin-Iceland.'" She identifies its official name in a familiar tone I know means there's a further point to follow.

"You know you're skating on thin ice by having that nasty witch and her stupid spawn over tomorrow. I don't know what you hope to gain by doing this, but really there's nothing worth it. You're putting yourself at risk of getting hurt in ways you can't imagine. And you're making her dinner. So unless you have some devious plan to take her out with a cyanide-laced cake, this is stupid. There's still time to change your mind if you want to."

"I've already told you, I can't," I snap. Her warning lessens the pleasure of the warm water bubbling around my feet. "Besides, you of all people should appreciate hospitality being extended to an adulteress. You've been the other woman for how long?"

"This is exactly why you should listen to me, Grace. You are going to be the one that gets hurt the most, not Marc and certainly not that skank. It isn't right or fair, but it's the truth. She comes out the winner in this threesome no matter what. I know from experience. I'll let you in on a secret about why women stay with married men." She stops our conversation to ask the nail technician if she can upgrade to the package that includes the heated thermal booties.

"Don't hold me in suspense—what's the secret?"

"The secret is, we care more about winning than love."

"What? That's not true. You love Max."

"I do, but not in the way you do with someone you want to build a stable or forever life with."

Her iciness sends shivers down my neck.

"Over the years, it's turned into this co-dependent competition—the wife vs. me. I'm addicted to being the one he wants to compliment, to fuck, to buy extravagant gifts for, to tell his deepest, darkest secrets to. Every time he gives me the best he has to offer, I get high from winning him over to my side."

"But you love him, right? We haven't covered for you all these years because you're addicted to winning?"

"It is what it is." She shrugs her shoulders. "I know it's wrong, but he needs me and I need him. It's that simple and that complicated. Max doesn't want to give up the adrenaline rush he gets from being with me that he can't ever get within the limitations of his marriage vows. He loves Leslie, but he worships me."

"It's different with Marc. He wasn't prowling about on the hunt for a scandalous affair. He got caught up in nostalgia, a sentimental attachment to his first love. Since she was the one who broke up with him, this is his way of getting closure so he can move on. It's not like she's some random woman he met at a bar or a secretary at his office."

"Doesn't matter. She's the other woman."

"Would it make a difference if you met Max's wife and children? Would you end the relationship if you got to know their personalities and dreams? If you knew you were causing harm?"

"Grace, I've met Leslie, little Max Jr. and their twins, Peyton and Haley. And here is what I see—an exhausted, boring mom raising three spoiled brats. I know it sounds heartless, but I don't give a shit about Leslie. She and Max made a choice about what they want to do with each other, and I'll stick around for as long as I feel like the most desired and adored."

"Marc doesn't see me that way, and our kids aren't spoiled brats."

"I'm not saying you're boring, and I'm not saying anything derogatory about your kids. Don't be stupid. I'm telling you she'll always be the forbidden fruit Marc longs for."

"And I'm the carrot?"

"Or worse, the Brussels sprout."

"He doesn't hate Brussels sprouts. You do."

"I'm just saying you'll have to figure out how long you can take being the Brussels sprout, constantly rejected for the peach."

"This is seriously the stupidest conversation I've had in a long time. I don't want to be the Brussels sprout, carrot, or peach—I just want Marc to come to his senses and realize we're his family, and she's not. And I want her to see it too, so she'll leave us alone."

"Let's hope, for your sake, she isn't anything like me."

Christina reaches for her feet to stretch and poke the paraffin-filled booties. Before I can make a snide comment, a woman sidles up to my chair and informs me that before they apply color to my toenails, she will be waxing and sculpting my eyebrows. Scarier than Fiona, she's a tall, postapocalyptic-looking Goth wearing a white lab coat with the name Gia stitched above the left breast pocket. Gia pulls over the silver trolley holding the waxing equipment and tools and inspects my face, running her gloved finger along the sides and below my nose, which makes me feel incredibly self-conscious. It's even worse when she presents her findings: "You have quite a bit of peach fuzz above your lip and sideburns that really should be removed."

I cringe at being told sideburns and a mustache are not only present, but noticeable. However, the fear of pain, coupled with the knowledge that I won't be paying for the extra hair removal, necessitates a polite decline of her offer to do more than what was originally agreed upon.

"I really think you'll be happy with the final result if you let me take care of this issue for you. You can't possibly feel good about yourself walking around with all that hair on your face." Gia looks at me with pity, as if I am the abominable snowman asking for a trim.

"Go on," Christina pipes up. "Don't scrimp on your

beauty treatment today of all days. You want to look your best for your dinner guests, don't you?"

Insecurity shoves its way to the front and agrees to spend the extra money to ensure I take first place in the facial-hair-removal category. The next seven minutes transport me back in time to experience the gruesome terror of medieval torture. Like clumps of weeds gripped and ripped out of the dirt, unwanted hair is pulled out by the root, section by section, stripping away protective layers of skin. I try my best not to howl, whimper, or cry, but there is nothing I can do to prevent the tears from welling up and streaming down the sides of my cheeks. Gia must have been trained to be completely oblivious to any signs of suffering, as never once does she acknowledge the repeated cringing and moaning. Not even spasmodic flinching distracts her from creating a completely smooth canvas for make-up. I don't want to sound overly dramatic, but I would honestly choose the pain of childbirth over hot wax treatments. At least something beautiful came out of giving birth.

I'm not sure how Gia can smile as she shows me the final results of her work. Can she not see the bright red stenciled-in Wolverine mutton chops, Yosemite Sam mustache, Bozo the Clown nose imprint on my chin, and the one very hungry hot-headed caterpillar crawling across both eyebrows? I know she can't feel the stinging sensation tap dancing across my face, but surely the speed with which welts are forming should be somewhat concerning? The hot wax may have removed all traces of hair, but there is nothing discreet about how this was accomplished.

"The redness disappears once it cools down," Gia promises. "You won't regret having this done and will want it included as part of your beauty routine from now on."

Chapter 8

"Vanity is but the surface."
-Blaise Pascal

The alarm clock's Arabic dial announces I've had at least seven straight hours of sleep. I have been out of the conscious world for longer than I planned or wanted.

"Mom? We're going to be late." I dreamily hear Kelsey's voice on the other side of the door. "Are you up?"

"Sugar balls! Yes! I'll be out in a sec."

"Okay. Hurry up. It's close to ten," she scolds me. "I heard your alarm ages ago, so you should've been out a long time ago."

I'm not only embarrassed at being reprimanded by my child for tardiness, but cross with myself that catching up on sleep has also cost me valuable prep time. The plan was to get up early to assemble the lasagna, garlic bread, and salad in advance. Thankfully, I cleaned the house and set the dining room table last night, but now I'm going to be rushing to get the food ready before Marc, Emily, and Birch arrive this evening. What do they say about the best laid plans?

Part of me wants to skip church and stay home, but Bailey and Kelsey will be gravely disappointed in me if I do so. We used to attend the Catholic parish I grew up in, but after Dad's funeral, I just couldn't go without having a complete meltdown. I'd end up immobilized by depression. Everything about me would completely shut down, and I'd stay in bed for days. Sympathy quickly morphed into resentment when two days turned into a week of Marc taking over my role and responsibilities, and then after one seventeen-day streak of being bedridden, he insisted we take a break from our Sunday routine. It gave us an excuse to drink coffee and lazily read our favorite sections of the *New York Times* instead of going to church. We told ourselves God was everywhere—including our living room. This became the preferred way to practice our faith.

Shortly after Marc moved out, Bailey asked if the three of us could try out her friend's church. I didn't have the heart to refuse her anything, so she picked a Sunday, and we were introduced to an entirely different way of worship. Her friend, Holly, promised Bailey it wouldn't be anything like St. Theresa's. It was the understatement of the decade.

Holly's church has given the worship experience an

extreme makeover, taking a Mall of America approach to invite outsiders to experience what it means to be a Christian. The cathedral has been replaced with a contemporary modular building, versatile, functional, and stylish; however, gone is the spiritual beauty of stained-glass windows expressed in lyric color.

The choir and hymns have been retired and replaced with a rock praise band belting out worship songs, percussive and amplified. Lyrics penned centuries ago are missing, but you can find and order a chocolate-sprinkled cappuccino with extra foam and then stroll over to the bookstore to browse through the CDs, books, jewelry, and other items for sale while waiting for the service to start. Worshippers sway in their designer jeans in the auditorium and call out or raise their hands in response to words, phrases, or notes meaningful to them.

My comparisons are trivial and surface-level, but for someone my age who has had a traditional Catholic upbringing, the service is unnerving. I know what is expected of me at St. Theresa's—when to make the sign of the cross, kneel, and respond with "Lord, hear our prayer." Now I am unsure of what to do with my hands, when to sit and stand, or what to say when someone tells me I'm on the right path by just showing up. This or some other saccharine version of "Welcome to the God Club" makes me want to gag and become an atheist, to flee from religion, separating myself from anyone who thinks speaking this way has the power to convert a nonbeliever or bring a believer back into the fold.

There are two reasons for coming back to this congregation—my children and the pastor. I know I'm lucky Bailey and Kelsey enjoy our new Sunday morning routine, church service and IHOP pancakes. They want to see their friends, and I've come to look forward to Pastor Lottie's messages.

I tuned out the first service I went to until she preached, "Some think church is only for the perfect, a place to celebrate and strive for perfection. I'm here to tell you it's not. It's for the broken. And since all of us are broken, there is no one among us who doesn't belong, who isn't welcome here. You and I, we are here to support each other in our weakest moments and be lifted up by God's unconditional love."

It was as if she was speaking directly to my unaddressed fears of no longer having a place at the table. I didn't want to show up without Marc, to have my failing marriage out in the open for all to see, to sit among the righteous when my heart was breaking and everything I once had faith in was being questioned. Pastor Lottie took me out of my comfort zone to look beyond the surface glitter of a weekly worship resort drawing in visitors and dollars with caffeinated beverages, up-tempo rock concerts, and big screens flashing high-tech graphics and videos. She helped me give it a chance. I go back because I find myself overwhelmingly curious about what she has to say next.

I catch sight of myself in our bathroom mirror. It doesn't matter if Pastor Lottie were to give away free trips to the Holy Land for everyone seated in the audience, I want to jump back into bed and hide under the covers. The majority of my face has broken out in misshapen red splotches and uneven patches of bumpy blemishes. I don't think anything in my makeup bag will conceal what was done yesterday. I knew I shouldn't have listened to Christina and Amaya.

"It's not that bad." Bailey's words are comforting, but the expressions on both girls' faces are not.

"Yeah," Kelsey agrees, "I barely even noticed until Bailey pointed it out."

Bailey gives her little sister a shove, not wanting me reminded of her immediate reaction to the dermatological damage done by the beauty ambassador at A Cut Above Salon. Kelsey rushes up to her room and returns with her beloved Yankees ball cap. She hands it to me . Thank goodness Apex Community Church's dress code is casual. I could never get away with wearing faded jeans, an unironed linen shirt with a cactus print, and a baseball cap at St Theresa's. Or keeping my head down and avoiding eye contact with parishioners.

I put my hand on the back door latch and catch sight of my red, pimpled mustache reflected in the window.

"You know, we could go straight to IHOP. Get some blueberry waffles. I'd even let you off dish duty tonight."

"Mom, you said looks don't matter, it's what's inside that counts, so this will be a good test to show us if you really mean it." Bailey summons an annoyingly maternal air. "Stop being a baby, and let's go. You'll be fine. No one's going to be looking at you anyway."

Ouch. I don't know what's worse—being ridiculed or overlooked. Normally my fragile ego wouldn't want anyone to respond to my existence with either of these extremes, but today I'd give anything to have the power of invisibility, starting at the point of walking out the door. Ian is in the front yard carefully pouring gas into his lawnmower. I give the visor a downward yank and Ian a hurried, sideways arm wave, but in doing so, I somehow trip on the uneven pavement and fall on my knees. A grass stain scrapes across my jeans, but Ian miraculously misses my klutzy stumble. I quickly grab the door handle and pull myself up to swing into the car.

Bailey and Kelsey squabble about which actor's voice is featured in an animated movie, oblivious to their mother's pain. I rub my knee, which aches.

"Come on, Mom!" Kelsey shouts from the back seat. "You're fine, let's go!"

"Ya." Bailey crosses her arms. "You're not getting out of this." They might not be spoiled brats, but they're certainly bossy ones.

Thankfully, we arrive at a time when I can easily

escape into the darkness. My face is burning, and my knee is throbbing. I wonder if it would be wrong to pray for a miracle to have these superficial ailments disappear before the lights are turned back on. This query is swiftly answered in the form of a guest speaker who gives a short and impactful presentation about an organization with a mission to stop human trafficking. I am a self-centered punk praying for the trivial.

Pastor Lottie walks up to the podium and offers gratitude for the speaker and his work. I expect to hear a lecture about how we need to do more to serve those in need.

"I don't want you to use these tragic stories to minimize your troubles. I'm guessing a few of you are sitting out there feeling guilty for not having life or death problems, but you, my friends, are falling into the comparison trap. Most of us know comparing ourselves to those who have talents, attributes, and possessions we lack can cause all-consuming jealousy. But did you know comparing the magnitude of our troubles also initiates resentment and self-pity? We should pray for others. We should answer the call to act on behalf of the vulnerable, for the least among us. But we should not compare their pain and suffering with our own because it's another destructive way of distracting us from our purpose in life. It robs us of being genuine, of getting real with ourselves and others. Don't take my word for it. I've got the Bible to back me up, so here we go!"

The spotlight follows her around the stage as she effortlessly weaves memorized scripture into her case for removing the need to compare yourself to others—to basically mind your own business. I can't get over how she never refers to notes and is able to match her words with movements that accentuate, never detract, from the points being made.

It is also dumbfounding how Lottie, herself, is not a distraction from her own message. The spotlight draws attention to the fact that she is preaching barefoot. She is not anything like the clergy I grew up with. She's an unconventional Harvard Divinity School graduate with a silver toe ring and dragonfly tattoo on the back of her shoulder who forces me to confront my many hang-ups with religion. I'm bothered by being bothered at taking spiritual advice from someone who doesn't look the part—who doesn't have white whiskers, wrinkles, and, quite frankly, a penis, which is a terrible thing to admit, but is my distorted truth.

Chapter 9

"How old do you think Pastor Lottie is? In her late twenties?" I ask Bailey as we drive home.

"God, no. She's old. Your age, I think."

Huh. And there you go, a penalty incurred for making assumptions based on mistaken guesses. Not only has a snarky teenager reminded me that I'm no longer a spring chicken, but I'm also confronted with my stereotypical hang-ups trapping me in my own prejudices.

"But you are right mom, the purple hair makes her look at least ten years younger than she really is," Kelsey comes to my defense. "She's a real-life kitsune."

"A what?"

"Kitsune, everyone knows is from Japanese folklore," she enlightens us. "A creature with supernatural powers to ward off evil—a hundred-year-old fox who can shape-shift into a beautiful young woman. That's Pastor Lottie—old disguised as young."

"Of course, Kelsey the nerd would come up with some made-up beast that only D&D dorkoids know about to describe Pastor Lottie. But maybe I really am the only one who has no idea what a kitsunami is. Mom? Did you know about this mythological foxy lady?"

"Never heard of it, but really wish I had the power to shape shift into a fox right now to hide what that evil Gia has done to my face."

"You can keep my baseball cap for as long as you need it," Kelsey offers.

"Or how about we glue clumps of fur on your face," Bailey flippantly proposes. "And tell everyone you're try-ing your Halloween costume out early."

"I can download instructions for making animal ears and a tail we can stick on your head and bum," Kelsey joins in the fun. "We can paint your nose black with mas-cara. No one'll know it's you—not even Dad!"

"Great. Thanks for helping your poor old mom out," I groan. "Guess this is what I get for allowing myself to be bullied into getting a good look at myself in that mirror magnifying every flaw—and for letting your aunt talk me into doing something so stupid. Never again!"

"Or how about next time, why don't you give yourself more time to recover," Bailey advises. "It probably wasn't the smartest idea to mess with your face the day before you're in charge of having people over—even if they're family, 'cause you know we are def-o going to have the most to say about your stupidity."

"Thanks for that, Bailey." As she catches my overstated frown in the rearview mirror, she gives me two thumbs up.

I'm glad we kept to our new worship routine. The girls continue chatting and laughing, and all three of us are enjoying each other's company. It's probably blasphemous to confess I find these moments more spiritually meaningful than any of the times I've spent on my knees in a church. I just know a belief in and reliance on a higher being is intensified by my constant monitoring of Bailey and Kelsey's well-being. There is never a time I'm not praying for their safety, health, or happiness. Motherhood has made it impossible for me to be an atheist.

* * *

At home I check my email first thing. Maybe, just maybe, Marc has emailed and cancelled. It would make more sense for him to text or call if that were the case, but I hold onto my delusions until they are utterly dashed by the contents of my inbox.

Among the usual buildup of mail from places I don't remember signing up to get mail from, receipts for online shopping, and school email announcements, I see an email from Mary Anne.

> *Grace,*
>
> *Patty was right about you. There are some people who come into your life who are so special you'll never ever forget them—and you are such a person. It was only because I desperately wanted your help that I shared*

*what I did. I wasn't sure what to expect, but you held my
story with a respectful tenderness. And then you took
my measurements without making me feel ashamed of
what I've done to myself. I want to thank you for this but
have to do it in an email because I'd cry like a baby if I
told you in person. I can't tell you how much it means to
me that you've said yes to the dress—to my dress!*

*You are a fairy godmother who has made me incredi-
bly happy by making my dream come true.*

With gratitude,

Mary Anne

*P.S. If you'd like an Oreo blizzard, stop by anytime for
a freebie!*

Her email makes me teary. I want to be compassionate, caring, and supportive, but I'm only like that as a
seamstress. It hasn't transferred over into my role as a
wife. I don't want to follow where love has led me. I want
to follow Christina's advice and cancel this evening's
plans. She was right. I've misjudged what I can handle. It
was a very bad idea to invite all my worst fears to dinner,
but it's too late to back out, and now I am forced to do
everything to make the best of a bad situation.

With the help of an online beauty blogger, Kelsey fig-
ures out an alternative to wearing a Halloween costume
to conceal from Emily and Marc the volcanic eruptions
etched into my face. It takes up time I don't have.

The onions need chopping, but then so do the green

peppers and parsley. Where's the 13 x 9 pan? Is it in the dishwasher? And the frying pan? Is it in the drawer under the stove or the sink? The Italian sausage needs to be browned with the onion and garlic, but not the peppers. The peppers are for the salad, so I should really chop up the cucumbers, tomatoes, and carrots while I'm at it. Maybe I should've sliced the bread on a dry cutting board, but that's now covered in vegetable guts, so I will need to find another one. Will anyone notice if I stamp slices of butter with a decorative wheat design? Is it a waste of time or a value-added detail? Wait. Should I only focus on the lasagna right now? What time is it? Where is the timer? How am I possibly going to get everything done in two hours?

Shredded mozzarella and parmesan cheese cover the last layer of rigid noodles, and I sprinkle a bit of dried parsley on top for color. Hands on hips, I stand back and admire what has been accomplished in spite of the countless setbacks. Surely Emily will recognize the amount of effort put forth, which will transfer to an awareness of how determined I am to keep my family intact, and this will make her change her mind about moving in with Marc. And, as a result of her retreating, this will turn Marc's attention to repairing our marriage. Yep, it will be worth going through all this hassle if this is the end result.

Christina calls. She tells me this thinking is a "delusional mindfuck." However, I'm confident my make-believe luncheons with Jacqueline Kennedy Onassis and Halle Berry have successfully prepared me to outclass the competition. I hold my head high as if these famous and beautiful women have actually taken me in as one of their own.

Kelsey lets an overly rambunctious Moby in through the back door. I trip over the four-legged speed bump just as I swivel to move the lasagna from the counter into the oven. My wish to save the uncooked lasagna is not enough to override my body's instinct to protect itself from falling. As I release the sides of the ceramic dish, layers of red sauce, cheese, and meat spill and splatter across the floor, wall, and cabinet surfaces.

Moby starts to run out of the room but quickly turns back to lick and gobble as much of the meat mixture as he can before he's shooed away. It doesn't really matter if canine saliva is added to the ingredient list. Even though I have a flash of a thought of scooping the slop back into the pan and calling it an Italian casserole, I'm fully aware it is not salvageable.

"Mom, don't cry. It'll be okay." Kelsey forcibly leads Moby back outside.

I cry anyway.

She rushes back and finds a sponge under the sink to start the cleanup activity, but her frenzied circular wiping motion smears the mess around so our cabinet doors look like the finger paintings she used to create in her kindergarten art classes.

"We can order a pizza," she says. "Or just serve what's in our fridge or go out instead. It might be better anyway if we all meet at Perkins or wherever."

It is tempting to swap a restaurant for our home, but the whole point is to immerse Emily in what she is endangering if she stays with Marc. Everything I planned has been overturned. My knee throbs again. I wish I hadn't brought Moby home from the humane society. I regret the thought instantly. How can I think like that about an innocent animal? The weight of my thoughts keeps me down on the floor.

I hear Bailey coming in the front door with the dog. "What idiot left the gate open?" she shouts at us. "Good thing I was walking back from the corner store getting your stupid blocks of butter because I found him sniffing around the neighbors' yard and he was . . . Whoa! What happened here?"

Moby procures a second helping of his late afternoon snack.

"Change of plans." I pull myself off the floor, ignoring my knee screeching at being the target of impact for the second time in one day. I limp over and retrieve a tissue to wipe my eyes and blow my nose.

"Can you call your dad?" I ask Bailey. "Tell him I've paid and placed an order with Noah's, but we need him to pick it up. We'll keep with the Italian menu. It just won't be me cooking tonight."

Bailey calls her father and then calls in our order. She

takes care of adding decorative details to the rooms, which elevates the informal dining experience on the outskirts of a suburban neighborhood to noteworthy levels. Kelsey and I work furiously to remove the lasagna shrapnel from the kitchen surfaces.

Kelsey rises up on her tiptoes to reach the edge of the cabinet above the stove with a soapy dishrag. "Do you think she'll like us? I mean what if she doesn't want us around? Emily, I mean. What if she wants him all to herself? Do you think Dad will give us up if she ends up hating that he already has kids?"

Chapter 10

An anvil drops from my throat to stomach. I stop what I'm doing and turn Kelsey so she can see my face. "You are the light in the darkness when we are at our very lowest points. Both you and Bailey remind us of the best of who we are. You two are the greatest gifts we could ever receive from our marriage, and no matter what happens, neither one of us will lose sight of what a privilege and honor it is to be your parents. No one, and I mean no one, can ever, ever, ever change or take that away from you or your sister."

She squirms and turns her face away, eyes wet. I gently direct and lift her chin toward me. "You will always be loved by your father and me. One of the villains could pop out of your comic book and rip out our hearts and chop our brains into a million pieces, and we would still find a way to let you know you're forever loved."

"I don't read comic books."

"Well, a bad guy from *Star Trek* movies then."

"Don't watch those either."

"Nasty He-Who-Must-Not-Be-Named in *Harry Potter*?"

"I'm not five."

"The White Witch in *The Lion, the Witch and the Wardrobe*?"

"Again, not a junior reader."

"I know! *Interview with a Vampire*, those vicious villain-ous viper vampires."

Kelsey is giggling, and I give her another hug.

"You get my point."

"I do."

We return to scrubbing. Miraculously, twenty or so minutes are granted us to breathe before our guests arrive. The three of us nestle into the sofa cushions, me in the middle with an icepack resting on my knee. We take time to review and assess our eventful Sunday. As I thank the girls for their help, Moby, not wanting to be left out, jumps up and plops himself across our laps. I grip his face in my hands and give him a fierce kiss on his forehead before sending him back to the floor where he belongs.

Bad, unruly dog. But good, sweet dog.

A few moments later, Marc stands on our porch and rings the doorbell. My brain tells me to open the door and let the man in, but I can't come to grips with the formal seeking of permission to enter his own home. He's used his key to help himself to leftovers in the fridge, leave dirty dishes in the sink, fix the leaky sink, or hang out with Moby countless times since our separation. On this occasion, he chooses to knock on the dang door when I don't respond quickly enough to the doorbell chimes.

Kelsey shoves past me and greets Marc. He looks sheepishly uncomfortable holding three oversized plastic bags with our carry-out meal and a plastic-wrapped bouquet of daisies and yellow roses. He passes the flowers to our daughter.

"Emily and Birch aren't with me. They're on their way from a Target run. Birch needed contact lens cleaner or something."

I suspect they agreed in advance to come separately. Good. I'm glad they found it awkward to arrive together. They must know at some level there is something wrong with what they're doing. My plan for the night has a good chance of working. Things are starting to look up.

"I'm glad we have a couple minutes before they get here anyway."

My breathing comes to an abrupt standstill. Bailey takes the food from Marc and disappears into the kitchen, leaving us to continue our bumbling conversation in the narrow vestibule. We are so close, I lean into the scent of the cologne he applies every morning after his shower routine. I pull myself back when I start to feel faint.

He stalls with a little cough, and then does it again to clear a path for the words to make their way over to where I can hear.

"I wanted to thank you for going through all this

trouble for me. There aren't many women who would agree to something like this. You've gone way above and beyond what anyone else would've done." He frenetically rubs the side of his nose with the right knuckle of his index finger, a tell that he's beyond nervous. "You should know I think you're amazing and appreciate your effort to not make this more awkward than what it already is."

"Well, I ruined our homemade dinner and made you pick up a new one, so guess I'm not that amazing."

"Well, okay. Let's call you amazingly clumsy and inept in the kitchen then." He steps back and feigns bracing for some type of physical punishment for his insult. I accept his invitation and playfully thump his arm. I can't look him in the eye or I might punch him in the balls or kiss him on the mouth, either one with passionate fury.

A car door slams outside, and I can feel his energy rearranging and changing direction to chase what is in the driveway. Whatever confidence I had dissipates into thin air.

Emily's son, Birch, slouches up the path, head bobbing to whatever music is on his earbuds.

"Take those out," Emily hisses at him.

He grudgingly follows instructions. The sides of his head are completely shaved, so the central line of about fifteen spikes of dark hair is the focal point. This impressively tall mohawk is accessorized with several piercings, including a vertical bar crossing his left eyebrow, a ring looped in his lower lip, and circular, black-framed windows in his earlobes that look like they were made with an oversized hole punch. He assumes that slumped over adolescent posture. Any evidence of physical resemblance to his mother has been disguised, but he can't alter the shape of his nose and mouth, which are identical to hers. Birch lets Emily go ahead, not wanting to be the first to reach the porch.

Emily's nose twitches ever so slightly as she greets me with a wide, friendly smile. There is not a single trace of nervousness in her approach. It's as if this meet and greet in my home is a common, everyday occurrence.

"I'm so happy to finally meet you, Grace." She hugs me. I am being hugged by Marc's first love, embraced by a woman who doesn't seem to mind that I still hold the title of wife. I'm not sure how to respond. I don't want to be rude, but I'm not particularly interested in reciprocating affection from a woman who will soon be sharing a bed with my husband. She squeezes once more before releasing me. I can't detect anything insincere in her opening move, but I'm suspicious regardless. Is she purposely trying to throw me off my game?

She takes a purple gift bag from Birch. "We picked up a little something to thank you for your grand gesture of hospitality. When our Marc told me I was cray-cray for wanting to gather us together for a meal, I told him I didn't care. I know as a mother you'd want to know who your girls would be spending time with when we move up here. And why not try and be friendly? So this is my thank you for making it possible."

I am dizzy. She hasn't even stepped into the house and already everything I assumed has been thrown overboard. I can't imagine Marc willingly incorporating "cray-cray" into any of his sentences and am shocked and horrified to hear this wasn't his idea. I knew it was out of character for him to do so, but because I was convinced this outrageous request was an unconscious test of what I would do to make him happy, I said yes. Why hadn't I ever considered the possibility he didn't think this up? If I had known it had everything to do with what she wants and nothing to do with Marc and me, I would've followed Christina's advice to abort all effort to make things nice.

"We're happier'n all git-out to be here." The foundational pronunciation of her sentences signal she was raised in the Midwest, but an odd hybrid of Southern accents and phrases are selectively turning up now and again. "Aren't we, Birch, darlin', no, yeah?"

Birch grumbles too low to hear and gives an apathetic shrug as his mother nudges him forward. I realize we haven't moved from the porch because everyone is waiting for me to make the first move. I hold the front door open. Birch wordlessly makes his way inside with an upward tilt of the chin I assume is his thank you.

"He's tired," Emily apologizes on his behalf. "We've been on the constant go for weeks, and since he didn't want to leave his friends or Florida, it's been that much harder for him to make this move, so he's a smidgen grumpier than the average moody teenager at the moment."

I get a good look at my competitor as she moves past me. She is exactly as I remember her from what I discovered in Marc's childhood bedroom and his sister's description. What I couldn't predict from any of the photographs is how her in-person presence crackles and sizzles with Hollywood pizzazz. I can't help but understand why she is attractive to others, including Marc. She's everything I'm not—a movie star Reese Witherspoon look-alike with a God-given ability to sing.

Chapter 11

Emily stops in front of our upright piano in the living room. Family photographs are displayed in a hodgepodge of silver frames on the top of the piano and on the wall behind. Our framed check from the marriage license office sits behind the piano lid's hinge, and the center photograph on the wall is my favorite one of Marc and me on our wedding day. In a white lace cocktail dress, I am standing face forward with the tips of my aquamarine stilettos pointed together as Marc, who has a sideways-leaning stance with both hands in his pockets, is tenderly kissing me on the cheek.

"Is this a Kemble?" Emily asks, running her fingers along the closed fallboard. "Love, love the crimson color."

"Yes. It was a Christmas present from Marc's parents for the girls," I tell her. I wonder if it's uncouth to let her know the instrument is connected to my in-laws. How is it that all of a sudden, I feel responsible for making her feel comfortable? It doesn't seem right or fair, and I briskly go ahead to see what is happening in the kitchen.

"Are you okay?" she asks, observant of my limp. "Did you hurt yourself?"

I give a dismissive wave and explain, "Just a minor incident involving the dog. I'm okay, just bruised up a bit."

Bailey and Kelsey have separated the laminated lids from the restaurant's foil containers and have plopped serving spoons into the contents. It's helpful—but contrary to our efforts to impress. As I find more appropriate serving dishes from the sideboard, I glance over at Bailey and Birch standing in the corner of the dining room. They are sharing his earphones—she has the left and he has the right earbud. Their heads bob in unison.

"This is the kind of music my band plays back home," he shouts. "See why I'm pissed about giving it up to move here?"

Marc swiftly comes from out of nowhere, taps Bailey on the shoulder before removing her earbud, and I hear him tell her he needs help bringing in things from the car. I wonder what else he has brought—dinner, dessert, and hostess gifts are on the counter. I see his face and I know he's lying. I bet he doesn't want Birch to influence anything our daughter does or thinks. He should have thought of that before making the decision to move them into our lives.

"Let me help you with that," Emily offers. She reaches for a serving dish, the one with a barefoot Chinese fisherman figurine sitting on the edge opposite two gaudily disproportionate frogs, a most unwanted birthday present from Erika, my battle-ax sister-in-law, a superfan of Emily. The doorbell saves me from confessing that the bowl only comes out when Erika visits and vehemently directing her to leave it where it is. Instead, I excuse myself, saying I have no idea who it could be as we aren't expecting anyone else.

Kelsey beats me to the door. Ian stands there with a shamefaced Moby.

"Hey there," Ian grins. "Found this guy running close to the busy road as I was driving back from a Home Depot run. Luckily, he jumped in the car without a fuss. I think he knew I'd get him back home safely."

"Bad Moby! Bad dog!" Kelsey scolds and grabs Moby by the collar, leading him to her bedroom where we keep his crate.

"I don't think we've met," Marc says, extending his hand out to Ian from behind me. "I've seen you a couple of times coming and going but haven't had a chance to come over and say hello."

Ian reaches forward and they shake hands, with me in the middle of the two, making an awkward sandwich.

"I meant to catch you as well," Ian responds apologetically and asks, "So you're a Cowboys fan?"

"Ya, ya. What makes you ask?"

"I noticed you loading a Dallas Cowboys tailgate table and dart cabinet into your car the other week."

"Oh right. I figured Grace was sick of seeing them in the garage and thought I'd better move them into the apartment before Emily arrived." No further explanation is requested or given as to who they are in relation to this property. They are more interested in exchanging their opinions about the NFL season's stats and predictions.

When Ian discloses that, as a student at the Art Institute of Pittsburgh, he became an avid Steelers fan, Marc jokes, "Well, I was going to invite you to join us for dinner, but no way that's happening now."

"He doesn't want to anyway," I respond, not meaning to sound impolite. "I'm guessing you have better things to do with your time than hang out with us."

"Actually, I'm on my own for dinner. Caleb is out with friends and mom is at a church event, so I'm free and starving. Whatever you've prepared smells absolutely delicious so if you'll have me, I'd be most grateful for the dinner and company."

I don't think there is much more the universe can throw at me. This is the most bizarre event of my life. The table comfortably seats six, not seven, so I squeeze in another place at the corner and move the piano bench over as a makeshift dining room chair. Ian insists that since he's the last-minute addition, he is happy to take this custom-built place setting.

"And who is this tall and handsome stranger?" Emily addresses Ian. She has floated in from the kitchen into the dining room carrying a pitcher of water—sliced cucumbers and lemons are floating amidst cubes of ice. Her loose-fitting charcoal grey sweater has slipped to the side exposing a bare neck to shoulder line, which, after putting the carafe in the middle of the table, she adjusts to a more modest position. I wish she would disappear or at least instantaneously develop a small grouping of zits and maybe a wart or two around her chin and cheeks.

Ian doesn't react to the compliment with anything but courteous charm and answers, "Thank you for your generously kind way of asking who has crashed your party. I'm the sort-of-new neighbor who has been lucky enough to snag a last-minute dinner invitation. Are you a friend or relative of Grace?"

The adults in the room are silent.

"It's complicated," Kelsey announces, "Would anyone like ranch dressing for their salad? I only put the raspberry one out, but we have others."

"Basically, my mom is their dad's girlfriend." Birch expands on Kelsey's discreet version of our situation. "And because they can't stand the long-distance thing, we're moving from a sunny paradise to this corn-and-pig dump. She doesn't care that all my friends are back there because—joy, joy—we get to come to dinner today to meet our new family." He puts family in air quotes.

Ian's line of vision swings from me to Emily, from Emily to me, from Emily to Marc, and then back to me. "This isn't the first time you've all met, is it?" His voice registers panic.

"Glorious stuff, ain't it?" Birch scowls but appears quite pleased with himself.

"It is," I admit.

"I'm really sorry. I had no idea," Ian stammers. "I have a couple of frozen pizzas . . . and bread . . . really, I can get my own dinner."

"No, no, don't be silly," I say, resigned to the absurdity of the situation. "We ordered enough to feed a small army, so the more the merrier."

"Lasagna, chicken parmigiana, a chicken pesto pizza, and two orders of ravioli," Bailey lists what she ordered from the carry-out menu. "And Mom made her famous Baileys tiramisu for dessert. That's Baileys Irish Cream, not me-Bailey . . . ha ha. She doesn't make it often, so better get it when you can."

Chapter 12

Ian stays because he can't figure out a way to escape fast enough. At first, I didn't want him here either, but it turns out that having a guest who's not involved with our drama works in my favor.

"I hear you're fixin' to be a judge," Emily says as she passes the basket of garlic bread in Bailey's direction. "Why law?"

"I'm interested in helping people take notice and understand the fine print in society's terms and conditions," Bailey replies, with an answer I recognize from her working draft of an essay for college applications. "I thought about being a public defender, but I know I'd get fed up working with adults who know better but still choose to break the law."

"Your dad tells me you created a rulebook for all the neighborhood kids and enforced every single one." She laughs and looks at Marc for confirmation. "And she wasn't quite ten years old, isn't that right?"

Marc nods and says, "That's our Bailey, a fan of justice and order . . ."

"I think the police and all lawyers are corrupt," Birch interrupts, "but Judge Judy's a sexy broad. I'd stand at attention in her courtroom."

Marc frowns, ignores Birch talking with his mouth full, and points out, "But as I also told you, while some accused Bailey of having an overly strict interpretation of the rules, everyone also thought she was very fair in her rulings on the matters at hand."

My heart is pulled in two directions. Emily's well-mannered inquiry about Bailey's career interest assures me Kelsey needn't worry their father will be forced to choose between his current love interest and them. But imagining the where, when, and why of Marc describing our children to her obliterates my appetite. I try to look as if I'm eating, but I am merely flipping the same ravioli over again and again with the fork and knife.

"My wife loved pasta." Ian wistfully tosses this fact out and then gives us one more thing to digest. "Oddly enough, she hated the texture of udon noodles and barely tolerated Japanese cuisine. When we lived in Japan, she'd make special trips into Tokyo to eat at Italian restaurants."

"Did she move on to Italy then?" Emily playfully asks about her whereabouts. She sprinkles extra parmesan over three slices of pizza, a pile of salad, and a conglomeration of each pasta dish messily arranged on her plate. I think she can't possibly eat like this all the time and stay that skinny. Maybe she's eating out of nervousness.

"We never made it to Italy," Ian sighs sadly. "Always thought we had plenty of time for her dream trip, but she was diagnosed with pancreatic cancer and was gone in a matter of months."

Emily stops sprinkling, and all clinking of tableware is silenced before Ian can say, "It's okay. I shouldn't have brought up my sad story. All this food reminded me of her. I've never ordered from Noah's. I'll have to, now. I've tried everything, and it's all absolutely delicious."

Only the sound of cutlery breaks the silence that follows his attempt to circle back to an impersonal topic of conversation. Even Birch is quiet. He keeps his mouth busy chewing and swallowing.

"Mom thinks her biological father's Italian," Kelsey announces as if it's some deep dark family secret. "She's made up his name, given him a hometown, a job, four children, three dogs, and a couple of chickens."

"You have?" Ian sounds relieved about the change in subject.

"It's really my fault," Marc explains. "Since Grace's family tree is an unknown, I used to make up scenarios about her lineage—like what if one day, a messenger shows up at our door to announce she's really a princess, and the time has come for her to accept the role as ruler of some unknown and remote island."

"Or how about the one where she's the secret love child of Bruce Lee and Isabella Rossellini? And the *National Enquirer* finds out and our life is taken over by the paparazzi?" Bailey brings up the one she feels would benefit her life the most. "But the good thing is that we get invited to the Oscars and become famous like the Kardashians!"

"Gross!" Kelsey shrieks. "I like the one better where Mom was kidnapped as a baby by underground ninjas who brought her to America for a top-secret mission—which will be revealed as soon as they feel she is physically and mentally prepared. She's still here, so they must feel like she has more work to do before they can give her the assignment."

"I've been the main character in their make-believe stories for a long time." I smile in Ian's direction, but the ease with which the four of us are able to recall our past bedtime ritual pulls painful longing into my body. I want my family back, for things to be like they were before Emily, Birch, and even Ian became part of our story.

But as much as I'm wishing and bargaining for their disappearance, they remain seated around the table. I watch the interaction between Emily and Marc. A respectful distance is maintained, and yet their restraint emphasizes curtailed public displays of affection. When she lets it slip and calls him E.T., a term of affection she's obviously given Marc, she apologetically blushes and quickly removes her hand from his forearm. I pretend not to notice and turn my attention to the others. Birch and Bailey are jabbering on about music festivals, Florida, and friends, while Kelsey and Ian are making plans for her to join Caleb and him for their Godzilla movie marathon night.

I'm not included in any of these conversations, which is why I can hear muffled retching sounds coming from Kelsey's bedroom. I excuse myself without giving a reason and go to Moby, who has vomited in his crate. I didn't think I'd be grateful to be called away to care for a dog who has done exactly what I felt like doing most of the evening—but I am. After cleaning up the mess, I sit on Kelsey's bed with Moby, stroking his head on my lap. He occasionally looks up at me with sympathy. I choke back tears and self-pity. The back of my head rests against the wall as I half listen to the ebb and flow of sociable inter-actions from the other room. I don't move from this spot until Bailey shouts they are starting dessert with or with-out me.

When our guests leave and I am alone with the post-dinner chaos, it's that final half hour spending time with the dog on my own that I remember most about the dinner party I never should have agreed to host. There is too much time to think about every single detail of the evening. I admit Christina was right but decide to keep this to myself. I can't handle the told-you-so look I know I deserve. Next time, I'll take more time to think when my gut instinct says no. At the very least, I won't make more work for myself than necessary. I'll hire a caterer or make a reservation at a restaurant.

As the last plate is loaded into the dishwasher, I force myself to identify one thing I'm grateful for.

At least nothing caught fire.

Chapter 13

nother two weeks pass. I decide not to switch therapists. Like a lot of things in my life, once things are set up, inertia sets in, and I acquiesce to the routine. I like to call it an energy-efficient management of time. This is preferable to calling myself a despicable lazy oaf who is always pathetically satisfied with the status quo no matter how horrible it is. I must be making incremental progress under Dr. Bennett-Hill's care since I followed her suggestion to find softer ways to describe my perceived weaknesses.

Yay me.

When I come home from my therapy appointment, there is something tucked into the crack of the back door. I pull it out, fully expecting a flyer for window washing or lawn care.

"The Prospect Drive Skywalk" announces the header. It is a single page with two columns of print. Most of it is an article on the history of the neighborhood. The by-line says Ian Hino. He came up in therapy today. I had already let go of my irritation over the prayer flags and the stone pagoda, and Dr. Bennett-Hill had helped me make peace with the dragon statue. I am not nearly as annoyed by the Buddha statue as I had been. In a few months, I might even be neutral about it. As neighbors go, Ian is not bad.

The rest of the paper is filled with a short yet wordy article on the longitude and latitude of our neighborhood—filler if I ever saw it. I hear a car coming up the drive and set the newsletter—though it lacks anything that can be called news—on the kitchen counter. I peek out the door and down the front drive and steel myself. Emily has come to drop off Bailey and Kelsey. Again.

The girls have taken to walking to their father and Emily's apartment after school, relieving me from school pick-up duty, which I appreciate. But I'm not sure it is worth the price of Emily's presence.

Kelsey and Bailey bang through the door, and Emily breezes in after them, laughing and chattering. "Hey you!" she exclaims when she sees me. She gives me a side hug with much shoulder squeezing. I tolerate this, but only because I still haven't figured out what to do about it.

"Neat." Kelsey holds up the newsletter, which she has replaced with her backpack on the counter.

"No backpacks on work surfaces," Emily trills. Kelsey moves it to the floor, which in my opinion is a trip hazard, but whatever.

Bailey leans over to see the newsletter as well. "Cool," she says. A little of Birch's monosyllabic nature seems to have worn off on her of late.

"What a great name!" Emily enthuses.

I agree, but only because it is objectively true. Ian had married the name of our street with our downtown's most notable feature, a tube-like system connecting buildings and protecting people from the weather elements as they walk to their desired destinations. And from which you can see what's happening on the street below. To me, it looks like a giant hamster cage.

I clear my throat, "We-ell I'm sure you have a lot to do . . ."

"Oh no, love, I got nothin' but time." Emily is rummaging through my cupboards for her favorite mug. She has a favorite mug at my house. It is not in the cupboard because I donated it to the Goodwill today, right before therapy. She settles for her second favorite mug, which, darn it, I like. I may have shot myself in the foot here.

Bailey charges up to her room, but Kelsey opens the fridge and stands in front of it in contemplation.

I gently nudge the door shut, "Decide what you want, then open the fridge." It's good advice I rarely manage to follow myself, but this is the sort of thing you have to say as a mother.

Emily laughs her tinkling laugh. She's brewing coffee in the French press, and my own preferred mug is sitting next to hers.

"I brought some cookies," she says. "Why don't you have one of those if you need a snack?"

Kelsey finds the box of Chips Ahoy! and takes three of them up to her room.

When I turn around, Emily has made herself comfortable at the kitchen island. Next to her, my mug is full, and the box of cookies sits between her and what is obviously my spot.

Emily and Birch are now living with Marc. I wonder how she takes care of my Marc. He has come to enjoy and expect having a dash of cinnamon added to his morning coffee, his towel warmed in the dryer and waiting for him after his morning showers, neckties color coordinated and hung with his shirts, and never having to worry about any of the household chores or bills. To get through the first weeks after he moved out, I repeatedly told myself that this was time allocated for him to miss what I did to make his life easier, all the little things he took for granted. I also told myself the cliché thing everyone believes after being dumped—no one can possibly love him the way I do.

"How's that wedding dress coming?" she asks as if I am the Thelma to her Louise.

"Good," I say. I pick up the coffee cup but do not sit down.

She lets out a puff of air. "I wish I could do that kind of thing. I can't believe what you can do with a little bit of fabric. It's just gorgeous."

How does she know what Mary Anne's wedding dress

looks like? Oh yes, she has been in my studio. Some-times, after she drops off the girls, she follows me down there with her coffee and tells me about her great parent-ing woes with Birch.

"Didn't you say it was—what was it—Muslim?"

"Muslin," I correct quickly.

"Not the finished thing, just like, a practice run. I can't wait to see how it looks in that scrumptious fabric down there."

Me too, but I'm not saying it. I have tried everything I can think of, but this woman will not take the hint that I do not want her here. I have implied she has better things to do, said I shouldn't keep her, told her that it would be boring if she stayed because I have to answer urgent business emails, and slapped my knees and said "Welp," which on the part of the host is midwestern for "Get the hell outta my house." But she's been in Florida too long or something, and she doesn't seem to speak Iowa nice anymore. Some might call it passive-aggressive, but the rest of us call it polite.

I sit down next to Emily, because if I'm going to endure her, I need a cookie. I look out the window above the sink and squint. Emily is holding up the conversation just fine without me. I don't even nod or say uh-huh. I notice something different outside. I stand up and walk over to the sink like I'm about to wash dishes.

"What the hell?" I say out loud and with vehemence.

Ian's side yard—with the rosebush and birdhouse I like—had been utterly and completely defiled.

"What?" Emily asks. "What's wrong?"

"He's put a goddamned panda out there."

Emily blinks in confusion, but I do not enlighten her. I am attempting to light the thing on fire through telepathy.

Emily comes to stand next to me.

"Oh," she says. "It's cute."

Which it is, if by "cute" you mean "sickeningly creepy."

"It has thumbs," I offer as a counterpoint.

"What?"

"Thumbs," I say. "Look! It's got regular paws on its back legs, but its front legs have hands. With thumbs." Each hand holds a piece of bamboo. It does not appear to be eating the bamboo, just posing with it whimsically. "Bears should not have thumbs. Or if they are going to, they should be anthropomorphized evenly, and have feet, not paws."

"I don't think pandas are bears actually." She pats my back. "I mean, not like related to bears. That's just what we call them 'cause they look like bears."

"Pandas are bears," Kelsey says. When she arrived, I do not know. Hopefully she has not heard me cussing out Ian's lawn ornament.

"Oh." Emily turns from the window to my child. "Interesting. Do you need something?"

"I heard Mom yelling."

I take a deep breath and shut my eyes—and there is the stupid panda burned into my retinas, laughing at me.

Chapter 14

One good thing about having a break from living with Marc is that I can do my own thing without feeling self-conscious or guilty about it. I didn't realize how much of my day was spent taking care of Marc's needs, but it's not his fault we slipped into roles reminiscent of Ozzie and Harriet, except with daughters, not sons. The way we settled into our relationship evolved as a result of my decisions to drop out of school, have babies, work from home, and make Marc so happy he'd never leave. Our schedule was based on Marc's work calendar and personal preferences, including the time of day we got up and went to bed. Marc requires a minimum of seven hours of sleep to function at full capacity during the day, but he's a very light sleeper—the slightest movement or sound disturbs him.

My insomnia attacks made sleeping in the same bed extremely difficult at times. I'd lie on my back, forcing myself to not move. I would concentrate on recalling the tiniest of details about places or people to help pass the

time. I'd count out how long I could stay still, not moving my toes, fingers, or head. Other times, I'd entertain
myself by imagining I was a *Project Runway* contestant
tackling the assigned weekly sewing challenges. That
kept me entertained for hours. Exercising the brain
distracted my legs from their desperate urge to run
away. Marc claimed he couldn't get a good night's rest
if I went into another room, and so because I thought it
was incredibly sweet that he couldn't sleep without me, I
stayed.

Now, I'm still quiet, so as not to wake the girls, but am
free to wander the house as I please when I can't sleep.
For over half a year, I've been working with, rather than
against, my natural biorhythms, and I've never been more
productive. Piles of laundry sorted and tossed in the
washer at midnight. Reruns of *Family Ties*, pages of celebrity gossip in magazines, or characters in a borrowed
library book might keep me company. Or alternately,
pots and pans washed, bills paid, a skirt pattern pinned
and cut, toenails painted . . . all completed by three
a.m. There's never a shortage of interesting things to do
during these restless nights.

Tonight, I decide to do the dishes, which I had not
done after dinner because I couldn't face the panda. I
stare out the window, hands in warm dishwater, eyes
on the shadows and outlines of Ian's side garden. In the
dark, the panda is just a blob among blobs, surrounded
by other dark blobs.

While staring at those blobs, I decide to face it. Emily is not leaving. Marc is falling back in love with Emily. She's the archetypal girl next door and I'm not. I consider the possibility that she's winning him over because I'm not a natural-born citizen.

A couple years ago, Marc and my sisters got into a discussion across the table about what qualifies as being an intolerant individual. The topic morphed into a debate about whether "reverse" placed in front of racism and sexism was necessary or valid.

"You get to use the race and gender card, don't you?" Christina nodded in my direction. She meant it as a benign joke and complimentary observation, but I took it as outlandishly distasteful. Even though I was fuming, I didn't want to initiate a verbal fencing match in front of the others because I knew it had the potential of escalating into an embarrassing screaming match. She fights to win, and it does not matter if, in the victory, she only takes away particles of dust and air as the prize.

When I asked Marc what he thought of Christina's comment about how I could benefit from racism, he shrugged his shoulders. He thought all our conversations, no matter the topic, publicized how all the Solberg sisters were off their rockers. Then, in a way that was completely out of character and is fondly stored in my bank of memories, Marc came up with an impromptu poetic telling of who we are:

"You and your sisters are elements of the sea. Amaya

is the ocean floor. She is deep and mysterious. Where light cannot penetrate and the pressure is great, Amaya will defy expectations by creating and nurturing life even though it doesn't seem possible. Christina is the water, but stormy waters. She can be worked up into tumultuous and destructive waves. At her best, she challenges the most skilled fisherman or surfers; at her worst, she obliterates everything that gets in her way."

"And what am I?"

"You are the salt," Marc answered ignoring my crinkled brow. "You influence the movement of ocean currents and marine life. You are the essence of the sea. Without salt, it's just an ordinary body of water."

It was probably the most romantic thing he ever said to me.

Marc was curious to know if I agreed with Christina's controversial stand that it is the sole responsibility of white men to eradicate racism. I thought the entire deck that included the race, religion, and gender cards should be tossed in the garbage and replaced with the dream of being solely judged by the content of character, nothing else. If this was the starting point for all conversations and interactions, it might give us a fighting chance to address and fix race relations in our country.

He snorted and dismissed this as an incredibly simplistic solution to a complex problem that only a naïve hippie would think could work in the real world.

I stand by what I said back then, but I'm guilty of

pulling out the race card to explain and justify my recent thoughts and actions. It works to my advantage to maintain that Marc's preference for blondes is the cause of all our problems. I am disgusted with myself for succumbing to the relief this horrid untruth provides, but I also can't deny it alleviates my pain, guilt, and fear.

It hurts too much to delve into other reasons why my husband no longer finds me good enough. I'd much rather blame what I can't control, like where I was born, for why he is falling out of love with the woman I was and am.

Chapter 15

I decide to skip work for a couple hours for a field trip to the botanical gardens. It's a place I regularly escape to when I need to figure out what comes next. One time, I entered the conservatory in a complete state of panic. Out of fear of having nothing in the pipeline, I accepted an assignment to design and construct a formidable armored-robot costume inspired by a client's favorite video game. She wanted the "mother of all mind-blowing costumes" to wear to an interview for a gaming company in Seattle—and believed this would win her the open position, but I had absolutely no clue how I could bring to life what she had in mind within her budget and short deadline.

By the time I passed the tumbling waterfall and made the final lap around the trails, I had a plan that made the client and interviewing committee gasp in awe—and a success posted on my website. All the credit goes to off-site brainstorming. For personal and professional quandaries, this is where I come. I have arrived with the intention of figuring out how to save my marriage, not interacting with anyone—and certainly not my neighbor . . . again. Ian is standing outside the gift shop talking to another man who is also wearing a dark, three-piece suit, but this man has a Principal Financial Group pin on his right lapel. I attempt to sneak by, wishing for invisibility. My wish is not granted.

"Thanks so much, Andy, for meeting this morning. I look forward to working with you," I hear Ian say and then, "If you'll please excuse me, I see someone I need to say hello to. She owes me lunch for rescuing her dog."

I force a smile and introduce myself to Ian's friend, who is not his friend, but a volunteer-work colleague. He is a tall, thin man with a sharp, hooked nose, and looks the type who enjoys having an insufferable reputation. His name is Andy Campbell, a senior vice president and chief risk officer. He feels compelled to inform me that not only does he serve on the botanical gardens' board of directors, but also the board for the local Habitat for Humanity affiliate. He brags that all his volunteer activity for the week has now been taken care of at once, and then goes on with a list of all the organizations depending on his donations, contacts, and expertise. I inadvertently roll my eyes but am able to turn my head in time so that he does not see. Ian does, and he gives me a stealthy nod of agreement.

I throw Ian a bone.

"I've only just met Ian, but he has already caused a

stir where I live," I inform the senior VP. "In a very short period of time, he did what others talked about but never did and started a newsletter to bring us together as a neighborhood. As the owner of a successful small business and a very active community volunteer, I'm impressed by his initiative and follow-through. You must be thrilled he's joined the botanical gardens' staff."

"You're right, he'd be great here, but I am just as thrilled he was hired to run Habitat for Humanity's local ReStore," Andy smugly corrects my incorrect assumption. "I want to be able to report quadruple sales to the board by the next fiscal year, so I expect great things from our new ReStore manager. The last one wasn't on the same page as me, and she didn't last very long, but I am sure that won't be the case this time."

He winks, and I am left with nothing else to say.

"I think I owe this lovely lady a lunch for giving me such a ringing endorsement in front of my new boss, wouldn't you agree?" Ian lightheartedly closes the conversation. "And since I don't start for another week, I'm going to take a long lunch break while I can. Grace, would you care to join me?"

"Sure, why not?" I shrug and accept his invitation, but only because I am afraid if I don't, Andy will keep talking. At this point, I would agree to open-heart surgery without anesthesia if it meant I didn't have to carry on a conversation with the pompous jerk.

"I'd stay as well—the food here is sublime—but I need

to get back to the office," Andy says, declining an invitation he wasn't given. "Nice meeting you, Lucy. And Ian, I'll email you the financials in the next couple of days for you to review."

I don't bother correcting my name. I make sure he's gone before I breathe out, "Wow. Do you really have to work with that?"

Ian and I walk toward the café. I smell Chinese black pepper—either from the kitchen or Ian's cologne—and realize I'm hungry.

"I bet he called me Lucy because he was thinking of Lucy Liu," I scowl. "What an idiot."

Ian laughs at me before confessing, "I'm a little nervous, but the executive director I report to is a guy I've known a long time, so I should be fine."

"It's okay unless Andy Campbell turns on him or you."

"Yikes."

"Yes, yikes."

Ian orders the bánh mì pork sandwich and a Bloody Mary. His order annoys me—not the Bloody Mary, but the main course. *What is wrong with me?* I ask for the Iowa honey crème brûlée followed by the health-nut salad. I can't break my habit of starting my meal with dessert.

"So are you an active community volunteer?" he asks.

"No," I confess, blushing furiously.

"I didn't think so."

"How'd you guess?"

"Two kids, a dog, and by the number of strangers

coming to your house, which I'm assuming are your clients, I figure you don't have time."

"Are you watching me?"

"You are right next door, Grace."

Something about this exchange catapults me into an uncomfortable tailspin of being flattered and exasperated at the same time, confused as to how I ended up having lunch with the neighbor I've been trying to avoid. We are sitting across from each other, but I refuse to look directly at him because I'm afraid of what I'll see, and I can't help thinking people seeing us must assume we've immigrated to this country together.

He continues, "Why didn't you just stick with the successful small business owner?"

"I was trying to help you out, and you're welcome."

"Thank you."

"You're welcome."

I get the feeling he thinks it's his calling to irritate me by pointing out my lies. Something in me wants to shove him back—and hard—so I ask, "Are you worried you might not be able to meet his aggressive goals, and you'll get fired? How did you get this job anyway? Bailey told me you were a graphic designer, not a salesperson or store manager."

"Well, I can't afford to fail or get fired." A fearful vulnerability shakes through his words. "A favor was called in to get me this job. I used to be a graphic designer but got fired. Self-sabotage at its worst."

"Really?" I can't help but be curious. I lean toward

him. He smells nice, of sandalwood and cardamom. I pull myself back. "What did you do?"

"I inserted a bunch of profanity and a couple compromising photos of my boss at a Vegas bachelorette party in a brochure I designed and sent it to the printer without going through the regular checks and approval process. The printer, who had worked with me for years and trusted me, didn't review the file and printed and mailed them to over 50,000 households across all of America. This was the last straw, but really I had been screwing up for, let's say, the last two years before my firing."

"Whoa," I say sympathetically, but am also grinning.

"Yes, I know—it's terrible. An old family friend stepped in and took over to save me from completely destroying not only my life, but Caleb's too. She said it was enough feeling sorry for myself and that Jenny was looking down from heaven pissed off. I was behaving badly—and selfishly.

"Everything came together. Maureen arranged for me to get this job, which meant moving from Arizona to Iowa. My friends thought it was crazy to move from the sun to snow, but oddly enough, it felt like the right place for starting over—after all, the field of dreams is located in this state, so how bad could it be? I couldn't afford to buy a house, but Maureen found a solution to that problem as well. She called my mom in San Francisco, tattled about the severity of my latest indiscretions, and informed her I would need help with the mortgage and raising her grandson. And so here we are."

I manage to mumble, "I'm really sorry about your loss."

"You're losing your husband as well, just in a different way," he says gently. "I'm sorry."

The words sting. Hearing my updated status in an unfamiliar voice, it comes across as an inevitable sentencing, not an unlikely option. Panic pokes my stomach as I wonder if this lunch distraction is a deliberate sign from the universe that it is a complete waste of time to come here to think of a solution for Marc and me. There is absolutely nothing I can do or say to change his mind.

"For the record, I think your husband must be insane." Ian points the tines of his fork in my direction. "Anyone who would let a woman as beautiful as you get away has to have severe mental health issues."

No one has called me beautiful. Pretty, yes. Cute, many times. Attractive, once. Never beautiful. I am taken aback by the compliment.

"You are beautiful," he assures me, "but I think you don't know it because you haven't figured out who you are yet—maybe you're unaware of what makes you unique and extraordinary."

"Thanks, Dr. Phil," I snort. Not wanting him to think there are self-esteem issues, I say, "Being ordinary isn't the worst thing to be in this world, and besides, I'd rather be average than arrogant. I'm really okay with it."

"That's exactly your problem."

Chapter 16

Mary Anne has become a repeat client, coming to me for a couple of new outfits and a number of clothing items requiring alterations after losing nearly thirty-five pounds. Her nearly completed wedding dress remains in my workshop, ready to be tailored down as many sizes as required a week before the ceremony next spring. But tonight, Mary Anne is here to drop off folded yards of wool, spools of thread, and buttons for a winter coat inspired by the one in the ice-skating scene from *The Man Who Came to Dinner.*

Emily is hanging around at my house after dropping off Bailey and Kelsey. She doesn't even take her leave when Mary Anne arrives.

"Can I get you both a cup of tea?" Emily offers as Mary Anne takes a seat on the sofa. "I'd love to stay and find out what you're making with those gorgeous buttons, if ya'll don't mind."

"I don't mind," Mary Anne says before I can politely

inform Emily that my normal practice is to see clients in private. "Are you working for Grace?"

Oh my God, do I really have to explain how Emily is related to me again?

"She's just a family friend," I say without thinking.

"Aw! That's so dang sweet," Emily squeals while she purses her lips and thumps the palm of her hand over her heart. "You have no idea how nice it is to hear you consider me a friend."

My face flashes the immediate effects of a shock-and-awe surprise attack. "I . . . I don't . . . we're . . . we're . . . I mean, we have the best interests of our children in all this," I stammer.

"Of course, of course," Emily grins, happily ignoring everything I said after calling her a friend. "We're in this together, of course."

Mary Anne looks confused, but I pick up a hint of bemused acknowledgement in Emily's favor. I'm ready for all non-residents to exit my home, but it's apparent they aren't going anywhere, especially after questions about the coat lead to the wedding dress and a spirited ranking of what they include in their list of the top five Bette Davis movies. Then there are the follow-up questions about the engagement, wedding plans, and Herbie.

I return from the kitchen carrying a tray balancing two cups of decaffeinated Earl Grey tea with splashes of milk, the sugar bowl, spoons, and a plate of almond shortbread cookies as Emily admires Mary Anne's engagement ring. It's bling at its finest and most sophisticated, an art deco crossover gold and platinum ring with over a carat of diamonds set at an angle so the sparkle will never go unnoticed on her finger.

"It's stunning," Emily whistles admiringly. She dips a cookie into her tea. "I've never seen anything like it."

"It was custom made," Mary Anne blushes, holds her hand out, and tests Emily by acknowledging, "to fit my finger."

"That middle rock alone must have cost your fiancé a small fortune." Emily doesn't know she passes with flying colors. "He has excellent taste in jewelry and women."

"Sometimes I'm embarrassed to wear a ring that costs more than some people's cars," Mary Anne admits. She scoops sugar into her tea and stirs vigorously. "He has good friends who have a passion for finding one-of-a-kind antique jewelry to sell in their shop. They helped him pick out this ring after he told them how we met and why I was the one he wanted to spend the rest of his life with. It's so romantic and sentimental that it's easy to focus on that instead of the expense."

"Well, Herbie sounds like a gem of a man," Emily exclaims and giggles at her own joke. "What's his last name?"

"Heith. His first name is Herbert, but I call him Herbie."

"Mary Anne Heith, that has a nice ring to it." Emily

again laughs at her own joke. "And how did you meet Mr. Heith who put a ring on it?"

Emily's sincere interest in Mary Anne makes me think it might've been entirely possible we'd be good friends under different circumstances. Even though she's been granted an excessively unfair distribution of desirable qualities, she is quite likeable. I noticed at our first encounter she does more asking than talking, and it is the same tonight. She asks a question, listens and hears the answer, and then waits for non-verbal cues to know when and how to continue. Emily has made Mary Anne the star of the conversation without making her feel she's being interrogated.

"Herbie grew up in Carroll, Iowa but he moved to Des Moines when he was in his late twenties to start a career in pharmaceutical sales and coursework at the AIB College of Business. He ended up juggling work, school, and family obligations that forced him to commute back home on the weekends. It started to take a toll on his health, but after receiving a sizeable inheritance from his grandfather's estate, he could afford to focus solely on completing his degree and having a social life, which made it possible for him to meet me.

"I didn't have much of a social life or many friends. I got this email about the "piss-poor level of customer service" one of my customers received when she ordered an ice cream cake for her granddaughter's birthday party. It took a while, but I worked everything out. The customer, Rose, and I started texting and emailing. She asked if I wanted to do something called 'contra-dancing.' I thought Rose might not want to be friends with me if I mentioned all my limitations and insecurities, so I flat out rejected her first invitation. But Rose knew what I looked like. She'd seen me. And she said it was a perfect event for single women because, as she understood it, no one was ever left out from the line. Every folk dancer was guaranteed a partner.

"Neither of us realized someone had to invite you to join the dance line.

"I found myself fuming from the sidelines as Rose never left the dance floor, and I was forced to stand awkwardly alone and lean against one of the floor-to-ceiling barn beams because the seating didn't seem sturdy or wide enough to support me.

"I was ripping myself a new one for being so desperate for friends that I put myself in the worst possible nightmare situation—judged and rejected at the school dance as a grown-up. Then this guy makes his way over to me and asks if this was my first time contra dancing. I was suspicious of his motives at first, but before I knew it, we had been talking effortlessly for over an hour. That was when he asked me to dance, and I happily accepted his invitation."

"He likes to dance?" Emily asks. "That man's a keeper for sure!"

"We've been together ever since." She flashes her

signature light-up-a-room smile. "Rose turned out to be awful. She only wanted a friendship to try and steal my business, but it all worked out in the end. I don't have many friends, but I have a best friend because of her."

Emily's phone buzzes, and she quickly scans the message before informing us, "Didn't realize it got so late. Tomorrow's a workday, so I should really scoot, but I've got a fab idea."

I know that text is from Marc, a harsh reminder of why I can't and won't ever be friends with Emily Brandt. I can feel my lung tissue crumpling into a tight ball in response to the stress from what I imagine he has typed.

"Where do you work?"

"I'm a social worker at Mercy."

"You are?" I gasp. "I thought you were a music teacher."

"I used to and can teach private music lessons, but I'm putting my master's degree in social work to good use," she adds modestly, "which was my back-up plan if I didn't make it as a musician. Since I wasn't good enough, this is what I do to pay the bills. I love it. Maybe more so than being on stage with Celine Dion, but don't ever tell her I said that." She winks mischievously.

"You know Celine Dion?" Mary Anne hiccups and squeaks at the same. "Wow! Wow! Woweeeeee! You actually were close enough that you could touch her? I love that woman!" She can't help herself from belting out hit-and-miss notes with lyrics from "It's All Coming Back to Me Now."

Unveiling this part of Emily's past life not only keeps my uninvited guest from moving towards the door, but also brings Bailey and Kelsey out of their rooms to join the impromptu karaoke night. Bailey brings Celine to the party via YouTube on her laptop, and I am now living out my own worst nightmare.

Between their theatrical renditions of the *Titanic* theme song and "If You Asked Me To," Emily suggests, "I think all us girls should get together once a week for a bit o' fun—go for coffee, bowling, see a chick flick, whatever. But just us, no boys."

Everyone but me wholeheartedly agrees to Emily's horrific idea.

"And speaking of boys, I'd better go. Birch's been fast and furiously texting me because I promised I'd bring him a Big Mac meal for dinner, and that was nearly four hours ago. Thank God there's a twenty-four-hour McDonald's on my way home 'cause my kid's a rarin' to turn me in for neglect."

Bailey finds "Goodbye's (The Saddest Word)" to play in the background as Mary Anne and Emily gather their belongings and get ready to leave, but not before Mary Anne throws out, "I just heard about this new place in West Des Moines that hosts group painting classes. We should all go."

As the Brush with Greatness class dates and times are quickly researched and confirmed online, I absolutely cannot believe how bizarre my life has become. Emily and Celine taking center stage in my living room is not what I imagined for my grown-up self. Being of a mature age was supposed to include reaping the rewards of following the rules and making good choices, so I'm struggling to understand where I've gone wrong to end up agreeing to a Friday night date with my daughters, the mistress, and a client.

Emily is to blame. She's making things messy and complicated, not unlike an experiment I tried with a Brazilwood extract to transform a bolt of off-white silk chiffon into the perfect shade of red for a formal gown to be worn at a Valentine's Day charity ball. In heavy-duty plastic buckets filled with water and dye, the scarlet mixture bled its way into the fabric fibers until no traces of its former color were visible.

This is exactly what Emily is doing to me. She's creeping into my life, permanently altering the original into something I would prefer to keep as is—as it was—and I need to quickly figure out how to keep her from destroying the family I had and always wanted before I either accept this as my new normal or, God forbid, I end up being friends with the woman.

Chapter 17

During my last session, I spent the majority of my time crying and finally felt comfortable enough to call my therapist by her first name. Beth has been paid to listen to complaining and crying, which I'm sure is boring for her and useless to me. I still do not know how to save my marriage. If I continue to carry on aimlessly in these sessions, it's going to be a complete waste of time and money. Therefore, at 3:32 a.m., mid-insomnia attack, I wrote down a list to take with me today so nothing is skipped or missed.

I miraculously arrive a couple minutes early, slightly out of breath from running up the four flights of stairs and down to the end of the hall. There isn't a receptionist for the office. A nondescript framed sign hanging on the wall by the door instructs you to buzz in and then sit until your therapist comes out and retrieves you from the waiting room.

Once the audio signal grants me permission, I enter into the oceanic oasis where six other patients have already arrived. I hate this part the most—picking my seat and hoping I don't see anyone I know for fear of them finding out I'm in need of psychological assistance.

I also can't stand the ocean music playing in the background. It tortures and taunts my bladder, but there is no point going to the bathroom, as it defeats the point of rushing to get here on time. This is confirmed when, before I can sit down, Beth opens the secondary door to greet me and lead me into her office. Splashes of yellow, green, and grey run through the room centered around a starfish theme. Beth apologizes for the obstacle course left over from her previous client, a child, and moves the Fisher-Price activity table to the side. I find my way over to the beige loveseat with throw pillows stenciled with words of affirmation.

Beth opens with, "So tell me, was there something that popped into your head as you drove here that you'd like to discuss?" She moves her reading glasses from the rim of her nose to the top of her head, the turquoise oval frames resting like a queen's crown in the swirls of her short white hair.

I set aside my list to answer her question. "How funny you would ask me that because on my way here, I had a wish pop into my head that I could go back in time to fix what I was doing wrong before Marc started to drift away. It doesn't seem fair that I was never given a warning he was so unhappy with me."

"And what do you think you would do if you could time travel?"

I'd stop my heart from breaking. Why can't Marc just give me a chance to make it right between us? *Why? Why? Why?*

Damn it, I'm not keeping to today's plan.

"I wish we'd never met," I hear myself saying. "If I knew it would end up like this, I never would've married him."

She waits.

"That's not true," I sniffle "I knew I wanted to marry him after he called me out for being a fake foreign exchange student."

Beth cocks her head at "fake foreign exchange student." I barrel forward lest we get caught up in more of my pre-Marc life.

"It's Emily," I say, "I'd make it so he never met her. Even though he met her first. When Marc called home to tell his family I was coming to Thanksgiving, I heard him say 'Yep, first girl since Emily to come to a family holiday.'

"And then he talked to his sister, Erika, about where I would sleep. He wanted to know if I could sleep at her house. She must have asked about me because Marc told her I wasn't another blond bimbo. He told her my Dad's side of the family was Scandinavian and my Mom's side has Irish, French, and English roots. But it didn't matter because I was adopted from Korea." I laugh a little. "And then he said, 'What? Why would I care if your friend is dating a Thai girl?'

"When he got off the phone, I asked if it was too late for us to spend Thanksgiving with my family instead. I was joking, but not completely."

"Marc kissed and embraced me tightly before he dropped me off at his sister's house the night before Thanksgiving. The house was the last place his family had all lived together under one roof. When their parents decided to downsize and move, Erika and her husband bought the place to raise their own family."

After a short pause to catch my breath I continued, "Erika is the female battle-ax version of Marc—shorter, wider, and less patient. Her eyelashes, stubby and light in color, always have at least three or four coats of jet-black waterproof mascara applied, which tends to overshadow all other facial features. A high ponytail wrapped in a colored hair band swings aggressively to and fro, no matter what she is doing. When she marches about, it is without movement in her knees and yet so fast-paced and aggressive in manner, it feels like if you dare fall behind, she'll spin around and kick you to keep up.

"I was Erika's first houseguest. She was seven months pregnant, living in chaos, and slowly sorting out the place. As an outsider looking in, you might say it was sweet that Erika had prepared Marc's room for me, especially since she hadn't finished the nursery or redecorating the master bedroom.

"She set his yearbooks in order and upright in the bookshelf, washed and made the bed up in his Star Wars bedding, placed his threadbare blankie with the puffy terry-cloth sheep on the chair, and left his beat-up Teddy Ruxpin by the pillow." I didn't want to stretch out the story for Beth, but the details were important. "There were cardboard boxes of his childhood belongings stacked against the wall, which she gave me permission to explore. She thought it might be fun for me to rummage through them so I could piece together the kind of kid he was. On the surface, she was polite and thoughtful, but there were jagged shards of unfriendliness piercing through her welcome that I didn't know how to take or interpret.

"She nudged me toward the desk and directed my attention to the assortment of photographs pinned to the cork board above. They were all of Emily and Marc—the two of them at the freshman dance, debate practices and tournaments, with the entire family, some of the family or with random kids they knew at one time or another. There were pictures of Emily as Eliza Doolittle in *My Fair Lady*, Nellie in *South Pacific*, and her breakout performance as Laurey in *Oklahoma!* with neatly cut out copies of newspaper reviews stuck together with a red thumbtack posted near the corner. What looked like more recent pictures of Emily at the beach with her friends and other candid shots of Emily having fun in several different countries were also included in the scrapbook shrine."

I stop for a moment. Beth leans toward me encouraging me to continue.

I take a deep breath and blurt out, "She said, 'I thought it might be fun for you to see Marc's first love.'" I sniffle again. "Yeah, right.

"I felt her watching me for a reaction, and I tried to be cool, but I blushed anyway.

"Erika told me that he was madly in love with her. She broke—no, she obliterated—his heart into a million-zillion pieces. She was,"—I make finger quotes—"too talented, beautiful, and driven to be tied to anyone back then. She told me Marc and Emily had kept in touch for a while, and she handed me their letters."

Beth raised her eyebrows in surprise. She asked, "What did you do then?"

"I desperately wanted to be gracious. I tried to compliment both Emily and Erika by telling her that I loved anyone who was special in Marc's life. I even said that I hoped to meet Emily someday and thank her for breaking up with him so he could make room in his heart for me.

"She told me Emily was one of Celine Dion's backup singers, and then said if I wanted to get in touch with her, I could ask her and Marc's mom if she had a current address because she kept in touch with Emily's parents.

"I don't think I ever really forgave Erika for putting tall, gifted, blonde, and perfect Emily in Marc's old bedroom for me to view and compare."

Beth sat back in her chair.

I confessed, "When Marc and I talked about it later he was a hundred percent positive Erika meant well—there was no way she wanted me to feel insecure and ugly. Emily was engaged, and the only time he heard from her was at Christmas when she sent a card, and it was always addressed to the family, not to him exclusively. Emily was talented, but she was also incredibly selfish and self-absorbed—qualities he despised. He promised he didn't have any residual romantic feelings for Emily. Even though there was something in the way he looked at her in the photos that fired up fits of jealousy, I told myself it was the magic of an impulsive first kiss, a first love ecstasy, the thrill of being each other's first intimate relationship—it was merely a milestone connection. She may have been his first, but I was his forever love. This is what he told me, and I believed him."

I crumple up my damp tissue. My eyes are completely dry now. I throw the Kleenex into the garbage can next to Beth, making a perfect basket. "I also believed him later, when he told me it didn't mean anything that he accepted her friend request. She was one of a million high school friends who invited him to reconnect via Facebook. I was just being paranoid, kicking up a fuss about his regular check-ins and likes of Emily's hourly posts of updates and pictures. After all, he didn't keep it a secret and, since we were Facebook friends, I could see all of his activity.

"Even though my gut had it right from the start, I was caught completely off guard when Marc announced he had fallen back in love with Emily and was moving out. I assumed our marriage vows were safeguarded by going to church, having two children, a joint bank account, a house with both our names on the mortgage, and 'I love you' said every day. It seemed out of character for Marc to abandon his conservative family values. I thought it must have been a temporary lapse in judgement brought on by an old-fashioned mid-life crisis—a fear of dying—and running back to recapture his youth by picking up where he left off with an old flame."

I fiercely fought back the inclination to dissolve into tears again. "I'm fully prepared to forgive him. He needed a reason to give himself a break from the duties of fatherhood and marriage. I can understand why he would need a breather from being constantly bombarded by female hormones with no place to escape in his own home. All that matters to me is getting Marc back with us, to resume where we left off, but make it better."

Chapter 18

The pause speaks. I am a delusional wackadoodle. Beth does not say that I am nuttier than a fruit cake, but only because she is a complete professional. Emily has moved to Iowa. With her child. Into my husband's apartment. Emily and my husband sleep in the same bed.

"I knew I loved Marc more than he loved me when we married. I made up for it by making it easy for him to stay—smoothing every little relational wrinkle, shaving off every bit of me that caused friction. As long as we both loved each other enough, what did it matter who loved more?"

It was like a scab begging to be picked at. "Marc is not going to come back to sleep next to me now that he sleeps next to her. He's traded up. I am store brand ibuprofen and she's goddamn Advil. Plus she sings. All for a cheaper price—one kid instead of two. No crazy midwestern clan. No lace-covered bedroom. She gets places on time and does not cover every surface with thread and fabric and pattern pieces even though she has a whole studio for that in the basement. She doesn't beat him at HORSE even when she is intentionally trying to lose. She is not driven irrationally insane by the neighbors' lawn decor."

Beth looks at her watch. "I'm afraid that's all the time we have today."

I think she really is afraid. She's hiding it well, but she is worried. She walks me to the door and says, "You know, you don't have to stick to every two weeks. I could make time for you next week as well. Lots of my clients come every week during times of extra stress."

God bless her heart says Emily's southern-midwestern mutt of an accent in my head. *God bless her heart.*

"Next week is pretty packed," I say, "But it's good to know I can come in if I want to."

Honestly, I don't know that I should come back in two weeks. I'd much rather not hear my own crazy mouth, let alone have an extremely well educated and observant listener.

When I get home, I almost trip over a gift left outside our front door. My heart skips a beat or two, hoping it's from Marc, which considering the revelation I just had is more proof that I am delusional.

The girls are home already, and Emily is sitting at my kitchen table humming and encouraging the girls to finish their homework.

"Gra-ace!" she exclaims with a music that suggests that seeing me is the best part of her day. Me. Her boyfriend's wife. I am not the only one who is a few crayons short of a box in this situation.

"What's that?" Kelsey points to the gift bag in my hand.

"Is it for one of us?" Bailey asks.

"I don't know yet. It was outside the door."

"Can I open it?" Kelsey jumps up and down.

"Knock yourself out." I pass the bag over to her.

Bailey opens the card. "It's from Ian." She holds it out. "For you."

Kelsey carefully lifts a bonsai tree with its roots firmly planted in a glazed cobalt blue ceramic pot. The ornate greeting card has a cherry tree in blossom delicately cut into the front cover and inside is a line of ornate Japanese hand painted character. Underneath Ian has written:

Dear New Neighbor aka Grace,

This roughly translates as "Even Buddhist teaching scrolls have brush slips." In my case, the scroll was a business school brochure and the brush slips were intentional!

Thank you for not judging me harshly for one of my biggest mistakes and treating me to lunch the other day to celebrate my fresh start. I hope you will let me reciprocate, but in the meantime, here is a little something to express my appreciation for making me look good in front of the board chair.

Warmest regards,

Ian aka New Neighbor

Ian's handwriting is a work of art and the sentiment is spot on. His gift is generous and thoughtful, but I'm an ungrateful recipient.

"Booooooring!" exclaims Bailey. "I thought it was going to be something cool, but it's so not."

"Can I have it, Mom? Please? Please?" Kelsey begs me. "You keep the card. I want the bonsai for my desk. Please, please, please?"

"Take it. It's yours, sweetheart."

I put the gift and card in the same category as his garden décor. However, I do make a mental note to thank him for his thank you.

Kelsey runs upstairs to squirrel away her treasure.

"I bet it'll be dead in a week," Bailey says. "You have to, like, prune it, and take it out of the pot and trim the roots and stuff. He totally overestimated you, Mom."

"Gee, thanks."

Emily's face folds into perturbed lines. "Your mom is a smart woman, young lady. And hard working and responsible. You give her some respect."

Bailey looks from Emily to me quizzically.

"My general airheadedness has been the subject of good-natured teasing between Marc and me for so many years . . . She wasn't being disrespectful, just teasing," I explain.

Somehow this makes her delicate little face wrinkle up

even harder. Like a fairy crossed with a pug, so cute it's ugly and a little unnerving.

She leaves not long after that, before I can begin a passive-aggressive midwestern whisper campaign to make her believe she's unwanted.

I head to the grocery store. The list is useless at keeping me organized. In the cereal aisle, I remember I need cheese. I return to the dairy section and throw packages of shredded mozzarella cheese in the cart but forget the ricotta. And then when I'm in the bakery, I realize I missed picking up not only bottles of salad dressing, but spinach leaves as well. Now I'm standing in the middle of the frozen food aisle not knowing why I'm here.

"Grace?"

I startle, surprised to find myself face to face with Mary Anne.

"Hi. How are you? Is Herbie here with you?"

"Oh no. He hates grocery shopping," she excuses his absence. "He's either at the gym or Home Depot. Anywhere to avoid being here."

She aims and tosses a bag of frozen peas so that it lands next to a couple of Lean Cuisine meals. There is an invisible line dividing her cart into two sections. At the front, there are packages of peeled baby carrots, stalks of celery, apples, oranges, and bags of lettuce beneath an assortment of lightweight items with earth-colored packaging boasting of their fiber and vitamin content. Pressed and stacked at the back under the child's seat is the section of items that are fun for the taste buds but bad for medical checkups. My eyes are drawn to the party-size bags of M&Ms, a variety bag of Hershey's miniatures, a couple packages of Pepperidge Farm Milanos, three bags of vanilla cupcake goldfish crackers, and a tub of Twizzlers.

"Some of this is for Herbie," she defends her sugar-packed purchases. "He's skinny as a toothpick and doesn't need to diet like me."

I place my hand on top of hers, give it a gentle squeeze, and say softly, "You don't owe me or anyone else an explanation for what you buy. I'm not judging you, I promise. Even if all of that is for you, it doesn't change the fact you're going to be a stunning and gorgeous bride on your wedding day if I have anything to do with it."

None of what I say is a lie. All I see is a beautiful spirit struggling to be set free from indescribable pain. I'm determined every stitch of her wedding garment will shelter her from harmful elements. And as she steps into the dress of her dreams, my wedding wish is that her past will lose its power to inflict shame and self-hatred. It's a lot to ask of one dress, but I have absolute faith that it can be done.

"Thank you," Mary Anne says with a smile. "You truly are my real-life fairy godmother."

Chapter 19

"The problem is that I am who I want to be when I'm with Marc!" I snap at Mathew over the phone. And then I start crying.

Mathew makes a strangled sound and says something along the lines of "don't cry."

"Screw you," I hiss. "I'll cry as much as I want."

"Sorry, just, hold on, I'll be there—Just don't wake up the girls."

It is that time of night when I feel most vulnerable. Not midnight or three a.m., but ten, when I wash the dishes and brush my teeth and call Mathew in case he's started drinking again. I'm sure I would be able to hear it in his voice if he did.

By the time he arrives, I am no longer crying. I'm drinking coffee. I'll sleep when I'm dead.

He arrives loaded down with AE chocolate milk and Oreos. When he gives me a hug, I feel a half empty pack of cigarettes in his front jacket pocket.

"I thought you were quitting," I say while scrunching my nose in disgust.

"Too stressed this month. Can't do it."

"It's a disgusting habit, Mathew. Go get the patch or gum and quit."

"Hey, you try dealing with Nadia and all her bull. If you experienced a second of it, you'd be amazed I'm not smoking crack cocaine."

"You need to make a permanent break from her craziness, my darling." I kindly suggest what Christina has a million times but try not to be as mean about it.

"I could say the same for you, big sister. You know I could always kick his ass for you."

"I appreciate the offer, but I'm going to decline. Again. I could always beat up Nadia for you, though."

He shakes his head and smiles, sure it is a joke. It isn't.

Mathew has never been the steadiest. He loves his family with all his heart but doesn't feel quite the same way about himself. He got involved with Nadia during some of the most drug-addled years of his life. And then Nadia got pregnant. Nadia dropped the drugs and alcohol like a hot brick, and Mathew had been sober four months by the time Jacob was born. For a moment there, it seemed like Baby Jacob might save them both.

Nadia stayed sober—but not faithful. I don't know that she ever loved Mathew. He seemed to feel honored that she was even there, and assumed he deserved whatever treatment he got. He did not—and that is not how relationships work. He started drinking again when Jacob was three. Which Nadia claims is why he doesn't remember the talk where he agreed to an open relationship. Mathew was happy to be dumped on by her, but he saw monogamy as non-negotiable.

And so they have been on again off again since. Which makes figuring out custody a real bitch. Mathew is soberish and employedish most of the time.

Nadia has remained drug and alcohol free and is a talented and fully employed tattoo artist. She gifts Jacob with battery-operated toys, plushies by the busload, and the newest gaming systems and games, but Nadia does not, in my opinion, come through where it counts.

Jacob never goes hungry, but often the only thing he eats for a week is cereal, because that is all that he can make by himself. When I see Nadia with him, there are none of the behaviors that made my childhood better than average. No hugs, no hair tousling. He doesn't whine for her attention—he knows he won't get it, not truly. He is often in the care of Nadia's family members and not Nadia herself.

With custody entirely informal, Nadia is always changing her mind about when Mathew will see him, for how long, and under what circumstances. Sometimes Jacob lives with Mathew for months without seeing hide nor hair of his mother. Sometimes Mathew is only allowed a few minutes with his son a week.

The only lie in me offering to beat up Nadia for

Mathew is the "for Mathew" part. I'm with Christina on this one—he needs to grow a pair, drop the bitch, and take her to court for custody. I would beat her up for Jacob.

We eat on the sofa, sitting cross-legged side by side, watching reruns of *Three's Company*, snickering at the roommates' antics.

As kids, Mom forbade us to watch the sitcom because she didn't approve of single men and women living under the same roof. We also never would have been allowed to eat any of our meals away from the table. For a free spirit, she could be very old-fashioned. She believed children were *free to be you and me*, but also needed manners and morals. Breaking her rules made it feel like we were playing hooky—which is probably another reason why Mathew and I got such a kick out of watching Chrissy, Jack, and Janet.

By the time Mathew leaves, I am feeling calm and stable. Cheerful even. But I am not tired, even though it's midnight. So I check my email.

Advertisements and spam vastly outnumber client correspondence. After deleting these, there are three legitimate emails left to address. Two are inquiries: one is from a new homeowner wanting a quote for eighteen Roman shades to cover and adorn her windows and doors, and the other is from a parent who needs a winter-waltz dance costume for her seven-year-old daughter. After replying to both women who found my business,

Seams Perfect, from a flyer stapled on a grocery store's community board, I noticed Ian has sent me the newsletter from his new job.

In it, I find an article requesting volunteers who will be rewarded with authentic Laotian dishes served at the lunch break. And I have . . . a thought.

Most insomnia-induced ideas are one-night stands. They wander out from the shadows cloaked in seductive and tempting desires, impossible to resist. Once I decide to go home with this bad idea, I surrender to how good it feels in the moment. Usually, all that changes when the sunrise casts its light on the realization that it was a meaningless encounter best forgotten.

I turn off my computer, and I sleep on it. I wake up on cloud nine to discover I've slept for almost five hours and the thought has not lost its luster.

Marc is not leaving Emily. But Emily might still leave Marc. Seeing the family their relationship has destroyed didn't do the trick, but this woman is hanging out with her boyfriend's wife, for God's sake. I don't know why, but she must be lonely. Marc is handsome and charming—but emotionally intimate and supportive? No. I did all that work myself. And I'll do it again. I'm used to it.

But there's no reason for Emily to settle for it. If she met a sweet, widowed, kind, and gentle ex-samurai-looking kind of guy . . . why would she stick with Marc? She did say Ian was tall and handsome. He's also kind, funny, and charming in his own weird way. They have a lot in common, including holding jobs that help people in need and being single parents, each with a son to raise. Plus, they are both either oblivious of or undeterred by social norms and cues, brazenly inserting themselves into people's lives whether they're wanted or not. Both Emily and Ian are glass-is-half-full sickeningly cheery optimists. An article in *Psychology Today* (read twice in the therapist's waiting room) published findings that successful couples are ones that have a shared positive outlook on life. Experts in the field support my hypothesis. They would make the perfect couple. They are a rom-com waiting to happen.

True, Emily might end up as my neighbor, but I bet she could convince him to move the damn panda. Everyone gets what they want, and no one is rejected or unhappy. I won't have to sew Roman blinds for my kitchen window.

The genius of how I'm going about this is that it isn't obvious what I'm up to. I forward the e-newsletter to Emily and ask if she'd like to join me and the kids to build the Habitat for Humanity home for the Truong family. Marc has already informed us he will be gone that weekend and the following week for a tech conference in Seattle. He's never been interested in volunteering anyway. It's not that he isn't philanthropic, but he prefers to give money over time.

Within the hour, she replies with an enthusiastic yes including five paragraphs explaining why it will be good for Birch to be involved in an activity that is not self-serving, how his effort to form a new band has been all-consuming, bordering on obsessively selfish, and he needs opportunities to give back to others and the community to remind him that he is not the center of the universe. She also thinks I'd be interested to know she had been terribly sad her best friend wasn't able to visit that weekend, but she wouldn't have been able to join us if she hadn't cancelled so it worked out for the best in the end. Whatever the reasons they're in, it's all good.

I send Ian an e-mail asking if the five of us can sign up for his designated volunteer day. He calls because he feels badly Kelsey and Bailey can't work on the construction site, as the minimum age is sixteen, but there are three spots reserved for the rest of us. He offers to ask the partner family if they'd like help preparing and serving the lunch to the volunteers. I thank him and let him know the girls, especially Kelsey, would love helping with the meal if they are needed and won't be in the way.

We chat a couple more minutes about what is planned for our workdays before he politely excuses himself to direct a truck carrying donated furniture to the loading dock to move the new inventory into their charity resale store. It's pouring down rain, but at least there are plenty of volunteers who showed up so they can quickly move the inventory inside. That's his sunny take on the situation. See what I mean? Ian and Emily are kindred spirits. And I'm a genius.

Chapter 20

When Emily picks us up, we look like three bulbous clones of the Michelin Man stuffed in the back of her Prius, each of us prepared for the day's fluctuating temperatures by wearing several removable layers under our coats.

Before Iowa hibernates, this time of year undergoes an identity crisis known for causing what-to-wear confusion by bringing forth all four seasons each day. October is a particularly tricky month. Last year, Kelsey cussed Mother Nature out for forcing her to wear a heavy winter coat over her Halloween costume. The day started out sunny, but later turned snowy, making all the creative effort to go door to door as a samurai vampire a complete waste of time. That's just that way it is living here. Iowans will jubilantly warn, "If you don't like the weather, wait ten minutes. It'll change."

We drop Kelsey and Bailey off at the organization's headquarters. Ian arranged for a group of students to spend time with the Truong family cooking and serving a meal to thank supporters for their contributions. The volunteer coordinator and fundraiser took credit for and ran with this, as the media coverage benefited both of their departments. The girls will be just as busy as we are on the other side of the city.

Ian is waiting at the build site to welcome the twelve of us who showed up to work the morning shift. He gives a general shout out to the four of us who are his neighbors and takes a minute to praise me by name for recruiting Birch and Emily. I never want to be singled out in front of a group, but I hope by him doing so he notices Emily as the others have. She turns heads with her volunteer outfit—dark skinny jeans, trendy black Converse sneakers, long-sleeved T-shirt paired with a quilted biker vest, and an Oakland Raiders fitted baseball cap. She is dressed appropriately for working on a construction project, and yet looks like she could just as easily be on her way to stroll up and down Hollywood Boulevard. Adding to her intrigue is tall, spiky, sullen Birch, whom she leans against and hangs her arm around while listening to the opening remarks.

Ian finishes his speaking part and comes over to stand by us. I fake not being able to hear the speaker and move so Emily is closest to Ian. The site manager provides an overview of the goals and instructions. He then directs us to break into groups of three. Ian protests, but I insist that he join Emily and Birch in the living room under the pretense that I want to meet new people. I assign myself to what will be the bedroom for two of the younger daughters, working with a couple who eagerly tell me the name of the real estate company they own and run together as life and work partners.

The husband, Danny, a man in his early sixties, has gauzy grey hair swooping across his mostly bald head and falling out of his nostrils. The wife, Gabby, is an over-perfumed woman a good number of years younger than her partner. I'm guessing she's the second wife.

"We just love giving back to the community," Gabby enthuses. She is not dressed for a construction site. The shoes are closed toe and the sleeves are long, but the jeans are more like leggings, and the shirt has rhinestones on it, as do the shoes.

"Everyone should have a home," booms out Danny. I agree with the sentiment, but something about the way that he says it makes me think it might be the slogan for their real estate business.

"It takes so much time, energy, and money to build a house," Gabby says, as if she is being interviewed. "Not enough businesses invest in those who can't afford homes." She places a hand possessively on the pile of sheetrock we are about to hang.

"These things can't get off the ground without the financial support of companies like ours," Danny says.

"This is our first time volunteering," Gabby announces.

"We donated at the sponsorship level," Danny says. "And they asked if we'd like to volunteer as well." He says it like he'd really impressed them with his check-handing-over abilities.

"That's why our company is on all the signs around the house. They do that for all the sponsors."

"That kind of publicity is just good business," Danny agrees.

I'm not sure if they want me to compliment them for their selfless giving or for their shrewd commercial self-interest. I'm praying Emily is in the other room falling for Ian's good looks and charismatic personality.

"So Grace, I bet you were good at math in school," Danny says to me as the three of us look up at the ceiling. His breath emits the scent of burnt leaves and garlic as he speaks. "Because this is really a mathematics problem to be solved."

He is referring to figuring out the best way to measure, cut, and factor in openings for air conditioning vents and ceiling lights to hang sheets of drywall in the room. The site manager has told us an experienced volunteer team leader will join us shortly to lead the effort, but for some unknown reason these two want to start the job without assistance.

"This man here already knows I was never any good at math or science," Gabby admits in a high-pitched sing-song voice. "My best subjects were cheerleading and drama class, which won't be any use today. You two will just have to tell me what to do. Danny, you understand I'm hopelessly blonde and will need direction."

Her squeaky giggles and his bemused reaction constitute such a May-December relationship stereotype.
I want to respond with a gag-me-with-a-spoon gesture.
Instead, I pretend I'm searching for a good place to stash
my hat, scarf, and gloves. An industrial space heater in
the hallway is effectively warming the place, making me
regret my choice of putting on three tank tops under
my lined Simpson College sweatshirt and red polyester
puffer coat. It's only fifteen minutes into my shift, and
I'm already finding it is one too many layers. How long
can I stand being overheated in the same room with this
obnoxious duo? I create a word problem in my head:

*Danny can hang 4 sheets of drywall in 50 minutes. Gabby
can hang 4 sheets of drywall in 6 hours. Grace can hang 4
sheets of drywall in 30 minutes. How long will it take for
the 3 of them to hang 4 sheets of drywall together?*

The funny thing about Danny is he looks exactly like
my ninth-grade algebra teacher whom I didn't like either.
Mr. Neer scheduled a special meeting with my parents
to discuss my quiz scores and missing homework assignments. I barely had a passing grade for the semester.
It was his opinion I was purposely failing, that I understood the concepts and process, but didn't want my
peers to know I did and therefore exhibited disrespectful
behavior.

I "made a big show" of not knowing the answer when

it was my turn at the blackboard to solve the assigned problems. Yet he overheard me swiftly calculate how much gas could be purchased with only $20.00, with gas sold at $.98 per gallon and how much money needed saving if my friend moved to L.A. and her car got twenty miles to the gallon. It didn't make any sense why I was performing so poorly in his class. When my parents sat me down to discuss the matter, Dad asked if it was a clash of personalities or truly ineptitude. I claimed both and ended up with a C- in Mr. Neer's class.

The answer to my most recent word problem is *way too stinking long.*

Chapter 21

I go find our volunteer supervisor. He has just arrived and is dusted with feathers.

"Ah gosh, I'm sorry," he apologizes as he follows me up the stairs. "This morning I came downstairs, and Marvin was rolling around in feathers from sofa cushions and throw pillows he chewed up. My wife went ballistic. The couch is the first piece of new furniture we ever bought, and Marvin's a service dog in training. I don't think he's gonna graduate the program. He's probably just gonna be the family dog, unless my wife kills him first."

"Hang in there," I reassure him. "Our dog, Moby, also went through a maddening phase testing the strength of his jaws and teeth. At a family gathering, I thought it was the crunching of gravy bones we were hearing from the other room, but later discovered it was, in fact, Moby chomping on Marc's grandmother's false teeth. I almost traded him in for a goldfish that day."

The supervisor, whose name is Brad, laughs and says he works for his dad's drywall business, so he's hoping he can make Marvin the company mascot and take him to work so they can both stay out of trouble with his wife during the day.

It is obvious Brad has been shaken up by his morning because the instructions he gives don't make any sense for the project we are doing.

"Shouldn't we measure vertically from the floor to the center of the air conditioning duct in the wall, transfer the measurements to the sheet of drywall with a tape measure and mark an X where those two measurements coincide?" I ask, hoping I don't sound like a know-it-all.

"Sorry, right. That's right," he apologizes and says approvingly, "You have a job at MacAllister and Son anytime you want it."

"I just am thinking of approaching it in the same way I would in my own work," I explain and include a follow-up question to hand the reins back over to him. "Do we need to measure the center-to-center distance between wall studs as well?"

"Told you she'd be the one to figure out our mathematics problems," Danny boasts to his dingbat wife, Gabby, proud of his ability to size someone up just by looking at them.

Happily, I don't have to interact much with Danny and Gabby. They hang a couple sheets of drywall, then wander out of the room for extended periods of time doing who knows what, coming back every so often with updates about the progress going on in other parts of the house. Neither one of us asks or, quite frankly, cares if they want to help finish our assignment. We leave them to spend their time volunteering as they wish.

The rest of the morning goes by quickly. I enjoy talking to Brad about his Chocolate Labrador, work, and recent Hawaiian honeymoon trip while we create the walls and ceilings.

He and his dad started their drywall business knowing they wanted a charitable component included in what they did for a living. They first heard of Habitat for Humanity from watching an episode of *This Old House*. They admired their mission enough to volunteer one Saturday and have been coming back ever since. As long as they are able, they plan to donate materials and time, as it has never felt like an obligation, but a privilege to work side by side with families like the Truong family.

"You would not believe what this family has gone through. Changvang was asked to speak at a fundraising event. My family and friends, we all cried our eyes out, even my badass, tough-as-nails dad." Brad shakes his head as he tells me the story.

"Soldiers attacked their village with grenades and guns, forcing them to escape into the jungle. In constant fear of being tracked down and killed, his wife drugged their children to keep them from giving away their location with their frightened and hungry cries. They kept moving and survived on whatever scraps they could find to eat. After many days of traveling under these brutal conditions, Changvang's blind and elderly mother fell ill. One night, overcome by fatigue and resolve, she said to her son, 'My life is at the end. Your life is just beginning. I'd rather die here,' and begged to be given enough opium to end her life. Changvang was given the terrible responsibility of dispensing the drug, watching and waiting for her to die, tenderly placing her body in the hole he dug, and leaving her behind.

"After many days, they reached the river on the border where many others attempting to escape had drowned. It was reported that farmers would sometimes strip the dead bodies of silver and other valuables, then heartlessly toss them back into the river. Changvang, along with the remaining family members, made it across the river to the refugee camp. Then he was accepted by America to come with his wife, daughter, and infant son as refugees. Since ending up in the Midwest nearly a decade ago, he and his wife have overcome adversity and worked hard to achieve a better life for their children."

Brad finds and plays the YouTube video from the event on his phone, and I hear and feel Changvang's heartbreaking closing remarks: "Since the late morning when I put my beloved mother in that hole and covered and hid her body with dirt and branches in the middle of the jungle, I still remember her favorite food, her voice, and I still think about her all the time. The last thing she said before dying in my arms was that the hardship would be gone with her so my future would be brighter. She loved us so much she was willing to go so we could stay in this world. As I look out with a grateful heart and see all of you in this room who came out tonight to support this worthy organization, I know my mother is thanking you for helping us and other families make our future brighter with a home we can call our own."

There is a different feeling of satisfaction associated with this unpaid hourly job. It takes me by surprise when I need to find a tissue to wipe my eyes as we step into the middle of the where two of the Truong children will study, dream, and play.

The moment of satisfaction for a job well done is abruptly broken by Dan and Gabby. The shuffled clomping of her Marc Jacobs gemstone buckle and block-heeled boots (every female volunteer hears the story of how she found this fancy footwear marked significantly below the original 540-dollar price tag) announces they are on their way.

"There she is," Danny shouts as he bursts into the room. There are three other volunteers following behind Gabby. She smiles and points at me. I wonder if they need help with their drywall too.

"Here are a couple members of the family who have unexpectedly come out to help," a young volunteer wearing a red volunteer T-shirt and black striped stocking cap broadcasts loudly. He's also wearing a black sweatshirt underneath the T-shirt with its sleeves and hood sticking out the arm and neck holes. I bet he is uncomfortably warm.

As I wait for the purpose of this mini mob's entrance, a crinkly eyed woman who has two dark braids hanging well below her shoulders steps forward to speak on their behalf. "They still have difficulty expressing themselves in English, so we need you to come and translate for us."

Chapter 22

"Do they speak Spanish?" I ask with a straight face. "I took a couple classes in high school to fulfill a language requirement, so I might be able to help out with basic phrases and words like *hola* and *¿Dónde está el baño?*"

I see the guy at the back sheepishly turn as if he was never part of this group and walk away. The four remaining don't know what to do with the silence. Danny gives a disappointed look, as if to say he knows I could do better if I tried.

"I also tried learning French using Rosetta Stone tapes I borrowed from the library. Who knows? Maybe once I hear a couple words, it will all come back."

"Oh," stocking cap guy says, shifting on his feet uncomfortably to the right. "I . . . I think they probably don't speak Spanish . . . or French . . . I don't think so anyway."

"Guess I'm not the right person for the job then, but maybe there's someone else you can ask."

"Right, well . . . thanks anyway."

"Anytime. No worries."

Brad waits for everyone to leave before he bounces around and roars, "That was friggin' off the charts awesome! What friggin' idiots! I can't believe you were able to keep it together to put them in their place like that. Booyah!"

"I've had plenty of practice." I sound confident replying to his off-the-wall compliment, but my hands are shaking, and my stomach is twisted in knots.

We finish and make our way over to get lunch. I enter the conference room and see a *Register* reporter has taken Bailey aside to ask her if she thinks kids can make a difference doing volunteer work and, although unprepared, Bailey must be doing well. The reporter's head bobs up and down as he furiously records her answers. After the newspaper journalist finishes interviewing Bailey, he introduces her to two television reporters who also decide to focus on young people spending their free time volunteering in the community for their human-interest story clips.

Overall, the day is a resounding success. On the ride home, our kids are talking non-stop about what they did, how awesome it all was, and how they want to volunteer more in the future. Even Birch, who incessantly talks about how much he loved the food, also liked the building experience and would do it again.

"How was it working with Ian?" I ask Emily. "Is he fun or bossy?"

"I don't know," she answers. "We worked with this woman named Liz. She was absolutely fantastic."

Emily goes on and on about Liz, but I don't hear a word. What happened to Ian? Why didn't I ask where he was or how it went when we drove away after our shift was over? I guess I was too busy selfishly fuming about my own issues. Come to think of it, I didn't see him at the luncheon either. But this could have been because the organizers handed out random seating assignments to force mixing and mingling among strangers. What was the point of doing all this if those two didn't spend time together? I change my mind about the day and feel guilty, thinking this was a complete waste of time. But it was, based on what I wanted to accomplish.

Stupid one-night-stand ideas.

I forgot the clothes I stripped off and piled in the corner of the Habitat for Humanity bedroom. Ian emails, informing me he has everything and will get them to me in the next couple of days. His postscript is a complimentary summary of the feedback he received about us from various team leaders. In his last sentence, he says he owes me a pizza or a dinner of my choosing.

This gives me an idea. I invite my intended targets to our house for my own appreciation event before Marc is due to return from his conference on the west coast. Thrilled with a second chance to get it right, I take it as a good sign that Wednesday works with both of their schedules.

On Tuesday, Emily hangs around, watching me hem chiffon, which would have been a trial to my patience even without her demonstrating proper yodeling. Apparently the sweet little "lay ee odl lay ee odl-oo" Julie Andrews does in the *Sound of Music* don't even come close to right. It sounds a lot like vocal techno music to me. She leaves before dinner but calls again right after.

"I ran into Mary Anne MacDonald at the pharmacy and mentioned our plans tomorrow. She looked lonely, so I lied and told her you were planning on inviting her, but you must have forgotten because you were so busy, but now since we luckily ran into each other, I could do the inviting and asked if she was free. Mary Anne said yes, she didn't have plans, and there you go—I couldn't take back the invitation. Mary Anne looked really, really, really sad, and so I really, really, really, really was hoping including Mary Anne wouldn't be a problem."

"That's fine," I say, and it is, but I think my post-separation circle of friends is forming into a very odd bunch.

"Phew," Emily breathes for what I believe to be the first time since I answered the phone.

I immediately call Mary Anne to apologize and express my appreciation that Emily caught her just in the nick of time to extend the invitation.

Wednesday after school, I mix up pizza dough and let it rise. When it's ready to roll, I call Kelsey to come down and help me.

"Wouldn't it be easier to order these instead of going

through all this work?" she groans as she rolls the pizza dough into a flat circle on the counter. Flour dust covers her hands and arms.

"It won't be as special if we do the dial-and-deliver method. And as this is a thank-you party, it calls for the Hunter-family deluxe special, not Paul Revere's 100% Wisconsin Mozzerella Special."

"I can't believe Emily taped the five, six, and ten o'clock news. Do we really have to torture ourselves watching Bailey go on and on about how kindness and compassion do not belong to one specific age group if she isn't even going to be here? I don't think I can or want to listen to that sappy crap one more time. Once was more than enough."

I make noncommittal noises.

"Stupid old VCR," Kelsey mumbles.

While the world has long moved into the digital age, Marc keeps a VCR, for reasons neither Emily nor I can fathom. But the dang thing has finally earned its keep since Emily can use it to tape the news. We have been told by our children that there are easier ways to do this.

Kelsey and I finish assembling the pizzas but won't stick them in the oven until we're close to being ready to eat. Emily is the first to arrive and brings dessert, but not Birch. Birch and Bailey get to skip my gathering to see their friend perform at a local coffee shop's amateur open-mike night. Since I agreed to pick-up duty, Emily offered to drop them off before making her way over here. I open the door and quickly help by taking the VCR and one of the grocery bags she brought. She rushes ahead and drops the other overloaded canvas totes on the floor.

"I forgot to ask if Herbie was coming. Did Mary Anne say anything to you when you bumped into her?" I situate the VCR under our TV in the place where it sat until Marc moved out.

"No, but it sounds like he's always traveling for work, and she gets awfully lonely. I think this is why she looked so sad the other day." Emily gives me a hug after sliding a cake box onto the counter. I see it is a chocolate mocha coconut cake from a bakery I mentioned in passing that I wanted to try.

"Aww. I hate the thought of her being sad and lonely. Glad you invited her so she'll be with us tonight."

"It must be tough to be on her own so much, but at least she's got a wedding to plan."

"But it is a little odd we've never met him or seen any pictures, don't you think?"

"My guess is she's experienced some kind of childhood trauma which explains her struggle with weight and some of the other defense mechanisms she uses to protect herself from being hurt by others. I bet she doesn't take pictures of herself, even with Herbie. But don't say anything—it's just a guess."

Chapter 23

I am dumbfounded. Somehow Emily's eternally cheerful demeanor made me forget that she is not just intelligent, but observant and intuitive. Marc isn't good enough for her.

"Hey, are you talking about me?" Kelsey butts in, Ian and Caleb in her wake. "What do you guess?" Ian gives a round of hugs in the kitchen. He's an impulsive and inescapable hugger like Emily. He's clearly a better match for her than Marc. Good Lord, I have to save this woman from herself.

"Hey girlie, how'd ya guess we were talking about you?" Emily teases. "We heard a rumor you wanted to watch Bailey's TV debut fifty thousand times to make sure you don't miss or forget one word she had to say to her adoring public."

Kelsey rolls her eyes and pulls Caleb by the sleeve. "Let's get out of here before they really do hook up that thing and make us watch it."

Mary Anne rings the doorbell. Because she also read

the rave review by the local food critic in the Sunday edition of the paper, she has purchased a pink champagne cake from the same bakery as Emily. She jokingly suggests we use hers as the appetizer for our meal. We quickly agree this is an excellent idea. Half of the cake is sliced into hefty triangular wedges. The fact that we have purposely excluded Caleb and Kelsey from partaking in our pre-dinner party sends us adults into fits of giggles.

After the evidence has been hidden, I call the kids down. Emily's guilty gasp as she spots frosting on her nose in the wall mirror prolongs the merriment. She spins away from Caleb to rub it off with a paper napkin. The young ones are not privy to what is so dang hilarious, and as a result, the supposed adults are getting on their nerves. They choose to ignore our inexplicably immature behavior.

"How fancy!" Caleb exclaims as he holds up his personalized calligraphy place card. I made these for the table to make certain Ian and Emily sit side by side and fall for each other. I lift my champagne flute and lead a toast thanking Ian for an amazing Saturday.

"Where do you work?" Mary Anne asks as she fills her glass with more Prosecco from a pink glitter bottle.

Unfortunately, I didn't realize that by having Mary Anne sit across from Ian, they would engage in a lengthy conversation about their workplaces. No matter what I do, the conversation is divided into the following: Mary Anne and Ian, Caleb and Kelsey, and Emily and me. After dinner, Kelsey and Caleb impress us by shooing us out of the dining room so they can take care of the dishes. I can't interrupt Mary Anne asking Ian for details about making a donation even though I want to and am instead forced to half-listen to Emily as she connects the VCR to the television set.

"I'm glad Bailey isn't here because I wanted to show you something I noticed this morning," Emily says as she points the remote control towards the corner of the room. She pauses on a still frame of Bailey looking with puppy-dog innocence into the camera. I think this is when the reporter was waiting for her to answer the question about what she gave up on her Saturday to volunteer.

"Look here," she directs my attention to Bailey's neck, "above the collar bone. Do you see this little bump?"

I see it. My brain reacts with static fuzz blocking thoughts from coming or going. I'm filtering out most of Emily's sentences, but a jumble of words strung into incomplete fragments gets through: "you might want to," "probably nothing," "get checked," "better safe than sorry," "can get an appointment with," "don't worry." And the word I want to kick as far away from me as possible: CANCER.

I don't care anymore if Ian talks to Emily or anything else happens between the two. There is nothing more important than picking up Bailey and taking her straight to the hospital to find out if her cells are waging war against my baby. Emily must think tossing out statistics will ease my mind. But who cares if the survival rate is ninety-eight percent if it's caught early? It can't be very comforting to the two percent who don't make it. Flash-backs of Dad's last year are jumping forward from my memory bank. I start breathing in erratic spurts, and my vocal cords produce fluctuating squeaks, nonsensical whining, and whimpering at the same time.

Emily claps her hands in front of my face. "Stop it. Stop panicking. That won't help anyone."

And I do stop panicking. Emily hands over her laptop with several websites she has already pulled up for me to do some preliminary online research. I realize that she is not panicking now, because she has already panicked—possibly enough for both of us, considering the depth of the click hole she has fallen down.

She thanks the kids for cleaning up and, to shield them from what has just occurred, asks them to stay in the kitchen and pack three generously sized doggy bags. While they do this, a brief explanation is given to Ian and Mary Anne for my dithered state. I overhear Emily say the only reason why she brought the tiny lump to my atten-tion is she's currently working with young clients who are dealing with an early thyroid cancer diagnosis. Emily assures us Bailey is going to be fine no matter what, but first things first.

Emily won't let me drive and makes me promise not to say anything tonight. There is absolutely no need to cause worry when nothing can be done at this late hour. When she brings Bailey back home, I can't stop myself from running down the driveway and grabbing her as she gets out of the car.

"You're squishing me, Mom," Bailey moans and pushes me away. "Don't be such a drama queen. We're only an hour past your unreasonable curfew. I thought you were picking us up, so it's really your fault we're late."

Emily rolls down her window and calls me over to keep me from stalking Bailey. "Grace, I promise she's going to be okay. Look at me. I mean it. It could be absolutely nothing, and I'm being overly paranoid, but I have a lot of great contacts and even if it's something, we'll get the best care, okay?"

I blink back tears and nod. "Did you tell Marc yet?"

"No. I thought I'd tell you first and let you decide how to deal with him about this."

"Thank you," I whisper.

"Of course. Now get inside and act normal."

"Okay," I say and follow her directions.

Chapter 24

It was the first day of November when Mom and Dad went to Dr. Siegel's office to find out what was going on. They promised us it was nothing more than walking pneumonia that refused to walk away. Dad had repeatedly used this bad joke to avoid going to the doctor. But when the chronic dizziness, yellowing of his skin, and lumpy swollen glands flanking his Adam's apple wouldn't go away, Mom threatened divorce if he cancelled the appointment she made for him. He went—but let everyone know he was not happy about it.

He kicked up a bigger fuss when he found out that an X-ray, CT scan, and bloodwork couldn't be done in one appointment. Each technician was forced to politely listen to his unusually boisterous expression of his opinion that these costly tests were a scam to funnel monetary resources into a failing healthcare system and how he was now contributing to the problem, wasting time and money with multiple appointments for something so minor.

Dad insisted that the chronic cough had started shortly after the unwanted presence of Mr. Mewowgi and Clawdius, the scraggly kittens Mom rescued when they were tossed out of a truck window on a busy road. None of us believed for a second that the poor cats were to blame for his weight loss and fatigue, but he went to that follow-up appointment seriously convinced the doctor was going to tell his wife she needed to evict anything with dander from their home to alleviate his severe allergies.

Mathew and I were convinced he'd be hospitalized against his will to be given antibiotics intravenously because he had waited so long to be treated. We also knew that even if Dad was ill enough to require immediate medical attention, Mom would be the one who'd need the most care. The two of us offered to pick up soup and sandwiches so she'd have lunch and company waiting for her when she got back home. Amaya also believed a short-term hospital stay was inevitable and took time off from work to wait with us and help deal with our overdramatic mother.

We were surprised to see the two of them holding hands as they entered the kitchen where we were gathered. I knew something was terribly wrong from the expressions on their faces. The alarm clock on the counter marked the time in red as 11:18 when we received the news. Dad was facing stage IVB lung cancer. I initially thought that four was a good low number—everything is on a scale of one to ten, with ten being the worst, right?

Mom started to enlighten me, but she couldn't stop sobbing, making it impossible to understand a word she said. Dad took over and calmly explained what the stage actually signified. I angrily asked what sick-ass clown decided to number the stages from one to four instead of one to ten or at least one to five? Didn't anyone stop and consider this dimwitted numbering system had a good chance of multiplying the stress and confusion for the patient and family? It was infuriating to find out the number four accompanied by the letter *B* meant we were in the incurable hopeless stage.

This is what I think about as I listen to Marc's phone ring, waiting for him to answer.

I give him the short and sweet version of Emily's discovery and our concerns, knowing that when someone you love is in danger, being tactful is torture. Ripping the Band-Aid right off is the best course of action.

"I don't think we should make too much of Emily's hunch," Marc cautions. "She's just a social worker, and let's not forget she's a performer at heart, which influences how she sees things."

"I've got a gut feeling she's right."

He sighs, saying nothing for several minutes. I choose to remain silent as well.

"Take her in then, and we'll see who's right," he snaps.

I hear the phone being put down on a hard surface and then the unzipping of his toiletry bag.

"It won't do any harm getting it checked out," I hold my position, "but you're right, Emily's not a doctor. Let's hope she's got it wrong."

"I'm not worried." The electric shaver buzzes on and off. "Anyway, I have to get ready and go. I'll give you a call when I get back tomorrow." He hangs up without a goodbye. I look at the phone.

First thing in the morning, I make a doctor's appointment for Bailey.

I meet up with Amaya, Christina, Mathew, and Mom for lunch. This time it's just because we want to, not to mark a milestone of Dad's life. But we still eat at the A&W.

"Are you planning on inviting Marc's second wife to our Thanksgiving?" Christina goes straight for the emotional jugular as she squirts ketchup into a spiraled dollop by a pile of onion rings.

Amaya groans.

"Emily might get an invitation to our holiday dinners," I parry. Actually, Emily would fit right in with my family. "Bailey's life could be saved because she's in Marc's life." I'm able to refrain from bellowing out, "So there!"

"How so?" Amaya crinkles her forehead into skeptical lines.

"She may have identified an early sign of a serious problem."

"Oh?" Mom asks with such concern it stops her from taking a bite of her Coney Cheese Dog. Everyone else at the table looks just as puzzled. Now that I have their undivided attention, I explain Emily's concern.

No one interrupts my description of the bump on Bailey's neck. Amaya straightaway grabs my hand and holds it against the middle of her chest as I share my preliminary WebMD research about the causes, symptoms, and treatment of thyroid cancer. Christina pushes her plate aside to reach over the table so she can clasp my other hand.

"Well, fuck." Christina mutters.

Mathew gets out of his chair, crouches by my side, and rests his head against my shoulder.

Mom remains frozen in her chair but has the most dramatic response. "Shit! Shit! Shit!"

Everyone's jaws drop and it takes a moment for me to gather myself to say, "It's probably nothing to worry about, but I have to find out for sure."

"Of course you do," Christina, on the verge of tears, nods in agreement.

"I know they're going to ask about family history at the appointment," I slowly say as Mathew returns to his side of the table and my hands are released by my sisters. "And it's got me concerned."

"That cancer runs in our family?" Mom stutters out.

I take a deep breath. "In order for cancer to run in Bailey's family, it would have to come from me or Marc. They might want to know *my* medical history."

Mom's gasp at her faux pas is followed by rapid blinking, fluttering her eyelashes up and down. A paper napkin is pulled from the dispenser to swipe the surfaces below her eyes and nose. There are a couple of sniffles and a heavy sigh she releases for all to hear, but she will not look at any of us. Instead, she pulls at the petals of one of the fake marigolds while staring out the window.

"I've never cared about my biological parents, but this situation kind of calls for some information, don't you think?"

"What are you thinking? Doing an internet search? Like Mindy?" Christina says.

The four of us look at each other, confused.

"You know," Christina nods. "My client who—"

Amaya, Mathew, and I nod, so she doesn't have to finish the sentence and stir things up anymore.

"I was thinking the note left by the biological carrier of my DNA could be useful," I continue, keeping my voice gentle and undemanding. "The scrap of paper she placed in the box before abandoning me so I could have a better life. There might be a tiny chance there are clues left behind to help track down my medical history. The only reason I'm asking is to help Bailey and the doctors now. But also thinking ahead, as this information may be helpful if Bailey and Kelsey ever plan on having children of their own." I state my case and add, "Of course, I don't want grandchildren anytime soon," followed by a feeble chuckle at my own joke.

"Don't you have the one we passed around at the Homecoming Days?" Mathew asks. He passes a pack of tissues down the line to the other end of the table.

"It's a copy," I explain and gently make the request. "Mom, could you get the original note from my adoption records so I can borrow it for Bailey?"

Mom's face crumples. "No." She sniffs and raises her chin, tears glittering in her eyes. Generally, Mom is a free crier, but she is clearly attempting to keep the tears from falling.

"Mom," Amaya whispers tenderly, but firmly.

"No, I won't give you the original note."

"Mom!" Mathew barks at her.

"I won't because I can't."

"Why not?" Anger is starting to rise up and tear through my throat. "I hope it isn't because your insecurity is greater than wanting to help your granddaughter in her time of need."

"Is it because you've lost it?" Amaya asks for an excuse that isn't selfish.

"Because that note was made up. It isn't real."

Chapter 25

Shock circulates around the table at the same speed as a Formula One car racing around the track.

"What?"

"You heard me." Mom slowly pulls a tissue from the pack. She blows her nose and then confesses, "I asked the actress—you know, the one who played the White Witch in our annual holiday production of *The Lion, The Witch and The Wardrobe,* to help me translate what I wanted the note to say in Korean months before you were due to arrive from Seoul to the States."

"Why on earth would you do that?" Amaya gasps.

"Because I read countless stories of adopted children who struggled with the reason why they were given up, and I didn't want that for Grace. With Sin-Joon's help, I created a christening gift of closure."

"But you had no right . . . all these years . . . who does this kind of thing?" I struggle to string together coherent sentences.

"What does it matter?" Mom asks.

"Seriously?"

"I did you a favor! You were able to focus on living your life, not questioning the beginning point of your existence. It doesn't matter how you got here, you're here, and that is what I wanted you to know. Besides, it will be next to impossible to track her whereabouts. You were left in a box on the steps of a police station, taken to a countryside orphanage, and then transferred to a foster home where you stayed with this family until we adopted you. That's it. End of story."

"I don't know if I believe you."

"That is the truth, so help me God," she says matter-of-factly, holding her hand up as if she is taking an oath in front of a judge and jury.

"I want my records—everything related to my adoption. And there better not be anything missing or any fake documents in that file. If for any reason I think you've messed with anything in my records, you will regret the day you were born. I will do something equally as bad to mess with your life. I am so pissed off I can barely look at you."

"Grace, it's okay." Amaya pleads for me to sit back down.

"It is not okay," I shout in spite of being embarrassed that people are starting to stare. "You cannot tell me this is not a betrayal of trust, duty, and honor. I don't know if I'll be able to get over what you've done. It's that stinking bad. And let me tell you, Evelyn, if Bailey dies, so help me God, I will never ever forgive you."

I had never called my mom by her first name before. I instantly regret letting my temper get the best of me, but it's too late to take back my hateful words. Words that carry out a vengeful punch to the gut, but don't really carry truth. As it is no longer possible for me to be civil, I storm out of the restaurant and take immense pleasure in the tires squealing as I reverse and drive off.

* * *

Amaya calls later that night to check in and to let me know Mom has retrieved the document I requested from the attic. She dropped it off at Grandpa's house for me to pick up whenever I'm ready to do so.

Mom and Grandpa live ten minutes apart in bad traffic. Mom moved into our great-grandmother's house shortly after her passing. For the most part, the short miles separating them work to our advantage. Everyone and everything we need is within striking distance, making visits manageable and pleasant. However, there are often times when the ease of accessibility to each other's lives snuffs out niceties reserved for out-of-town guests.

"Don't be too hard on her, okay?" Amaya advocates on behalf of the matriarch.

"You agree what she did was outrageously horrendous, right?"

"Yes, but she feels horrible."

"Does she really?" I argue with my sister's lie.

"Yes, she's clueless, but she means well."

"Does she?"

"Oh Grace, we know who she is," she sighs in defeat. "We've always dealt with her antics one way or the other, so why would it be different this time?"

"But this time, it isn't annoyingly immature behavior we're dealing with. Making up a sacred document and then repeatedly flaunting the forgery at a holiday she made up to in order to supposedly honor the daughter she adopted is a cruel thing to do."

"I know, I know. But she loves you very much."

"She has a very strange way of showing it."

"Our mother is a rare bird, bringing great joy and sorrow wherever she lands."

"Yes, a crazy, self-centered cuckoo bird."

We agree to disagree about the punishment she deserves before saying good night. Amaya does have a point. One of our mother's crowning achievements was rescuing a dying theater company. It was clear that she recognized what made a great story. Even mom's costume designer, my beloved sewing mentor, who was loyal to a fault, believed Evelyn Solberg was crazy, but the kind of crazy that adds a magic sparkle to your life. It was the reason why Betsy and the other staff members tolerated their leader's erratic moods and decisions for as long as they did—and why my father was madly in love with her.

I wonder if or how he would have defended falsifying

the note. Did he know she asked one of her employees to do this?

For the first time since I started therapy, I look forward to going. My appointment is tomorrow, thank God. I laugh, thinking about the list of things I wrote down to talk to Beth about last time. I did not need one this time, that was for sure. I guess the upside of family drama is that you know what you're going to talk to your therapist about.

* * *

"Wake up Mom!" Bailey is on her knees shaking me by the shoulders. I can smell burnt toast and brewed coffee. She must have been making herself breakfast when she heard noises coming from my bedroom.

My eyes flutter open, and I hear myself gasping for breath. Kelsey runs to the other side of the room and jumps on the bed near my feet. They are both bouncing and shouting at me to stop dreaming.

Moby smears my cheek with dog snot and slobber.

"I'm up! I'm up!"

Kelsey crawls up towards the pillows to check if I am awake. Once this is verified, she curls up under the covers next to me.

"Are you okay?" She clings to my arm and nuzzles her head against my shoulder.

"You scared the life out of us," Bailey accosts me for

disturbing the peace. Moby, now bored by it all, jumps down to go check if food and water have magically appeared in his bowls.

"Sorry, just one of my nightmares." Still trembling, I apologize.

"Your therapy appointment is this morning, isn't it?" Bailey asks in the irritatingly authoritative way she does when she feels a need to take control of a situation.

"Yes, and your doctor's appointment is this afternoon."

"Can't you cancel? Or at least reschedule it for another day?" Bailey whines. "You've made it for the worst time. Now I'm missing two of my most important classes. And anyway, Dad says you're making a mountain out of a molehill."

Irritation is a better alarm clock than concern. I am now wide awake. Kelsey moves with me as I pull myself up and check the clock. There's plenty of time before it will become necessary to rush around.

"Well, you're going, and it's not only me who thinks you should be seen either."

"I know your dream was about me," Bailey snottily interrupts. "You are exactly like Grandma, always over-dramatizing every little thing."

"Oh my God! You did not just say that to me! You take that back right now!"

"Nope. It's true. You act just like her, and that's why you've gone all over-the-top about my tiny neck bump."

Kelsey slips out of my bed and gingerly tiptoes out

of the room. Bailey and I are left glaring at each other, but I catch a mischievous glint in the corner of her eye. I accept this as an apology and reward her with an affectionate headlock.

Bailey escapes from my tight embrace. As she scampers off, I call out, "I may be like my mom, but I promise you're going to grow up to be exactly like me. And I'm passing along the curse that has been passed down from mother to mother that you will have children just like you."

As she turns the corner, Bailey throws her arms up in the air and moans, "God help me if any of it comes true!"

I get dressed, and our weekday morning routine resumes as normal. The girls are off to school, and I have a couple hours to work before leaving for Beth's office. I'll stop by Grandpa's farmhouse after, then pick up Bailey from school.

Chapter 26

While pinning pattern pieces to the fabric for a ruffled taffeta bolero, I decide it's not worth tattling to Beth how aggravated I am with Marc for undermining my parental authority by telling Bailey that seeing the doctor is more for my benefit than hers. If there's any time left after the note drama, I want to pull apart my fear of cancer.

Entering her office, I see a new work of art that takes up almost the entire wall. A red-haired mermaid kissing a sea turtle hangs above her desk. The remarkable resemblance between the aquatic creature and my mother is unnerving. I'm unable to move away from the painting and stand there staring into the piercing green eyes looking down at me. Beth breaks the spell by asking if I'd like a glass of water. I decline as we settle into our assigned places and begin.

We exchange pleasantries, and then I run through what has occurred since the last session. There is so much. Beth doesn't tell me to slow down like she usually does. Instead, she crosses her legs, takes notes, nods every now and then, and lets me finish without interruption. She gets me to agree there isn't enough information to know how to address Bailey's health status. In a few moments, she tricks me into tabling this topic until our next session. But then, perhaps this is a counseling technique she's using to stop me from obsessing or worrying about an unknown future. She sits in silence for a moment, surely waiting for me to dive into my actual reality instead of my fears.

"How long has it been now since your separation?" she asks. Which is a weird way to get into it but whatever.

"Almost seven months."

"And how many times have you been together? Just the two of you?"

"Since our separation?"

"Sure." Beth shrugs indifferently.

"I don't know. He's been out of town a lot. Maybe six or seven times."

"So you'd say about once a month?" she confirms. "And how much time would you say you've spent with Emily?"

"The more time she spends with the girls and even me, the greater chance she'll pack up and leave. If she develops empathy for us, she'll understand how being with Marc isn't right."

"Uh huh." She gives no indication if she agrees or disagrees with my strategy. "And why do you think she's willing to spend so much time with you?"

"Guilt?"

"Do you think she feels guilty?" As Beth grabs her coffee mug from the end table, she turns, and I can see Prada marked on the side of her eyewear.

"I think she has to at some level, don't you?"

"Has she ever told you she feels guilty?"

"No." Beth's Socratic method seems like an unfair way to get me to do her job. I just want her to tell me what I need to do to fix things.

"Do you think Marc feels guilty?"

"I would hope so."

"And why is that?"

"Because he should know I want my life the way it was." Each word climbs towards a high-pitched screech. "Because he should know it's not fair if the family I've worked so hard for is taken away from me." I slow down and my voice drops an octave. "I want us to celebrate our fiftieth anniversary. We might have rough patches here and there, but the wedding vows are supposed to see us through until death do us part. It might not be easy, but I made a promise to Marc and God that I'd stay married forever. Besides that, I've been saving all these mementos starting with our first date in a big, huge box so I can bring them out at our golden anniversary party. I want our friends and family to lift their glasses and toast our enduring love—and for our children and grandchildren to be proud of us for not being like every other couple who gives up and gets divorced. There has been so much thought that has already gone into planning this celebration, it would be such a shame to think it was all a big frigging waste of time."

"And you think this party signifies success?"

"Yes, I do."

"Would the party celebrate love or endurance?"

I don't answer right away. She waits. My stomach growls, but I don't have anything to say at the moment.

"Tell me how you're spending your time when you're not with your children." Beth is testing me to find out if I'm letting myself go in Marc's absence.

"Work, of course, takes a lot of my time. Try to visit my family when I can. Trying out a yoga class, started volunteering a couple hours a week, hosting a book club meeting, oh, and planning to sign up for a women's group at church that looks good." I've passed her test with flying colors.

"Did you do those things when you were with Marc?"

"I never had time and didn't know I ever wanted to do these things until now." I fall into her trap.

She removes her glasses and places them on top of the clipboard resting on her lap before leaning over to ask, "Grace, have you ever thought you might not be trying to save your marriage but an outdated version of yourself?"

I must look as shocked as I feel because she then says, "Something to think about as you figure out if you miss Marc the man or the construct of who you are in this marriage."

I should have known the painting was a sign to talk about Mom. Why did I let her distract me with this marriage crap? My mom faked a note from my birth mother! I wonder if it's possible to ask for a refund if you aren't satisfied with the results from a counseling appointment. It doesn't seem right that I've paid to feel worse than I did before coming to see Beth. I would have spent my hard-earned money on the fantasy comic book drawing class I told Kelsey we couldn't afford this month if I'd known how today was going to turn out.

A Metallica song is playing on the car radio when I exit the Freedom Counseling Center's parking lot. I call this heavy metal band Marc's mad music, what he listens to when he is furious with work, the kids, or me. It has never been my kind of music, but I turn it up to drown out thoughts of my morning from hell.

Vinnie, the afternoon DJ, shares a piece of movie trivia about the song "More Human than Human" before playing it for his listeners, but I turn the volume down so there isn't even a tiny chance the White Zombie lyrics can be heard by Grandpa Joseph as I park the car outside his garage door.

I bring the letters from his mailbox inside and set the stack down on the dining room table. The ancient coffee maker is gurgling and sputtering, announcing it's nearly done brewing three large scoops of dark roast ground beans. It is customary for Mr. Coffee and Folgers to greet Grandpa's guests, but it isn't typical for the other appliances to join in unless a meal is involved. The oven timer calls attention to a buttery cinnamon scent that permeates the air with memories.

"Look, I've made a batch of your grandmother's famous cookies," Grandpa boasts while removing a tray of oatmeal-raisin cookies from the oven.

"Very impressive." I ignore the mess, which would have sent Grandma over the edge with exasperation. There are piles of excess flour, raisins, and oatmeal spread across the kitchen island. Sugar crackles beneath my shoes as I walk over to the sink to retrieve a green sponge floating in soapy water and give the small oval table a quick swipe before taking two mugs from the cabinets and a gallon of milk from the fridge.

"I thought you might stay longer if I baked cookies. I'll take a couple containers to the nursing staff later." There are disposable storage containers filled with layers of cooled cookies stacked near the silver Kenwood mixer.

"These cookies have been given to every car mechanic, teacher, postal worker, and farmer in Indianola, don't you think?" I recall Grandma's baking days.

A tin of these cookies was once delivered to the across the road neighbor as an apology for Mathew and me trespassing on his land to test out our makeshift sleds. We got caught because Mathew plowed through a barbed-wire fence and sliced his left hand, which bled across the snow as we made our way back to the house for help. It was fortunate neither one of us were hurt worse or killed. We escaped with only a two-week grounding for our carelessness. Mathew wears a jagged scar that runs from his wrist to the tip of his pinky finger.

Through the window in the lounge, the hill of terror is barely visible from where I sit in the bentwood rocking chair. Grandpa and I enjoy our afternoon snack in here, where we can't see the dirty dishes and messy surfaces. This room looks as it has for over three decades. The red gingham sofa, oval braided rag rug, and all-black Shaker-style accessories are in the same places they always were. Even Grandma's sewing table and chair remain in the back corner with the next pair of pants in line to be hemmed held in place by the presser foot of her sewing machine. The wood-paneled wall leading to the basement displays an edited pictorial history of us. Although the timeline is jumbled, the selected impromptu group pictures, formal family portraits, individual senior class pictures, and snapshots of special family pets, including one unusually charismatic guinea pig, do a decent job capturing the Purviance family tree in the oversized photo collage. There are two I'd like to have removed—my adoption agency photo, which looks like a criminal baby mug shot and one of me at thirteen with a frizzy perm and metal orthodontic braces.

"I understand, young lady, you're here to pick up a file your mother left with me because you lost your temper with her at the restaurant, and she's afraid it might happen again if she gives it to you herself. Do I have this right?"

Chapter 27

My feet propel the rocking chair back and forth a couple more times before I reply.

"It's a little more complicated than that, but I guess that is one way to explain why I've asked for what is really mine anyway."

"Did you scream and swear at her in public?"

"Yes."

"Do you think that was the right thing to do?"

"No." I hear the swish of wind brush up against the house.

"You are part of this family, and families are God's construction. We do not get to choose our parents. God does. And He has commanded us to honor our mothers and fathers because they have been chosen to carry out His plan. You may be going to that new-fangled fancy church, but I know you haven't forgotten what you were taught at St. Theresa's."

"Of course I haven't, and it isn't as different as you think it is there." I stop rocking to sip coffee from my mug before it gets cold and to prevent myself from saying something I might regret.

"No matter what she's done, she is your mother and deserves a basic level of respect."

"But Grandpa . . ."

"Wait a minute, I know you want to tell me what terrible thing she's done. But first, I want to remind you that God wanted you to be part of our family. He chose you for us. And therefore, as this is His will, we are stuck with each other. And that is that." He pauses for half a second before promising, "If the good Lord had given me a say in who was to be included in our family, I would've picked you every time out of everyone possible to be our first granddaughter."

There's not much I can say in response to that other than to whisper out a thank you and finish my afternoon snack.

"Gracie," he says gently, "we have a limited time on this planet, so don't waste it on anything that separates you from loved ones. It doesn't do you any good to hang on to hate and anger, even if it is justified. Our lives, our bodies, are so fragile and temporary we can never be sure what the next day will bring—for better or for worse. Look at your grandmother and me. Our love is present even if her memory of me and the two of us is not. She can't remember our first date, our wedding day, and all that came after, but every day I feel like I'm the luckiest man. She agreed to take a chance on a lad who returned from the war without any job prospects. And this hurdle we're facing now, well that's a reminder that we ultimately all belong to one family—God's family."

"When I have learnt to love God better than my earthly dearest, I shall love my earthly dearest better than I do now," I quote C. S. Lewis.

"Perfectly said," Grandpa compliments my choice. He lifts his mug and says, "Amen" before getting up to go into the kitchen for a coffee and cookie refill.

I rock in the chair for a couple more minutes and think about repentance and forgiveness. My thoughts also wander to when Grandma lost the memory of who I was.

Marc and I went to visit her at the care center on a rainy Saturday afternoon. We were dressed up because we were on our way to a wedding at the Living History Farms chapel. My high heels confidently clicked against the linoleum floor as I made my way from the door to the side of Grandma's hospital bed and gave her a kiss on the forehead. Her light blue cotton nightgown slipped off her shoulder. As I gently wiggled it back in place and brought the blanket closer to her chest, she asked if I was a new nurse.

"No, Grandma, it's me, Grace, your granddaughter."

"I'm afraid I haven't been to China," she shook her head sadly. "I'm sorry I can't speak your language."

"Grandma, it's me!" I shouted. "It's Grace, Gracie."

"Oh dear, I've upset you, haven't I?" She pressed her index finger against her lips as she always did when she was upset. "I just am so mad at myself for never going to China, but I am sure it's a very nice place to visit."

I looked back at Marc and he moved forward to assist by asking her, "Do you remember me?"

"Of course I do!" She smiled, relieved to see a familiar face and to prove she was of sound mind. "You are my handsome grandson. I always like seeing you in your church clothes. Are you on your way to Mass?"

I moved in closer to Marc so she could see we were a couple, but it didn't trigger recognition. She looked at me but didn't see me. She looked at me with the same vacant stare as a store cashier who gazes upon the next customer in line with obligatory courtesy. I backed up, not knowing quite where to go or what to do next.

"My, isn't my grandson handsome?" Grandma turned her head in my direction to ask and then, with confused concern, she tried to console me. "Don't cry little girl. I'm sorry I don't know how to speak your language. Maybe you can teach me some words?"

Marc laughed his head off when we got to the car. I couldn't stop the waterworks because I felt like we had just exited a funeral. I was mourning the loss of one of my biggest fans who went around to every fabric store and not only hung flyers on bulletin boards but went around to each store talking to employees and customers about her granddaughter's new business. No longer would it be possible to pick up the phone and reminisce about our many outings to museums, restaurants, or shopping malls. She wouldn't remember any of it. The woman who taught me how to scramble an egg, correctly direct a spoon in the bowl when eating soup, level a cup of flour with a knife, and identify poison ivy in the woods had gone missing that day.

When I visit her now, I go along with whomever she thinks I am on the day. Sometimes I'm a nurse's aide. Other times I'm a Chinese or Japanese girlfriend of one of her grandsons, but she can't remember which one. When I greet her with "Ni hǎo" and depart with "Sayonara," I figure this must be karmic justice for the time I pretended to be a foreign exchange student. It just doesn't seem fair that Grandma is glad to see me, but it's the same level of happiness as it is with any visitor or staff member who stops by her room. I've had three years to gradually accept the situation as it is. All of us, including Grandpa and Marc, are now also mere acquaintances. She knows we visit regularly but doesn't know why. The moments when we can see she's fighting through the disease to attach a name and memories to any of our faces, the pain is from feeling as if we're being forced against our will to read her obituary over and over.

Grandma believed life was set up as a series of fleeting transitions so we never take our blessings for granted. I don't think I ever took her presence for granted, but maybe I did, and this is why I miss her so much. Intellectually, I understand no one really can know or bargain for how long a loved one has to live or die. Yet, I desperately wish something could have been done to have been granted more time with Dad before cancer destroyed his body and Grandma before her memories vanished.

If Dad were here, he'd say no one gets to stay in one moment forever. You are born once. Just as you get used to being a child, the next thing you know you have to figure out being a grown up. A wedding day will come and go. Children will leave to start their own grown-up lives. Illness will end with either a cure or death. We are all nudged or pushed forward in the progression of impermanence whether we like it or not. That's what he would say about the matter—and tell me to get on with it.

I do get why Grandpa wants me to focus on what is good in my life and the good in others, not the pain and flaws. While I fundamentally agree with the point he is making, I can't and won't let go of the anger fueling my desire to get answers.

Chapter 28

I leave the farmhouse later than planned. I drive dangerously over the speed limit on the backroads to pick up Bailey on time. Her overstuffed backpack bounces up and down as she rushes from the school entrance doors to the curb where I pulled up in the car with approximately five minutes to spare.

"I was waiting forever." She slams the passenger door shut and struggles to free herself from the arm straps so she can toss her belongings in the backseat before buckling up.

"What took you so long? It was embarrassing standing there looking like an idiot. Everyone was asking what was going on, and I had to tell them my stupid mom was taking me to the doctor because she's obnoxiously super overprotective."

"Oh, you poor baby!" I drawl. "It must be terribly awful for you because who is the worst mom ever? Is it Joan Crawford? No, not mean enough. How about Norman Bates' mama? Oh no, not crazy enough. Let me see, who could it be? Who *could* it be?" I asked in the snarky voice I've used to play this game a million times before. "Oh wait, let me guess . . . could it be me? Why yes, Grace Miju Hunter, congratulations you are the winner of 'Who is the Worst Mother in the Universe'! Why? Because you want to take your daughter to the doctor to make sure she's okay, you mean, horrible, terrible, awful, wicked mother."

With a quick turn of my head to check if the lane to the right is clear, I catch her grinning as she sinks back into her seat.

"God, you are so stupid," she mutters as she lets out a thunderous sigh of exasperation. She starts rattling off all the reasons why it was a big deal missing the last three periods of her school day.

None of them are new or relevant. I focus my attention on the road and radio. We listen to Terry Gross interviewing Matt Groening, creator of *The Simpsons*, on our local NPR station.

"I am the Lisa Simpson of our family. She'd also be annoyed missing school to come here." We walk single file between parked cars toward the building.

There's only enough time to skim and swap three celebrity gossip magazines in the waiting room before being escorted to Examination Room 3. A nurse named Pam weighs Bailey and takes all of her vitals before informing us that Dr. Butt is seeing patients while Dr. Groves is away on vacation. After Nurse Pam exits the room, Bailey and I fall into a fit of Bart Simpson giggles. We use our wait to come up with possible names of other doctors in her practice—Dr. Cheek, Dr. Bum, Dr. Arse, Dr. Crack, and our personal favorites, Dr. Derriere and Dr. Gluteus Maximus, who we decide are gorgeous foreign men.

Dr. Olivia J. Butt enters the room, a stern woman with evenly parted chestnut hair gathered into a tight bun at the back. A white physician's coat partially covers black polyester pants and a royal blue crew-neck sweater. Her physical features are equally unremarkable, but she exudes professionalism and expertise, which is all that really matters. She doesn't look like she has a sense of humor, so we stop smiling and pay attention.

I explain why we are here and hand over a pocket folder filled with the research I printed and highlighted from several reputable medical websites. She cracks a sliver of a lopsided smile. She keeps a straight face while examining Bailey though. She asks questions but doesn't say much in response to our answers except "uh huh," "okay," and "hmm."

I sit on the worn blue plastic chair and become the back-seat driver of the appointment, inserting my observations when I think they are needed or appropriate to supplement what data Bailey provides to Dr. Butt.

"Okay then, I think we'll take some blood samples today and take it from there," she says, concluding the fifteen-minute checkup. "We'll get the results fairly quickly. You can expect a call in the next day or so."

Then turning to Bailey she asked, "Are you experiencing higher than usual levels of fatigue?"

"Maybe," Bailey said noncommittally. "I think it's just all the stress of studying for midterm exams."

"Hmm. . ." Doctor Butt said carefully looking at Bailey.

"Do you think its cancer?" I have to ask.

"Let's see what the test results tell us. If you don't hear from us in a couple days, feel free to call and check in with me," she says without a fleck of emotion. "The nurse will be back to get those samples, and we'll be in touch once we know something."

Dr. Butthole's bedside manner stinks. I think from this point forward, I may request another GP in Dr. Grove's absence, as I'd prefer warm and fuzzy, not cold and prickly when dealing with the body at its most vulnerable. The cheerful receptionist who takes payment for the deductible makes me feel better than the doctor did about our visit.

Bailey's evaluation is in direct opposition to mine. She thought Dr. Butt was great. Impressed by the use of a smartphone to record and research information during her examination, Bailey grew confident she was being seen by a more-than-competent physician. I decide to keep my opinion of Dr. Butt to myself.

While we wait in line at the grocery store, Emily calls to check how the appointment went.

"I don't know how I'm going to deal with the next forty-eight hours waiting for test results," I say.

"Tell me about it," Emily commiserates.

"Don't be such a drama queen. You're not the one who was poked with a needle for nothing," Bailey hisses. "And stop talking about me like I'm not here, for God's sake."

"That's the moody teenage hormones talking. Don't let her make you feel like a jerk for being a good mom," Emily says. "Call me anytime if you need someone to listen to your worries. We're all here for you. Marc told me about an hour ago he's about halfway to Davenport, and he'll call you when he gets to the hotel."

"Okay. Thanks," I say with a strange mix of appreciation and disbelief.

When I am at home boiling pasta for supper, Amaya calls.

"Mom is really sorry," she says after inquiring after Bailey's doctor appointment.

"She better be." I smack the top of the pot with a wooden spoon entirely unnecessarily.

"Absolutely," Amaya says. "She's not just sorry about the note, but about the way she told you and all of that. She loves you so much."

"Mmmm," I say, more a growl than an agreement.

"Thanksgiving is soon . . ."

"I am not reconciling with her just so we can all play happy family at Thanksgiving."

"Of course not. You're up for meeting Christina and her friend, right?"

I roll my eyes. "Lord, help us all."

"Most of her friends are great." Amaya is not wrong.

"Because they're too nice to realize what a bitch she is and fight back."

Amaya giggles and defends Christina half-heartedly. We idly chitchat until Kelsey finishes setting the table. I enter the dining room and notice Bailey and Kelsey are impatiently waiting for me to finish up on the phone. I fire off a goodbye and sheepishly sit down. Bailey says grace, and then we eat our dinner while sharing insignificant bits and pieces of our day.

* * *

Five hours after Bailey and Kelsey finish their homework and go to bed, I sit at the dining room table with a cup of decaffeinated Earl Grey tea, two of Grandpa's oatmeal raisin cookies, and a large gift box mom has ceremoniously covered in silver damask wrapping paper.

As I remove the shimmery ribbon and bow, I can't help but be somewhat amused that she has used leftover paper from wrapping Sin-Joon's wedding present. She must have forgotten I helped pick out the anniversary clock and gift wrap. How ironic that it comes with a reference to the woman who authored the farewell note. Granted, it was three years ago when we purchased these items together, so I don't think Mom purposely included her accomplice when she went overboard with the presentation of her recordkeeping of my adoption. It also isn't like I haven't seen the scrapbook before. Mom kept it, among other items she considered of high sentimental value, like Great Grandma's engagement ring, Grandpa's WWII Purple Heart medal, photos, sentimental legal documents, and letters, locked away in an antique military-style leather trunk.

She'd fetch me from my bed on the morning of my birthday to join her in the attic. A picnic basket filled with cupcakes, candles, a thermos filled with hot cocoa, paper plates, and cutlery was carried up with us as we ascended the stairs. Her present and card were always placed in advance on a makeshift table made from an upside-down milk crate. Before opening them, I was made to wait as she removed from her neck an oval gold-link chain holding the key that opened the trunk to bring the scrapbook out in the open.

Chapter 29

She turned the pages for a show and tell of "This was the first year of your life" and when the book was closed, she gave me as many reasons why she was glad I was born as I was years old. I was then asked to list the same number of things I liked best about myself. The birthday song was sung, wishes made, candles blown out, present and card opened, picnic packed up, and then we plodded downstairs to prepare breakfast for everyone else.

One of these mornings while she was mixing flour, baking powder, eggs, and milk together with a whisk, I granted Mom permission to sleep in the next year, as I was getting too old for a birthday picnic. Not a word was said until the first pancake was served—two halves of a heart arranged on a plate and thrown at my place setting. Spatula held high and hand on hip, she announced that no requests would be accepted for stars, numbers, or Mickey and Minnie Mouse—all pancakes would match the shape of mine. When Dad asked what on earth was going on, she told him he should ask his unappreciative daughter who was to blame for breaking her heart and promptly burst into tears.

Both Homecoming Day and this early morning annual event were created with the best of intentions, but honored what I knew separated me from normalcy. I was the only one in the family who received a private birthday party with Mom, and no one ever complained about it—not even Christina, although she did think it was weird that I never seemed to be bothered much about the scrapbook's contents or whereabouts. She cared more about it than I ever did. I was glad it wasn't easily accessible, as I never wanted it to be my life's showpiece and hoped it would eventually become the least interesting thing about me.

The only reason I wanted to take possession of my history was because I knew it would be painful for Mom to relinquish this item from her collection. Childish revenge to force her to sort out the facts from her fiction.

As I'm rustling through layers of tissue paper, there are a couple of light knocks on the door. Startled, I stop moving and wait. Another round of tap, tap, tap. It is three a.m. Sidling along the side wall to the corner, I grab the baseball bat Mathew loaned me for protection and stealthily edge my way to the front room. What if he has a weapon? I'll have to inflict as much damage as I can while I have the chance. I mentally prepare my defense for when the police arrive to ask questions. Where is my phone? It's on the table, completely out of reach, which means I stupidly forgot to dial 9-1-1. Well, it will have to be done after the skull bashing. Tightening my grip on the baseball bat's handle, I peer through the spyhole.

It's only Ian.

"I saw the light on and wanted to check if everything was okay. As the editor in chief of 'The Prospect Drive Skywalk,' I have to report any crimes, but unfortunately there's no room in next week's edition. The war of the gnomes between No. 2612 and No. 2616 has gotten vicious, and is taking up all the space."

"Ha, ha. You scared me to death knocking on my door this late. What are you doing up at this hour anyway?"

"Insomnia. I decided to take a walk around the block so I wouldn't wake anyone in the house."

I invite him inside for a cup of tea, but regret doing so when I recall what I was in the middle of doing. I gather torn wrapping paper strewn across the table and floor to take with me into the kitchen.

My worry over the album is replaced with sheer panic about what I'm wearing, which is a pair of flimsy shorts and a too-tight tank top. I run to the basement and grab a sweatshirt from one of the laundry baskets to throw on so he can't see I'm braless. Nothing more can be done to my ratty bedtime outfit without completely changing.

"Is it your birthday?" He waves to the album and wrapping paper sitting on my kitchen table.

It's too late and I'm too tired to lie, so I tell him what he's looking at and why I have it.

"Can I?" He reaches toward the album, and I nod. He removes the book from the box and flips through the introductory pages. He stops and takes his time at the faded, typewritten assessment where a social worker noted my preference for pureed fruit over cereal, and my habit of spewing the offending rice cereal all over whoever was feeding me.

It makes him chuckle imagining an infant storing ammunition in the crevices of her chubby cheeks and waiting for the right moment to fire off a cereal bomb.

"Do you still do that as your signature party trick?"

"Only at black-tie events."

Ian finds things to ask about in almost every document and photograph. I pull my chair closer to his and pour more tea in our mugs before taking a closer look. He points out details I'd forgotten or overlooked.

We scan through greeting cards from family members and friends of my parents. This was before Hallmark sold congratulatory cards for adopted parents, so they are all generic baby announcements with handwritten notes scribbled inside. Ian reads each one, and I somewhat patiently explain how the owners of the closing signatures are related to us. Following this section, we finally encounter a change to the book's contents. A clipping of a local newspaper article announcing my adoption and arrival is placed on the same page where the fake birth mother's note once was. Three photographs evenly spaced out in a vertical row have taken its place. I assume the bands of scratches on the paper surface surrounding the trio of images indicate Mom had a difficult time removing the forgery and covering it up with new material.

The top one is at the airport when she held me in her arms for the first time. A blue butterfly-print silk scarf is wrapped and tied loosely at the side of her head, holding her wild tawny locks back so the wide joyous grin she's giving the camera is prominent. The middle picture is one Dad took of the two of us at a beach in California. I'm wearing a red one-piece toddler swimsuit, and she's in a turquoise bikini holding my hand as my feet touch the ocean water for the first time. I wholeheartedly agree with Ian that these two original Kodak photographs circa 1973 are sweet and sentimental.

The one on the bottom, however, is a passive-aggressive reminder I am not perfect. It is a picture of the immediate family at Grandma and Grandpa's fiftieth wedding anniversary party. I was not in attendance because I was at an all-inclusive resort in the Dominican Republic. My decision to pick my boyfriend's family vacation over this milestone celebration caused a rift between my mother and me for a couple of months, at least.

Grandpa came to my defense telling everyone he thought Marc was "The One" and that I'd be returning with an engagement ring. That he stood up for me only made Mom angrier about my absence. She insisted the daughter who returned unengaged come with her to deliver the custom-framed photograph to the farmhouse. Grandma wouldn't let her hang it on the wall until she fetched a wallet-size school picture of me to insert in the corner. She gave Mom a defiant look and me a hug and said, "Now the family is complete." It was a sweet gesture that comes with guilt every time I pass by the crudely "Photoshopped" photograph. Of course this is the one Mom includes in her montage, replacing her wrongdoing with an example of mine.

"At least she tried to make things right?" Ian defends her intention.

"This isn't about making things right," I snap. "She's an absolute nightmare. If you met her, you'd know."

"When I do, I'll be sure to thank her for picking out two cute baby pictures and one of you looking all Madonna-like, which is priceless by the way."

When I shoot him a sideways scowl, he bites into half a cookie to hide his amused smirk. I pretend to angrily turn the page and discover a congratulatory letter from Father Gubbels has been tucked in the fold.

It is nearly 4 a.m. and we are only a quarter of the way through the story of my adoption. Light from the dining room's chandelier cocoons this part of the house while others slumber in the darkness. Neither one of us is tired, so instead of retreating to our beds, a container of Ben & Jerry's Oatmeal Cookie Chunk ice cream is retrieved from the freezer and scooped into two pasta bowls. Ian is carefully avoiding scraping the ceramic side with the metal spoon as he finishes his helping. I maneuver the spoon in the same way to prevent any clinking when stirring milk and sugar around in my tall stoneware mug. Steam from my third refill poured from the cast-iron teapot is pirouetting into the air as delicately as our whispered words. It's evident we are both experts in ensuring our nocturnal movements don't disturb others during our sleepless nights.

Chapter 30

"**S**peaking of mothers, I haven't seen much of your mom," I comment.

"That's because she misses the life she had in San Francisco and keeps going back and forth to see her friends and some of my dad's family. I think she regrets moving here with us, but she felt it was her duty as a mom and grandparent."

"There's nothing us moms won't do for our kids, huh?"

"God, when Caleb was born it was as if Jenny completely changed. She changed from this free-spirited California hippie into a fiercely protective and controlling tiger mom. She was so strict, but at the same time there was absolutely nothing she wouldn't do for him. It took her over a year to say yes to a first date with me, but only seconds to be head over heels in love with Caleb."

"It's a different kind of love. This primal instinct takes possession of your heart and mind during pregnancy. It's dominating but doesn't diminish the love you have for others," I defend the mother of his child.

"Jenny would say motherhood was like riding a wild, galloping horse. You hold on for dear life and try to stay on for as long as you can. It's a scary and bumpy ride, but you wouldn't trade the exhilaration of the unexpected for anything in the world. She was such a great mom. It made her so mad that she wouldn't be able to give Caleb a sister or brother. But between you and me, I know she really, really, really wanted a daughter. She would have adored your girls, especially sweet and gentle Kelsey."

"I'm glad Kelsey has such a great friendship with Caleb. He is a great kid—and no wonder, as he comes from two amazing parents."

"Thank you," he says softly.

Ian's image is reflected in the silver shabby-chic wall mirror above the sideboard. Both his height and exotic facial features catch the attention of admirers, including Kelsey, who swears he looks exactly like a Japanese model and actor she discovered in an updated Godzilla movie. This superficial comparison is accurate, but until now hasn't changed how much he annoyed me. Tonight, I see who he is and why he is a good father and friend.

"Motherhood scares me to death, but I'd never give it up. I've looked through this scrapbook before I was a mom and after I was a mom, and I don't get it." A lengthy pause ensues. I'm not sure I want to say aloud what I have only ever thought before.

"What don't you get?" he asks.

Growing up, I think to myself. I thought parenting was a

glorified version of being a teacher. Parents were responsible for instructing and enforcing their rules and values
while providing for your basic needs. They loved you.
You loved them. It was that simple. I wasn't prepared
for the nine months of pregnancy and certainly not for
childbirth, which shocked me into the realization I was
not accepting a simple eighteen-year assignment. It was
much more complicated than I ever imagined.

I know how wrong I've got it when I can't stop myself
from missing my children when they're only five miles
away staying and sleeping at their father's place. Or when
they're at a week-long summer camp, and I go overboard
with worry they might get sick, scared, or lonely. I'm sure
parenting experts would agree it's perfectly reasonable
to be concerned about your child's safety and well-being.
It is, however, completely irrational to be afraid I might
forget the sound of their voices or the way they laugh at
my bad jokes. But I do, which calls into question whether
I'm a good mom or just a very insecure one. And waiting
for Bailey's test results, I find myself desperately bargaining with God to spare her from harm. I've offered my
business, home, and even my own life in exchange for
a clean bill of health for both girls because the thought
of being permanently separated from Bailey or Kelsey's
presence is unbearable. If they were ever taken from me,
I would wish for instant death.

I don't tell Ian any of this. He has found the locks from
my first haircut tied together with a thin red ribbon and

taped down with a yellowed strip of Scotch tape. As I listen to him read Mom's description of how I cried at the first snip of the scissors, it reminds me of how I wept both times my babies' umbilical cords were cut.

"I don't get how any woman could ever voluntarily abandon her child. It doesn't make any biological sense. I'd never do it, and your wife didn't do it by choice," I blurt out.

Feverishly blushing, I retreat back into private mode. Ian doesn't fill the silence with words. Instead, we listen to insomnia's symphony at sunrise.

Chapter 31

I have two more restless nights on my own wrestling with a potential cancer diagnosis since the night Ian came over. I'm tired, but I still manage to get to Starbucks at the time Mathew and I agreed on. I order a chai latte, read the paper, add notes and dates to my planner, call a couple of clients to confirm appointments, and anything else to keep from looking like I've been stood up.

I call Mathew for the third time since I arrived and get no answer. Again.

"I have a ton of work to do back at the house," I tell his voice mail. "Meet me there when you're ready."

At home I get a phone call, but not from Mathew.

"Grace . . ." says a serious, monotone voice. "Dr. Butt."

I grip the counter like it can keep me from drowning. "Yes?"

"I have the results of Bailey's tests. She has mono."

The room spins as I breathe for the first time in weeks.

"Yes, yes, yes!" I scream into the receiver. "That's fantastic!"

Dr. Butt yelps in pain.

"Sorry, sorry!" I'm still shouting. I take a deep breath. "That's wonderful," I manage in a quieter voice.

"Mononucleosis should not be taken lightly," Dr. Butt says.

"Yes, yes," I say and listen to her instructions quietly.

When I get off the phone, I dance around the room. There is nothing that can or will spoil my good mood—including having wasted most of my morning waiting for Mathew.

He calls at last.

"It's mono!" I shout.

"Who has my niece been kissing?" Mathew teases.

While he drives to my house, I call Marc and then the school. Mathew arrives with Ho Hos he bought at Casey's to celebrate. We eat, have coffee, and chat for far longer than either of us intend, and I have to hurry him out the door because a client will be over soon.

Before he leaves, I hand him an envelope with two fifties inside.

I've been giving Mathew a small monthly stipend for years. When Marc discovered the same amount of money was being regularly taken out of our joint account, and that it was being transferred to my lazy bum of a brother's bank account, he went ballistic. It made him beyond angry because 1) it should have been a shared decision, 2) I didn't tell him about it, and 3) it was wasting money on a lost cause. I agreed with his first two points, but strongly disagreed with the last one. It hurt me that he didn't understand why I needed to support my little brother. He made me swear I wouldn't transfer any more of our money to him, and I didn't. I kept my promise by withholding earnings from clients who paid me in cash and gave this to Mathew in an unmarked envelope. It has been our secret that we don't need to keep any longer.

"Sorry it's not as much this month. I didn't have as much work, and Marc made a substantial withdrawal from our account this month. I need to ask him about that, but anyway, I hope it still helps you cover your rent." I apologize for giving him a hundred dollars less than usual.

"I always appreciate whatever you can do to help us out." Mathew hugs me, and I hug him back. He jogs out to his truck and drives home before my client arrives in her Lexus.

Chapter 32

essica is one of my best customers. She pays well and provides a steady stream of income I can depend on. She also is high maintenance. She will get an idea—like a peacock—in her head but won't be able to describe what that means. Is the dress long, short, strapless, voluminous, fitted? I've reviewed magazine pictures with her and asked targeted questions, moved forward, only to be told what I've come up with wasn't even close. This has been said even at the final fitting, which has resulted in starting completely over with a new concept, pattern, and fabric. Expenses are always covered for the rejected articles of clothing, but it doesn't change how frustrated I get with all that work thrown out the window. I don't how I might react if it turns out I've wasted all that time fastening over a thousand green and blue beads on this dress.

As Jessica changes out of her Diane von Furstenberg silk wrap dress into my creation, Emily arrives early with Bailey and Kelsey in tow. I dart up the stairs to give an estimated number of minutes left in my workday.

Emily claps her hands like a Disney Princess. "Is this the dress you've been beading all week?" Bailey, Kelsey, and Emily exchange longing looks. I sigh and head back to the workshop.

"Jessica," I call into the blue velvet curtain of the dressing room, "do you mind if my girls and a friend come down to see you in the dress?"

"I don't mind at all. I'm almost ready, just putting my shoes on."

I call Emily and the girls to come see the work of several months—not weeks—months. As they make their way down from the kitchen to the basement, Kelsey's squeal starts on the eighth step and doesn't stop until she gets to the bottom. Bailey and Emily gasp and applaud. Jessica savors every second of her red-carpet moment, twirling around on the wooden platform in front of the full-length mirror. I watch from one of the armchairs, reveling in the knowledge that this is the final fitting. If there was any question about it before, Emily and the girls have definitely convinced Jesica she is the prettiest peacock.

* * *

After Jessica leaves, I break the news to Bailey that she has mono, and that she is housebound to rest and hydrate until her low-grade fever resolves. Behind her, Emily is doing an "It's not cancer" dance, which makes it hard to keep a compassionate look on my face while I tell

Bailey that this means she will not be coming with us to A Brush with Greatness

"You just want me to be sick so you don't have to take me with."

"I could get a Netflix subscription so you can watch movies to pass the time," I offer.

"I don't intend on using my sick days as a lazy vacation."

Instead of being appreciative that I've made preliminary arrangements with the school to have her assignments sent home for the next couple of weeks, Bailey is annoyed because I've supposedly made her look incompetent at taking care of her own business.

I get Bailey settled unhappily on the couch and retreat to the kitchen. Emily has already brewed two cups of coffee. I take the place next to her at the island.

"I'm ready for a Friday night out." I mean it, even if my plans take me well outside of my comfort zone with a very strange mix of company. "But I don't know how I feel about my first attempt at painting happening in a room full of strangers."

"And some of your best friends," Emily says. "Who cares about those other people? We'll love you even if your painting turns out"—she drops her voice—"looking like a platoon of penises on parade in a cabbage patch." I choke on my coffee, and Emily looks mighty proud of herself.

"You sketch for your job all the time," Bailey shouts

from the living room. "For the love of God, get over yourself. You're just being a big drama queen baby over nothing."

Emily rolls her eyes and whispers, "Lord, teenagers."

We make chicken and porcini ravioli with the occasional demand or complaint from Bailey to interrupt us. Emily starts washing knives and cutting boards while I babysit the pasta water. She pulls open the shade above the sink.

"Oh," she exclaims. "There's that cute panda!"

I give it the finger behind her back. "Isn't it just," I say. Who am I kidding? If she'd gotten together with Ian, she would have added eight more panda statues, not gotten rid of it.

* * *

At supper Bailey asks if she can order a pizza because I've added too much garlic and too many onions, making her dinner inedible

As I calmly refuse, she makes a big show of gagging and spitting a piece of chicken into her napkin.

"If the doctors hadn't already restricted your weekend activity, you'd be grounded by your mother for having a poor attitude," I inform her.

"Amen," Emily says from her side of the table. Bailey glowers and picks at her pasta.

I can't say I'm sad to leave Bailey at home. I didn't

think anything could ruin my mood, but she's pushing me awfully close.

We walk into A Brush with Greatness to discover it's the three-month anniversary of their grand opening. Bottles of champagne and non-alcoholic sparkling apple cider rest in ice buckets, and empty plastic champagne flutes are lined up in rows on an oblong table near the entrance door. The adjacent oval table has a five-tiered cake stand holding all sorts of frosted cupcakes, petit fours, and cookies, and there are photographs of previous classes scattered across the surface of the black cotton tablecloth.

The cement and steel studio looks like a factory sweatshop, but for entertainment purposes. A brushed concrete accent wall behind the drink and dessert tables displays over fifty different unframed canvas paintings. Grey cafeteria-style tables in the middle of the room are segmented into individual workstations, each with an easel, blank canvas, paper plate palette, a ceramic cup holding brushes, and paper towels.

Mary Anne has saved three places for us at the farthest table from the front. She has replaced her stool with a wide, sturdy wooden bench to support her weight. It looks out of place. There must be at least fifteen other class participants circulating in the room, but not a soul is anywhere near Mary Anne. An eerie silence has settled into her space. Relief flashes across her face when she sees we've shown up. I wave and smile, hoping she didn't have to wait long on her own.

Poppy Cartwright, one of the owners and our instructor for the evening, comes over and introduces herself to us. She recognizes Emily from the hospital where she volunteers weekly in the children's ward. Poppy nervously runs her fingers through her bleached pixie-cut hair as she shares her plans for creating a pop-up studio to take to hospitals, schools, and care homes. I note that her cherry-red triangular cat-eye glasses extend inches beyond the ends of her penciled-in eyebrows and match the color of her five-inch pumps. She looks like a single tulip blooming in the winter snow. I'm so enthralled by her style and appearance I don't take notice of the couple who walks in behind three members of a bachelorette party.

"Oh no, not her," I hear Kelsey whisper under her breath with disgust.

I look up and see Mathew's Nadia—with Ian. It's obvious they are on a first or second date by the cautious way he guides her to a place for the two of them to sit. Nadia turns toward Ian with a lopsided grin as she holds onto his arm for balance, swinging her leg onto the other side of the bench. She's wearing silver hoop earrings, leather leggings, a frilly lace top, and grey suede over-the-knee boots—an expensive tacky hooker outfit. She gets settled and ready to paint and flirt, as does he. Both are unaware we are seated six rows behind them.

"Should we go say hi?" Kelsey asks.

"No way. Stay put," I hiss, frightened of giving our coordinates away by being too loud.

"What's going on?" Emily asks as loudly as if I'm stand-ing across the room rather than from less than two feet away.

"Nothing, shh . . ."

"Shh? What do you mean shh?"

"Everything okay?" Mary Anne checks with Emily.

"I think so, but she's shushing me."

"Yes, shh . . . The class is getting ready to start."

"Oh right," Emily says as she pops up and scans the room for the teacher. "Y'all, let's get ready for the fun to begin."

Lately I've noticed Emily's Southern accent and col-loquialisms are activated based upon the type of audi-ence and situation. She's mostly returned to sounding like where she's from—Ohio—but I bet if she moved to England, she'd adopt their accent and slang words quickly. She's the type that easily adapts and slides into her surroundings, which is evident in this class. A paint-brush is stuck between her teeth, and she's squinting ahead at her blank canvas as if she were on the streets of Paris preparing to paint the Eiffel Tower for a tourist.

Poppy stands at the side of the room and starts giving step-by-step instructions. Each brush stroke builds on the others, eventually creating a pumpkin and harvest moon looking as they should. It is easier and more rewarding than I anticipated.

I grit my teeth when I catch Ian and Nadia leaning against each other to compare what is materializing on their canvases. My neck and jaw muscles tighten when I hear his laugh in response to her irritating giggles. Kelsey paints a frowny face on her paper plate and points to it when we both catch Nadia playfully kiss Ian on his cheek.

Before the fifteen-minute break is scheduled to start, Poppy has an assistant pour champagne for the adults and sparkling cider for the minors. She offers a brief general word of thanks and invites us to toast their early success.

Nadia springs up from her spot and turns around. As she does so, we lock eyes. Hers widen and mine narrow, messaging a mutual disdain for each other.

Chapter 33

Ian is surprised when he turns and sees Kelsey and then me, standing in an unorganized line for the champagne and cider. He waves and comes over to chat with us.

"Hey there! Have you been here the whole time? How'd we miss each other? Then again, who would've guessed there'd be so many wannabe artists in our city? They've packed us in here like sardines to make as much money as they can, don't you think? But guess this is a good way to meet people while we paint our masterpieces." He laughs genially. "Speaking of meeting people, let me introduce you to my date.

"She came into the ReStore looking for a kitchen table. After we struck up a conversation, she agreed to donate a silent auction item from her business for our fundraiser, a generous $1,000 gift certificate and piece of artwork. You'll never guess from where . . . her tattoo studio! Can you believe it? I think this will be the first of its kind in our auction items, and I'm not quite sure how it will go over. But hey, I might be surprised, and a board member might have the winning bid. Remember meeting Andy Campbell? Maybe he'll show up with a neck tattoo at the office. Anyway, she invited me to come out and give this a try tonight, and I thought 'Why the heck not?' . . . Where'd she go? I want you guys to meet her. She's quite the character. She has this incredible Ryū tattoo on her leg. You've got to let her show you."

Nadia is pouring herself another glass of champagne and takes the bottle with her as she saunters over to Ian. "Hey cutie, I thought you might like some as well," she says while interlacing her arm into his.

"What are you doing, Nadia?"

"Don't be stupid, Grace. Obviously taking a painting class just like you."

"Uh right, so do you two know each other?" Ian asks.

"Where's Jacob?" I ask instead of answering Ian's question. "Who is watching Jacob while you're out tonight?"

"None of your business."

"It is my business because he's my nephew and I know you are supposed to be taking care of him tonight."

"I tell you what. How about you mind your own damn business for a change?"

"You told Mathew you and Jacob were taking an art class together and that's why he couldn't have him for the night. But he's with a babysitter, isn't he? You lied to my brother—again."

"Not that I owe you any explanation, but he's taking an art class at the community center."

"Bull."

"Look Grace, I don't care if you believe me. Jacob ain't your kid and never will be so stop butting your nose in where it don't belong."

"I would if you were a decent human being, but it's quite obvious you are a cruel pathological liar. I just can't for the life of me understand why you would make such a big fuss about having Jacob and not letting Mathew use those basketball tickets he won to take his son to the game tonight. You said it was because you wanted to spend as much time as possible with Jacob before you leave to go home for a month. But here you are minus Jacob, doing your own thing, caught in your own lie. Jacob isn't at an art class, is he? I'm betting he's with one of your shady part-time workers who's earning babysitting money to pay for their booze and drugs."

"Whatever, bitch. Look, I'll take care of my kid and you take care of your two pathetically boring kids. I don't need you nagging me about what you think I should or shouldn't do—you are not my mother, significant other, or friend. In fact, you are absolutely a hundred thousand percent nothing to me, so I don't really give a shit about your useless advice, judgments, or disapproval."

"You are a disgusting disgrace to all things decent. You

don't deserve Jacob or Mathew, and never have. They are both way too good for the likes of you and would be better off and a million times happier if you'd disappear forever because you are a nasty piece of work."

"And you are a fucking yellow belly chink who doesn't know when to shut the fuck up."

Ian and I simultaneously gasp in horror. He is paralyzed and stands frozen in place. I, on the other hand, move into action and grab the champagne bottle she's holding, place my thumb over the bottle opening, give it a good shake, and then spray the fizzy drink up and down Nadia's body and then finally back up again to pour the last dribbles on her head.

Kelsey sees and hears the commotion and rushes over holding a cupcake in each hand. Without thinking, I seize both and smear the pink frosted ends into Nadia's black top so it looks like her nipples have exploded through the cheap fabric.

Poppy's ruby-red heels strike against the polished concrete floor as she comes over to take control of the classroom brawl. The lead instructor comes in from my left, which gives me an opening to snatch the glass out of her hand and pitch champagne towards Nadia's face. She moves to retaliate, but Ian blocks her path.

I dismiss myself from class, walk for about three blocks to a coffee shop, and call for a taxi to take me home. I'm shivering because I left the studio without my coat, but the image of Nadia covered in champagne and cupcakes makes me feel warm and fuzzy inside. When I climb inside the cab, the driver says, "You look like you must be having a good night by the smile on your face."

Without an ounce of remorse for my actions, I'm thinking a visit to St. Theresa's confessional is probably required.

Chapter 34

Ian texted right away saying he offered to pay for a cab to take Nadia home because, as far as he was concerned, the date was over as soon as an ethnic slur came out. She refused the offer and stomped off.

She called Mathew, of all people, to come get her. Which I know because Mathew is yelling at me about it over the phone right now.

"She didn't even buckle herself in before she lit into me! She thinks I'm responsible for ruining her night by sharing details about our private conversations with my screwed-up family. Which I'm starting to think might be true. Jeez, Grace."

"She got what she asked for. I'm sorry it—"

"She threatened to take Jacob with her to Germany next week. The only reason she isn't is because I said you'd pay for her dry cleaning, get her a gift card to Merle Hay Mall, and send her an apology."

"Hell, no!" I yell.

"Gra-ace."

"Ma-athew," I mimick.

"God, Grace, take it."

"Nadia is a racist whore." I clank my cup down in the sink and yank up the blinds to glower at Ian's panda, shimmering with fall frost. "You should be suing her for custody, not licking her boots."

"She is the mother of my child—"

I snort. "Giving birth is not the same as being a mother."

"Just do it. So Jacob can be with us over Thanksgiving. You don't have to mean it."

"Oh, grow a pair, Mathew. Is it that hard to tell her that people who use words like 'chink' shouldn't be raising children?"

I hear a crash and the line goes dead. I have been hung up on.

Ian would understand. Ian would have the balls to stand up to Nadia. And he'd probably do it without using food-based assault. Or maybe he'd send her a pamphlet with dirty pictures.

I smile a little at the thought. And then I frown. What does Ian have to do with any of this? He's tangentially related to the situation at best. I give the panda a scowl. It continues to smile inanely, gripping its bamboo with its creepy little fingers.

If it wasn't outside my kitchen window, I definitely wouldn't think about Ian half as much as I do.

Ian texts that he offered to treat everyone to coffee and dessert. Mary Anne accepted the invitation, but Kelsey threw a massive hissy fit and demanded Emily take her home right then and there. Had Kelsey known I was home, I am positive she would've taken Ian up on his offer to extend the period of time away from me.

As soon as she sees me, Kelsey stomps off to her bedroom and slams the door shut. Emily enters the kitchen to check on me and give an account of what had occurred in my absence.

Sitting primly at the kitchen table Emily asks, "Grace, what happened with Nadia?" I just stare at her for a moment, and then groan.

Emily explains, "Mary Anne and I avoided high-calorie sweets during the class break by going out to peer into the different store windows in the shopping center. We completely missed what happened."

I respond by sitting down and burying my head in my arms on the table. I groan again.

"When we got back to the classroom." Emily continues, "Nadia was screeching obscenities and throwing dampened paper towels in Kelsey's direction. Then Ian lost his cool and reprimanded Nadia for taking her anger out on Kelsey, who was only trying to calm things down and make peace."

I lift my head long enough to see the genuine concern in her eyes. It is too much. I groan again and bury my head.

"A shouting match commenced between Nadia and Ian." Then a tone of defiance tinges Emily's voice. "Mary Anne and I joined in to help Ian clarify the difference between justified versus unjustified hostility. It got pretty noisy."

I lift my head again and ask, "What happened then?"

"Oh, Poppy took over and made all us hooligans step out into the plaza atrium and told everyone else to return to their seats to receive further instruction from Rosie. Poppy kicked our whole group out."

I sit up, not sure whether I should laugh or cry. "I never imagined we'd all end up being A Brush with Greatness dropouts with nothing to show for the fifty-dollar fee to take the class. It's difficult to say which would be worse—taking away seven identical paintings or going home empty-handed."

Emily grins, "I think the only person who genuinely cared about painting was Kelsey. The rest of us were there to cure our start-of-the-weekend boredom." Emily tells me that even though Kelsey's first instinct was to flee the scene, she felt obligated to finish the class, having promised to give her painting to one of the Habitat for Humanity families as a housewarming gift at their dedication ceremony. But as no one else in our group had a reason or wanted to stay for the second half of the class, she was forced to leave as well. And she's pissed. She not only blames me for turning a petty spat into a full-blown nuclear war but is also furious that I abandoned her to deal with the humiliating task of cleaning up the mess and apologizing profusely for her mother's white-trash behavior.

After Emily leaves it occurs to me that Kelsey has every right to be angry that overblown egos and tempers have wrecked her learning experience. But as horrid as this is to admit, it isn't enough for me to feel badly about ruining Nadia's date. I'm glad that for once, she didn't get her own way. I am also relieved to find out that Jacob isn't flying to Germany after all—the hassle and expense of changing things last minute outweighed Nadia's desire to punish Mathew.

Be that as it may, the weekend is filled with hard feelings. Bailey is still blaming me for her illness. I am still mad at Mom for lying about the note. Mom is aggravated by my lack of gratitude for the scrapbook and Christina's unreasonable demands to borrow her car for a trip to Nashville with a guy she met on Match.com. Grandpa is becoming more and more stressed out about everyone congregating at his house the following Thursday.

My thoughts are interrupted by an invitation from Marc. He asks if Moby and I are free Sunday afternoon for a walk around Water Works Park. He agrees to pick the dog and me up sometime after lunch.

We used to go to the park to practice what we learned in training classes when Moby was a puppy. It never went well. Marc and I were the new puppy parents screeching at Moby and each other when he wouldn't sit, stay, or come. Marc would accuse me of undermining his authority by sneaking undeserved treats to Moby when I thought he was too harsh. And I couldn't stand his draconian commands when he addressed the pup and me during these training exercises. I'd purposefully turn my back on Marc and scoop up the black and white bundle of fur and cuddle him until he wiggled free. All Moby wanted to do was run and play.

It is an odd location for Marc to pick for our outing. The last time we were there, an argument about the correct use of the whistle had resulted in a major battle between the two of us in the middle of the parking lot. As we scraped ice off the windshield, Marc had brought it to my attention that since it was my idea to get a dog, and as I repeatedly refused to do things right, he would no longer be responsible for our family pet. When I realized dog walks were no longer dreaded public displays of disobedience, it didn't bother me that Marc received all the benefits of pet ownership without ever having to pick up poop in the freezing cold or rain.

I wonder why we aren't meeting in the warmth and comfort of a restaurant or coffee shop. But I don't want to remind him of what didn't work between us. It doesn't matter if it doesn't make sense, and if the weather forecast makes it impossible for me to dress to impress. I might be invisible, but Moby is sporting a fashionable and functional quilted tartan dog coat which always garners compliments from admirers during our cold weather hikes.

"What on earth has he got on?" Marc shakes his head in disgust when he opens the door to let Moby in the back seat of his car. "Have you really turned our dog into a sissy snob? Good grief! Let's take it off before anyone we know sees us."

Chapter 35

We walk around the park crunching through the snow, Moby coatless and the two of us bundled up. Our voices follow the wispy trail of smoky vapor carrying the words out of our mouths into the open space. Moby tracks and identifies footprints not our own. I admire how the evergreen trees cradle drifts of unspoiled snow in their branches. We politely greet other park visitors, thank those who praise Moby for being so well behaved, and find things to point out within the park setting to sustain a conversation about nothing of real importance.

We reach the natural end of a conversation about the coffee shops of Indianola, and he clears his throat.

"So . . . I haven't had much time to work on the details of our divorce . . ."

I say nothing, and he stumbles ahead, "We're kind of stuck in limbo—not married and not not married right now—" He pauses for a moment at the place where I would, in different circumstances, appreciate his wit. He clears his throat again and then again. "And that's my fault. I said I would take care of all the paperwork and deal with the bank. Things are a little more complicated than I can explain at the moment. If it weren't for the pressure of making my business profitable, I'd devote more action to sorting it all out. I never meant for it to drag on like this. I'm going to re-focus my priorities to have things resolved in the next couple of months. I promise."

"All right." I pause for a moment to help Moby, who has gotten the leash looped under one leg.

"You know Emily and Birch are riding with me. I'll drop off Emily and Birch with her family for Thanksgiving, and I'll go to my folks."

"Emily told me." Emily had, in fact, asked. Which felt weird coming from a woman who sleeps in the same bed as my legal husband and spends an absolutely mind-boggling amount of time sitting where he used to in our kitchen.

"Oh." Marc uses his leg to edge Moby away from some others dog's poo, which Moby was seriously considering eating.

"You two are . . . close these days."

"Against my will."

"I just wanted to let you know that I made a fairly large withdrawal from our joint account. Over New Years, Birch's grandpa has a reservation at a dude ranch for himself and Birch, and they invited me as well, which meant upgrading the reservation, and the money had to be paid up front. I'm sorry I didn't ask you first."

We crunch along in silence, crushing salt and new snow under our boots. I screw up my mouth and relax it and don't shout or cry.

"I'd really appreciate it," I say evenly to Moby's backside, "if you could focus on finishing up our divorce. Please."

"I'm sorry, Grace."

"Yeah, well, me too. But I'm not the one who broke my marriage vows." I straighten and walk briskly down the path that loops back to the parking lot and my car. Marc doesn't try and keep up.

* * *

"Marc and I met in the first week of my freshman year at the University of Iowa," I say to Beth from the couch in her therapy office. I am not lying down, but it has not escaped my attention that there are five boxes of tissues situated within arm's reach. I don't plan on crying, but Beth clearly expects something else.

"I requested a single un-air-conditioned room in the dorms, hoping not to have to deal with roommates. I got assigned to a quad instead. But it had a kitchenette so . . ."

I don't think my feelings about my first dorm are really central to this story. But they feel a lot easier to talk about than Marc. The whole long sequence of events becomes vivid in my memory as I tell Beth the story.

It turned out to be the best room on campus. It had a ton of windows and a great view. The only person in the room when I got there was a blue-eyed brunette wearing a very thin fuzzy sweater, a short red plaid skirt, and a pair of beat-up black Doc Martens. A visible belly-button ring moved in sync with her erratic breathing patterns. She had several other piercings including a silver hoop located at the tail end of her right eyebrow, one tiny diamond stud on the side of her nose, and silver-lined black owl earrings in the center of each earlobe. A half-empty bag of peanut butter M&Ms was tossed next to a pile of books on what I presumed was her desk.

Looking up she asked, "Who are you?" like I might be lost, not her new roommate.

"Uh, your roommate, Grace."

"You are not!"

"Okay, I'm not."

"You are?"

"Yes, I am!" I asked her to help me with one of my suitcases, and she did. I started moving clothes into my part of the closet.

"They are going to be in for the major shock of their lives when they see you," she announced. "You are definitely not what we were expecting."

"What does that mean, exactly?"

"It's nothing bad. Don't worry!" Her mouth formed a circle of temporary horror. Then she snapped her lips upwards into a friendly smile. "It's just that we all lived here last year. The three of us got along like you wouldn't believe, but the other girl was an absolute nightmare. We were relieved when she decided to live off campus with her boyfriend instead of with us. But then we were contestants in the game of roommate roulette. Casey was a nutcase, but there's always a chance of getting the next level of crazy town. When we got our housing assignments over the summer, we called each other wondering who you were. Looking at your name, we all assumed you were a Dutch or Norwegian chick—definitely not Chinese."

"I'm not Chinese."

"Oh well, Japanese, then. Anyway, the rest of H465 went to get lunch. I volunteered to stay behind to meet you, but I had in my head I was going to welcome a blonde and blue-eyed Scandinavian farm girl to our group."

"Farm girl?"

"Don't you have an Indianola mailing address?"

"That's where my grandparents live. We used that as a permanent address because my family was in the middle of moving when I filled out the application."

"Huh, right," she grunted, obviously uninterested in why I listed Indianola, not Des Moines on the address line. She introduced herself. "I'm Cindy, by the way. Cindy Crawford."

In a moment of perfect timing, I told her, "Well, you

certainly are not the Cindy Crawford I expected to meet today."

She responded with laughter that spiraled around my rib cage, erasing any evidence of offense. Cindy declared, "We're going to have a lot of fun this year, all of us, but especially you and me. I can already tell we have a lot in common."

I thought we had absolutely nothing in common, but that is why Cindy Crawford—the communications major, not the famous supermodel—became my favorite roommate. She grew up in Chicago, was an only child and a Republican vegetarian, and wanted to run an upscale B&B someday but hoped her first post after graduating would be working for Oprah.

As Cindy predicted, the other roommates, Jenny and Tara, were shocked, but they were much subtler in readjusting their eyes to connect the name to my face. Jenny and Cindy noticed a family photo I pinned on the bulletin board above my workstation and asked how each person was related to me. In the process of providing this information, they were also granted the how and why I was adopted by a Norwegian family. I didn't think Tara, a psychology major, who opted out of looking at my family photos to put away her groceries, was paying attention until she piped in from the kitchenette, "Good grief, your mom's vagina must still be exhausted after having that many children. No one has more than two kids these days," and stated, "You have to be Catholic."

Cindy mischievously winked at me and said, "How rude, Tara! You shouldn't assume based on family size what religion a person believes in, especially when in fact, Grace's family follows the teachings and practice paths of Buddhism."

I nodded my head and laughed but told Tara the truth.

That night Cindy came up with the idea that ultimately led to me meeting Marc. I never would have gone along with anything like it before. For the evening I was to be Vivienne Tran. Vivienne was not my real first name. My Vietnamese name was too difficult to pronounce. Vivienne hadn't been taught English because she was from a remote village, but was such a brilliant mathematics student, she had been recruited to work and study with the department here. The university provided Vivienne with both a full-time interpreter and tutor.

My three roommates were assigned to be student ambassadors to make Vivienne feel welcome in America, Iowa, and Iowa City and introduce her to the campus nightlife scene at the University of Iowa before classes started. If anyone used or called me by my real name, the punishment would be dish duty for a week. If it was a repeated offense, the offender would have to do everyone's laundry for a month. We were to never ever break character, no matter what.

It was after midnight when we left the Fieldhouse, a popular campus bar. Our shoes were sticky from dancing on a concrete floor saturated in spilled beer and sweat, *our throats scraped raw from hollering to be heard over the excessively loud music and crowd of overexcited voices, and our egos stroked from not having to shell out money for one single drink. Each one of us either took or gave a phone number, confirming love or lust was possible for the upcoming semester. We were drunk on the camaraderie of hope and happiness—and youthful optimism.*

Cindy was eager to resume our foreign student game outside the noisy club. As we walked past a store window, she pointed to a faceless mannequin modeling a belted leather coat and gave an English lesson in very loud bursts of oddly spaced staccato phrasing: "Vivienne . . . this . . . is . . . a . . . store. Store. Stooore. That"
—pointing— "is . . . a . . . jacket. Ja . . . cket. Jacket."

I played my part and feigned limited understanding. "Ahh so."

I was their Vietnamese Helen Keller. Cindy led me by the arm and frantically pointed at this and that while pantomiming the essence of their meaning as she slowly and loudly pronounced the word linked to each object. The other two accomplices tried to keep up with us as we zigzagged from one learning point to another, with the aim of eventually making our way to the next bar. Cindy was egged on by our inebriated peers, who showered her with compliments for her patience teaching me to correctly assign the English words to everything from nouns such as window, bouncer, and puke to verbs like drink, smile, and skip—and a range of adjectives to start conversations with anyone who caught her attention.

"Gor . . . geous . . . gorgeous boys. Boys." Cindy's ultra-slow words slurred together as she pointed in the direction of a group of five guys standing around a blue and white striped food stand. Spirals of steam circled around the pedestrian mall, luring customers in with the intoxicating smell of sliced, salted fried potatoes and roasted pieces of lamb wrapped in warm pita bread.

"Are you talking about me?" A slender kid with freckles and sensibly groomed auburn hair pointed at himself.

Cindy grinned. This was the one she was hoping would say something. She sauntered over their way, and the rest of us followed.

"Is she deaf?" a friend of Cindy's redheaded target asked anyone who was willing to answer. I thought he looked exactly like Rolf Gruber from The Sound of Music, but this copy wore a NY Yankees baseball cap, and his name was Marc Timothy Hunter. The street vendor handed him a foil-wrapped gyro, which Marc grabbed along with a few napkins. He was looking in my direction when he took his first bites of the pre-hangover snack.

"No, she's Vietnamese with a name that is too long and difficult to pronounce so we're calling her Vivienne. Our Vietnamese Vivienne," Jenny, my bottom bunkmate, explained. She started to giggle but pulled herself together at the thought of spending at least one afternoon in the laundry room on her own as punishment if

she gave us away. "She just arrived today and doesn't know one single word of English. Her interpreter doesn't arrive until tomorrow, so we're trying to teach her as much as we can tonight."

"Vivienne . . . this . . . is . . . lamb. LAMB," Marc screamed at me. He must have thought the louder he bellowed, the greater chance we would have of leaping over the language barrier together. He bleated loudly and at length, much to my amusement. Then he mimicked the way he believed lambs jumped around in open fields.

I had an easier part to play than the rest of my comrades. I didn't have to say anything. When I suppressed fits of giggling, it just looked like I didn't understand. When I turned my head away, it was interpreted as diplomatic humiliation for not knowing how to communicate in English.

Being wordless was powerful. I was given grace and free food. Marc generously shared his gyro with me, and the others were given an easy opening to flirt and stay out late. Our first night as roommates, we didn't return to the dorm until shortly after the cafeteria opened for breakfast.

Forced to admit Cindy's idea was fun even though it was at my expense, I told her I'd be willing to be Vivienne again, but not that week. Classes were starting, and a high-pitched throbbing in the back of my head started as well.

"Start and Exit" is what I called the way I tricked my

high school teachers into thinking I was not intimidated by class participation. Sometime during the first week of class, I answered a question with an incredibly lengthy response. Most of the time, this was enough to get me through at least the first semester without being singled out. I planned to use the same strategy for my college career, starting with Monday's class.

To compensate for how much I despised being part of the education system, I developed coping mechanisms, like taking a couple extra seconds drinking at the water fountain, making tick marks with my pen on the palm of my hand tracking the hours left in the school day, or even something as silly as balancing on one leg and counting to ten or twenty while waiting in the hallway.

There were moments sitting at a desk when I panicked as my throat closed off air flow. I was less concerned about suffocating than fainting and falling out of the chair or collapsing into epileptic convulsions resulting in all my irrational fears and worries being exposed for everyone to see. I didn't want anyone to find out I was always on the verge of tears at the thought of being called on by the teacher and not having an answer or having the wrong one.

While students who signed up for the 8:30 a.m. Introduction to Political Behavior course were present for the first lecture, most were still caught in various stages of sleep, slumped over in their Schaeffer Hall stadium seats, but I was wide awake and prepared for any question

Professor Nelson planned to launch at us. After summarizing the course description, he asked, "Do any of you have any initial thoughts about the abysmal voter turnout in America?" This was my chance to stand out and then disappear.

I had guessed and prepared for a question such as this. Fortunately, he saw and acknowledged my raised hand. My answer was a four-and-a-half minute thoroughly researched synopsis of voter apathy, a notation of the attention Iowa received during presidential election years, a reference to the upcoming assigned readings including an interpretation of Max Weber's social action theory and a quote from Hannah Arendt:

"The sad truth is that most evil is done by people who never make up their minds to be good or evil."

I didn't take a breath between words. I could feel heads turning in my direction, but I didn't stop until I reached the concluding sentence. Professor Nelson didn't ask for my name when I finished. I don't think he could even see me from where I was sitting in the back of the auditorium and, to my disappointment, only said this reminded him that everyone should purchase the assigned texts by the end of the week. Lesson 1: College is significantly different from high school.

It was a superstitious ritual my brain couldn't give up, in spite of realizing circumstances had changed, merely functioning out of habit and not wanting the hours of reading and rehearsing to be wasted. After the class was dismissed nearly forty minutes later, I was still flushed from the release of adrenaline and embarrassment, so I rushed to escape. I didn't see the tall blond going against the crowd from where he was sitting six rows in front of me. He blocked me from moving out of the aisle.

"I just wanted you to know how impressed I was with how fast you mastered the English language," my Saturday night Rolf Gruber said with a tilted grin. "I think you owe me a gyro and a side of fries. What do you think?"

"And that's how Marc and I met and started dating."

Chapter 36

Beth walks in front of me on our way out. She reminds me she will be away for a conference for two weeks next month, and I should think about how I would like to schedule my sessions. Would I like two sessions in one week or to just skip altogether until she returns? She turns back and must sense my uncertainty because she says, "Think it over and let me know next week. You don't need to decide today." And with that, I am done with today's work.

On Wednesday night, one part of Marc's family was well on its way to the Buckeye state—the other was busily prepping to get its assigned items ready to take to a farmhouse in Indianola the next day. I had pumpkin and pecan pies baking in the oven and was stirring spiced cranberry sauce when Emily called to let us know they are only an hour away from her parents' house. Then Marc was off to Dayton. Bailey and Kelsey were occupied with assembling twenty-three personalized pinecone-turkey place holders for the dining room table.

After they speak to their dad, Bailey turns the volume back up on the *Everything is Wrong* album playing in the background. Moby snoozes under the table, catching glitter in his fur. Kelsey comes over for a hug, an act of forgiveness for my prior misconduct. If I don't think about Marc's sister taking pleasure in Emily's return, I felt quite happy with the way things are.

Thanksgiving is my favorite day of the year. It marks the start of a month-long break from dieting and of celebrating beloved family recipes. A guilt-free gastronomical extravaganza to delight all five senses scheduled for every fourth Thursday of November fits into my idea of a perfect holiday. This doesn't mean there isn't dysfunctional chaos associated with the harvest feast, as I'm reminded when we arrive today.

"Oh my God, you won't believe what Grandma did!" Ellie, my nine-year-old niece, screeches as I step inside the house. Her freckled skinny arms wildly fly up in the air.

Bailey impatiently moves from behind to carry the wicker basket with the two pies into the kitchen. Kelsey follows with the cooler filled with bags of ice, bottles of fizzy drinks, and side dishes. They enter pandemonium's hub. Grandma's fancy double oven draws the majority of our clan into the kitchen, where layer upon layer of dissonant conversations evict silence from the entire house.

I blissfully inhale the scent of earthy herbs and sounds of merriment circulating from room to room from this pre-dining rampage.

Amaya's third child has her hands firmly placed on her hips and blocks me from going in. She looks more and more like a miniature version of my sister every time I see her—a Carmen Sandiego explorer type with a little bit of Reba McEntire country music star mixed in—and just as determined not to be ignored when she has something important to say.

"She forgot to turn on the oven!" Ellie blurts. "That turkey is as cold as any frozen mummified Ice Age carcass discovered by random gold miners in Siberia. We won't be eating for hours and hours thanks to your mom. What do you think about that?" I assume her assessment of the situation is based on what she has learned from watching the Discovery Channel.

"Problem solved!" Kelsey announces as she parades through the crowd holding a pumpkin pie. Jacob follows her, clutching two aerosol cans of whipped cream. "Dessert first and the kids get to sit at the head table with Grandpa. We're mixing things up, people!"

And so it is. We let the children reset the order of things, and our Thanksgiving starts with pie and ends with turkey. This shake-up is the perfect icebreaker. Mathew brushes off my apology and admits he overreacted. Christina and Amaya organize an all-day movie-watching marathon at Grandpa's farmhouse. I fib and tell Mom she isn't a moron for placing a twenty-pound stuffed bird in a roasting tray on the bottom rack and then never checking on or basting the thing for over four hours but tell her the truth that her mistake has given us plenty to talk about for the next couple of hours, days, and months.

While we squirt whipped cream on the dessert of our choice, we unanimously agree this is the most memorable, if not the best, Purviance family Thanksgiving we've ever celebrated together. Although Mom asks for a second chance to be in charge of the turkey next year, we all let her know she is not allowed anywhere near the oven for any of our future gatherings. I swear a little smile twitches at the corners of her mouth, but she snatches it back into an offended pout. Ellie and Amaya volunteer to take over the turkey duty, and everyone cheers.

It is such a good day, I forget to be depressed we aren't with Marc and his family. I haven't wondered once if we are missed. This seems like a weird thing to be thankful for, but I am and make a mental note to talk to my therapist about it when I see her next. But for now, happiness is seeing all the kids seated at the head table with the patriarch of our family as he carves the turkey.

* * *

Bailey reasons since she's fever free and was with family yesterday, she should be allowed to go Black

Friday shopping with her friends. Partly because she has a convincing argument, but mostly because she's driving me crazy, I grant permission for her to get out of my hair for a couple hours. I'm in desperate need of some quiet time to recharge for a bit. Kelsey is off with Caleb and Ian to see an independent film at the Varsity Cinema, so I have the entire house—and the television set—to myself until Mary Anne arrives for her appointment.

Mary Anne has lost an impressive amount of weight since we first met, but constantly berates herself for not making as much progress as she thinks she needs to achieve an aggressive goal of losing 110 pounds in ten months.

She arrives early, catching me watching Corie and Paul's early days of marriage in the 1967 movie *Barefoot in the Park* while eating heaps of leftover turkey and cornbread stuffing. I confess how my obsession with classic chick flicks can take over an entire weekend or holiday break. It's a common occurrence to find me buried under mountains of tissues, empty boxes of Milk Duds, and microwave popcorn bags during one of my movie-watching binges. Mary Anne absolves me from my time-wasting sins, and we move into the dining room, which I've turned into a fitting room for my most loyal client.

"What did you do yesterday?" I mechanically ask while taking a blue tailoring tape measure and dressmaker's pins out of my concertina sewing box. Most clients will find a polite way to ask why I use this to store my portable equipment. The wood panels are heavily scuffed and marked, both lids are barely attached, and the multicolored pom-pom trim lining each compartment is not only hideously tacky, but severely ripped and frayed. The carrying case sat in Grandma's sewing corner for as long as I could remember, so I claimed it for my own projects.

"Not much. Got caught up on some cleaning and laundry," she answers and then takes a quick peek at herself in the mirror. After pulling off her woolly sweater, her hair responds by standing on end as if she's been holding onto a static electricity generator at the Science Center. She retrieves a hairbrush from her purse to smooth it back into place.

"What did you eat for Thanksgiving dinner?"

"I wasn't too bad. I had a Lean Cuisine pepperoni pizza and a couple of Skinny Cow mint ice cream sandwiches. I should've made a salad but didn't want to do any chopping or dicing. I know that sounds lazy. But I did get on the treadmill while I watched a full episode of *Nip/Tuck*, so hopefully that erased one of the ice cream sandwiches from the calorie board."

"Didn't you and Herbie have a turkey dinner?" Surprise pops into my voice. I look up and see Mary Anne looks distressed as she yanks the brush through a clump of hair. She is turning redder and redder by the moment.

"Well . . . Herbie was away," she starts to explain.

At the same time, I apologize by saying, "What an

idiotic thing to ask when I know you're dieting, which is the whole point of us getting together today." Then, "Wait—what? You and Herbie didn't spend Thanksgiving together?"

"He . . . he was away for the week . . . I mean . . . he's traveling for work so couldn't . . . so we couldn't, you know, be with each other for Thanksgiving . . . for the day . . . but really, it's not a big deal."

"But you should've told me you'd be all alone." I feel terrible that I didn't know she needed a place to go.

"It really wasn't a big deal. I didn't even remember it was Thanksgiving. This year has flown by so fast that the holiday kind of snuck up on me. And Herbie told me a long time ago he had to be in . . . to go to this thing . . . this conference or meeting thing out of town. And then he was in a rush, and we just left things as they were, without either of us really caring or remembering it was a national holiday."

"I really wish I'd known because we had plenty of room for you to join us. We could've added a dozen extra people, and none of my family would've cared or noticed," I insist.

"I think I might've felt a little awkward, but it's nice to know it would've been an option. It's so very sweet of you to care, but it's really okay. I'm used to being on my own. What I mean to say is that Herbie and I just aren't into celebrating holidays, and I'm fine with being in my own company."

"But what about your family? Didn't they do anything?"

Why can't I shut up?

"That's kind of a long story," she sighs.

"Oh my God, Mary Anne, I really don't know why I keep asking such nosy questions. What is wrong with me? You really don't have to tell me anything." I'm the one feverishly blushing now.

"No, it's okay." She hesitates and then comes out with, "They all went on a Disney cruise. I couldn't afford to go this year. The bills are piling up faster than I can pay them. I got an estimate for the food for the reception a couple weeks ago and nearly had a heart attack. You know how it is. To get what you want, tying the knot can be incredibly expensive."

"So I've heard, although I personally wouldn't know how much a wedding costs. As a little girl, I dreamed of getting married inside the Vatican City at St. Peter's Basil-ica.I even called a travel agent on my thirteenth birthday to find out how much it was to rent a villa for my guests. Can you imagine how much all that would've cost if I'd had my way?"

I sigh wistfully. "I don't know what would have hap-pened if my birth control hadn't failed my last semester of college. That positive pregnancy test was a precursor to Ian impulsively finding an engagement ring and hastily proposing, which ended up being more of a strategy ses-sion than a romantic invitation, but I was over the moon with happiness."

"You mean Marc, right?" Mary Anne asks.

"Oh no!" I gasp. "Marc. Of course I meant Marc. Two days after he asked and I said yes, we were holding hands while listening to instructions at the Johnson County's marriage license office front counter.

"He couldn't believe a marriage license cost twenty-five dollars, and we had to wait three days for it to be valid. He tried to argue with the clerk about it. He compared it to a gun license. She told him, 'Guns can cause harm, but so can marriages.'

"Marc refused to let it go. He called it a love tax. I was appalled that he was making a fuss about such a small amount, especially since Marc had convinced me that eloping was not only romantic, but practical. With the money we saved not having a wedding, we could make a substantial down payment on a really nice first house. The more he challenged the license fee, the angrier I became, thinking of the wedding dress we no longer had to pay for.

" 'Hey darlin', ' the clerk called out loud enough for everyone in front of and behind the counter to hear. 'Are you absolutely sure he's the one, sweetheart?'

"My face turned a thousand shades redder than a fire engine and a million times hotter than towering flames burning down a high-rise building.

"I was furious—but not at Marc anymore. At the clerk.

" 'Marc T. Hunter, this will be the best twenty-five dollars you'll ever spend,' I snapped some sense into him. 'Pay up and shut up!' And he did.

"We got the check back as a wedding gift from that clerk and everybody else in the office. They'd framed it. It's still my favorite wedding present."

Mary Anne laughs at my expense, which makes me feel better about my insensitivity. She also finds it amusing that I've created a catwalk with battery operated pillar candles leading from my bedroom to the dining room and a playlist to accompany this afternoon's fashion show.

Chapter 37

We bring her clothing into the bedroom, and I leave her to change into one of the first outfits I made for her—a black wool gabardine suit with a fitted jacket and wide-leg pants. We are both genuinely surprised and pleased to discover it will need quite a few inches taken in to fit properly. Emboldened by the tune "I'm Too Sexy", Mary Anne sashays across the floor as she models a red tiered corduroy dress with bracelet length sleeves. Her confidence skyrockets when I confirm that this one will need to be reduced by at least two sizes as well. Serenaded by girl-power tunes, we easily get into a groove of her coming and going and me marking and pinning.

With only a few more items to go, Mary Anne flinches when I pin the seam of an oversized button-down cotton shirt she claims is super comfortable and often wears with stretch pants and tall leather boots. This inadvertent wince shoots sorrow into my bloodstream. There has never been a word spoken about her past since our first appointment, but evidence of trauma haunts her body.

It shows up at every fitting we've ever had, and I feel a murderous rage for what those boys did to Mary Anne, which manifests itself into a protective and determined stance of wanting to make clothing that makes her feel beautiful. And, if possible, safe.

It ends up taking almost two hours to get through all the items needing a nip and tuck here and there. I feign exasperation about all the work it will take to reduce her garments by at least two sizes and lie when she insists on paying and tell her the work has slowed down so I need something to fill the time during my insomnia attacks. We agree to the terms and conditions of this appointment, and she commissions three new outfits. Once our appointment is over, we stop being business owner and client and are simply two friends trying to figure out what to eat for dinner.

My youngest courteously updates me of her whereabouts with a call, asking if she can go with Caleb and Ian to Noah's for pizza. Permission is granted as I glance at my watch and wonder why Bailey hasn't checked in. She was given specific instructions to let me know by a certain time if I'm the adult responsible for driving her and her friends home, and it's an hour past when I told her to do so. The girl is stepping all over my nerves as she tests her limits. Mary Anne comes to her defense with a guess that crazed, deal-seeking shoppers are shoving and pushing Bailey and her friends into areas of the shopping center where it's impossible to make a cell phone call either because of bad reception or excessive noise levels. I wish this were the case but think it's more likely she didn't want to ask permission to stay out longer with her friends and is keeping her cell phone out of sight to avoid seeing any of her unread texts from her nagging mother.

Ian rings to say his three-ring circus decided it was too crowded to eat in the restaurant, and would I be okay if they ordered and brought pizza back with them. Mary Anne and I are delighted to be included and add a couple salads, an Italian meatball sandwich (I don't want pizza), a slice of their famous chocolate blackout cake (which I quickly regret and say no dessert needed), and a dozen bread rolls to the order. Because the restaurant is so busy with orders, they don't arrive with the food until the credits are rolling for *Father Goose*, a Cary Grant movie I can't believe Mary Anne has never seen or heard of in all the years she has been on this planet. I was sure she'd like the classic movie as much as I do, but I'm not sure she did by the number of times she checked her phone for messages and how relieved she looks hearing the door open as I'm showing her the cover of *Breakfast at Tiffany's.*

Caleb brings in not a slice, but a whole chocolate blackout cake to split among the six of us. This is Bailey's absolute all-time favorite dessert, so I send her a text letting her know I'm holding her slice hostage until she contacts me.

"Mom, you will not believe what happened to us."

Kelsey punctuates each word with a follow-up gulping sound.

"Oh really?" A flashback of her at seven years old with the same amount of enthusiasm bursting into the kitchen to tell me how I had to come into the bedroom right at that second to see the most incredible thing I'd ever see in my whole entire life—Moby dressed up in one of her ballet costumes—comes to mind and makes me chuckle.

"No, Mom, it's huge. Unbelievably big. You will not believe it."

"So don't hold me in suspense then. What won't I believe?"

"Ian made friends with the movie theater owner's daughter when he bought Caleb and me popcorn at the counter, and now we're all invited to the theatre's private—yes, you heard me, private as in not everyone gets invited—anniversary party. Can you believe it? So very super cool, don't ya think?" she squeals.

"Impressive," I agree and wink at Ian before asking, "You didn't invite her out on a date, did you? Because if you did, make sure you tell me in advance where it is so I don't show up and get us all uninvited from the party."

"That's not funny." Kelsey frowns as she pours root beer into her glass. She glares in our direction before going into the freezer for ice cubes.

"I don't know." Ian pauses for effect and says in spite of Kelsey's disapproval, "Dull dates are the worst, and that last one of mine was certainly the furthest from being categorized as boring. I tell you what. If I get bored on my next date, can I ask you to be on standby to come and spice things up?"

"So not funny," Kelsey snaps as she takes her place at the table. "In fact, annoyingly unamusing."

"Speaking of which, where is your sister?"

"She hasn't called?"

"Nope, and I'm getting very annoyed now."

Kelsey utters a singsong, "Someone's in trouuuuble!"

"She's three hours past when I told her to be home."

"Double trouuuuble!" she sings.

It is half past eight and worry is creeping in. Mary Anne and Ian come up with a number of excuses for her lack of communication. I reluctantly agree to give her thirty more minutes to reach out with an update of her coordinates and ETA. But I can't wait. I sneak off to the basement to phone the police—not 9-1-1, but the non-emergency number. A nice lady sympathetically tells me a child has to be missing for twenty-four hours for something to be done. I knew this already but hope they might hear my panic and put out an APB or at least send out a couple available squad cars to patrol where she might be hanging out.

I send off three texts demanding to know what is going on. Then I worry it might make her afraid to respond so I leave a voicemail message hoping it conveys genuine concern rather than seething fury. Still nothing.

I fill the next hour with distractions. There is a dinner

plate filled with slices of pizza and most of my meatball sandwich wrapped in cling film waiting for Bailey in the fridge. Five dessert plates are rinsed and placed in the dishwasher. All kitchen surfaces have been wiped with a soapy sponge. The floor has been swept three times. From our street, I wonder if anyone has noticed how many times the curtains have been ever so slightly separated for me to see out. Probably at least fifty partings of the fabric panels occur before darkness falls. Fear has taken over all rational thinking.

While Kelsey is setting up a game of Yahtzee on our coffee table, I sneak off with my cell phone into the basement. Sitting in Bailey's chair biting my nails, I make a snap decision about getting Marc involved with my dilemma. I know where he is because Marc's sister hosts a Black Friday party for the family every year. They are the get up at the crack of dawn prepared to fight through crowds to buy all their Christmas presents for the lowest prices possible. Part of this eight-hour excursion is to find and purchase one particularly tasteless item to bring to Erika's later. If I call now, his mom will be sprinkling marshmallows into mugs of hot cocoa before they all draw names from a hat to determine the order of the gift exchange portion of the night. I really, really do not want to call Marc's sister's house, but he is not answering his cell phone and I know this is the best way to get in contact with the father of my missing child.

She answers her landline with a cheery, "Santa's direct line!" and "Hello? Hello?"

If I'd called half a second later or earlier, I might not have heard her signature laugh, a *fuffuffuffuffu* followed by a *horohorohoro*, in the background. I freeze up.

Marc's sister's shrill, "Anyone there?" shakes me out of my blackout moment so I can identify myself and ask for Marc before she gives up and hangs up the phone.

"What's going on, Grace?" Marc asks with a sharpness I know well. He hates being interrupted as well as getting caught in a lie.

I don't bother asking if Emily is there. What's the point? Instead, I run through the details supporting why I'm freaking out about Bailey's silence.

"You're telling me you let our sick kid run about when the doctor specifically told you she's supposed to be resting? I mean seriously, Grace, what were you thinking?"

"She didn't have a fever . . ."

"So? You don't let the kid tell you what she can or can't do. You are the parent. She is the child. It's that simple."

"I only gave her permission to go out for a couple hours and . . ."

"And what?" he snarls. "Did you also hand over your debit card so she could buy whatever she wants? I bet you did. Because you certainly wouldn't want her to be deprived of having anything she wants, would you?"

"Marc, it's not like that. I . . ."

"It is, Grace," he interrupts me again. "You let the girls get their way all the time."

"I don't let the girls get their own way all the time."

"You do! You always do. Every stinking time, you let them do whatever the hell they want. That's the problem.

You can't or won't tell them no because you don't ever want to be the bad guy. It's pathetic."

"I do tell them no, plenty of times."

"You wouldn't be in this mess if that were true. This whole thing is ridiculous. I can't believe you thought it was okay for her to be around crowds of people when she's sick. It's irresponsible and stupid. Anyone with the tiniest bit of common sense would know to keep their kid home. But no, our kid is out gallivanting about looking for a good time God knows where with Birch's punk-ass friends. Nice one, Grace. You let her go. You figure it out."

"I don't know what to do. That's why I called you."

"You know there's nothing I can do from here, so the only reason I can think of why you called is to check up on me."

"That's not true. I . . ."

"I bet it is," he snaps. "And just in case you're wondering, Emily is here because her parents were shopping at Fairfield Commons mall, and they stopped by for a quick drink before they go back to Athens. I know how you like to overreact, but don't forget Emily's parents are still friends with my family, so don't make more out of it than it is."

"I don't care," I said in truth. "That's not why I called."

"You don't care," he reiterated with bitterness. "I'd say this is exactly what the problem is between us as well."

He hangs up.

This is when I start crying.

Chapter 38

"Grace, you okay down there?" Ian calls down the stairs.

"I'm okay," I manage to squeak between hiccupping.

"I'm coming down," he gives notice as I hear him thud down the stairs.

He seats himself in Kelsey's chair.

"Hey, what's wrong?" His stupid samurai face is full of concern.

"I'm"—I paused to shudder-sob a few times—"okay." The scrap of silk I'm using as a tissue smudges snot across my face, making me cry harder. Ian pulls a handkerchief out of his jeans pocket and promises it's clean.

It wasn't my intention to divulge any details about that phone conversation, but I hear myself say, "He told me I didn't care, which is so not true." Then I can't stop myself from sharing the entire exchange. Ian's demeanor darkens, a mixture of confusion and anger with the occasional raising of an eyebrow and frown.

Hope for a continuation of my marriage is long gone,

but how did I miss that he held his wife and the mother of his children in such contempt? For how long have I been oblivious to the fact that I was failing at both roles? I always thought our daily disputes were normal marital spats, a way of working out our differences, so I let a lot of things slide. It didn't seem worth arguing about the small stuff. But did I need to fight harder to show I cared more? Maybe I gave in too easily to his requests for space and time and should've put up a bigger fight about Emily moving here.

I assigned the blame for all our problems to a mid-life crisis, a challenging life stage, but a temporary one that could be managed and overcome. It never occurred to me that he had been struggling with the dynamics of our marriage. And he thought I was the problem.

How could I have been so oblivious? Bad wife? Maybe. Bad parent? Huh? Although he must have a point about giving in too easily, or Bailey wouldn't be missing, right? What else had I overlooked about my part in all this? I am stubborn. I'm flighty. Oh, and I can come across as distant—and judgmental. What else? Irritatingly controlling? Or a pushover? Uncaring? Clueless?

"Have you heard from Bailey?" Ian interjects into my fault-finding monologue. When I shake my head no, he takes charge of the situation. "You were right. We should've done more earlier. Let's go find her, okay?"

He grabs both my hands and pulls me out of the chair. My head is spinning trying to think of where to start the search. I don't have any of the names or numbers for Birch's crowd, which underscores Marc's point of how stupid I was to not cover the basics before letting our daughter go with a flimsy promise that she'd check-in. And because Bailey isn't hanging out with her usual circle of friends, I have no clue where she could be this late at night.

It's Mary Anne who makes a suggestion based on what she's overheard from the younger demographic of Dairy Queen customers boasting about their "covert" hangout spot they use to get away from adults and cops. I suddenly remember watching a Channel 13 report about a teenager injured by a falling wall. The reporter warned parents to keep their kids away from the site. Birch laughed his head off and said nothing would stop them from hanging out there. As it is better than doing nothing, I accept Ian's offer to drive us there.

Caleb and Kelsey agree that we are majorly overre-acting, but also unquestionably believe Bailey deserves to be severely punished for staying out past her curfew. Right now, the focus is making sure she is out of harm's way. Mary Anne promises to call if Bailey returns before we do. Ian and I take off as the home team sets up another game of Yahtzee.

The navigation system in Ian's car leads us to the abandoned cement factory. Mary Anne's intel is good. I can see the sparks from a bonfire spiraling into the dark sky. We slowly drive past a row of beat-up cars covered in angsty bumper stickers, a sure sign of a teenage population nearby. The tires roll over the gravel with a crunching sound. I worry that kids hiding out from adults might scatter if they suspect a police car is driving up the road.

As if he's read my mind, Ian says, "Let's park here and walk the rest of the way."

He opens my car door and gives me a hand out of the low bucket seat.

"Thanks," I sniffle, my nose still running from crying.

"I'm using this outing as research about what Caleb will be up to in a couple years. He'll probably be a holy terror when puberty hits. I was. So thanks for giving me a chance to see this place. I'll know exactly where to pick Caleb up."

I laugh, though it is not really funny. "I'm glad this predicament benefits both of us as responsible and caring parents."

As we ascend the hill, my hands are freezing. Blowing on them does not generate enough heat to stop the cold from penetrating through the tips of my fingers. Marc would think that forgetting my mittens is another example of how I'm a complete moron. I've heard him say a million times that people failing to dress appropriately for weather conditions is laziness at its worst. People who ignore or don't check the forecast get what they deserve. Mother Nature must be on Marc's side, as it starts to snow.

Ian gives me his gloves. When I try and give them

back, he shakes his head and shoves his hands into his coat pockets. They are two sizes too big, but soft and warm.

Music, a drum and bass beat, is blared across the field and mixes with an ebb and flow of adolescent voices. We exchange furtive glances, nervous and curious about what we will encounter when we reach our destination. It is a half mile uphill climb to get to the roofless rotunda where we encounter the coming-of-age party taking place on the premises.

This hideaway is an adolescent's tip of the hat to freedom and rebellion—a modern-day peace, love, and happiness festival. A dozen or more underage trespassers are using nicotine and alcohol to fuel their extracurricular activities. This doesn't surprise me, but what does are the several volumes of poetry scattered on the ground or in the hands of a few of the Friday night orators. Sylvia Plath, Walt Whitman, and Khalil Gibran are a few of the poets they've selected to read aloud around the fire pit. Some are reading, others are dancing, a few are making out on a tatty burnt sienna sofa. They've somehow acquired quite a collection of cheap booze. Graffiti, a mixture of art and scribbling rants, covers most wall surfaces, and splashes of paint are splattered in sporadic locations across the gravel ground as well. Crushed Busch Light cans and cigarette butts have been tossed in a pile near a stack of red plastic cups. The place smells of berries, cloves, and puke.

This isn't Bailey's usual scene. She's a preppy, department-store kind of girl, not a bohemian, bargain-shopper type, therefore I assume she's somewhere else, not with these hooligans.

As I turn to Ian to tell him we should get out of here, I see facial features I recognize, but nothing else. Relief and disbelief lock my line of vision into place so the only thing I can do is gawk at a stark new version of Bailey.

Her hair, once dark brown and straight, is dyed a silvery violet color and twisted into dreadlocks. Intertwined into the rolled sections are strands of thin braids held together with tiny ornamental beads that snap against the middle of her back as she twists her neck to turn to the boy who wants her attention. This Ozzy Osbourne look-alike is holding a worn paperback copy of Herman Hesse's *Siddhartha* under his arm while he hands Bailey a pack of cigarettes.

I march over, smack the cigarettes to the ground, and take hold of her chin to see what else has been done. Someone has applied her makeup so she no longer looks like a child, but a vampy streetwalker. Even more deplorable, as these can't be washed away with soap, a silver ring and cubic zirconia stud have been pierced through her lip and nose. You would think there'd be some kind of penitent response for being caught red-handed, but Bailey looks at me as if I'm the criminal.

Chapter 39

Furious that she has made all these changes without my permission, I lose my cool and screech out high-pitched commands announcing to Bailey's peers that uninvited adults have invaded their space. The two necking on the sofa have disconnected their lips from each other and are staring openmouthed. Seeing this drunken couple takes irritation to a new level.

"Pull up your pants," I bark at a pimply kid guzzling a can of Red Bull. "No one wants to see your Calvin Klein underpants."

And then some kind of deranged maternal instinct kicks in, and I clean up their mess. I'm slamming bottles into a dented aluminum garbage can, satisfied by the sounds of glass hitting glass, and shouting obscenities while scolding all of them for frying their brains.

I snatch a Marlboro from a girl's mouth and snub it out on the "A" in the "Question Authority" scrawled out in red spray paint on the concrete wall. I observe Ian talking to Bailey. She nods her head, takes his set of car keys,

and starts walking towards the cavernous opening opposite from where I am. Ian rushes over before I can follow
her and leads me by the arm to another exit. "Grace, I
know you're upset," he calmly validates my feelings. "But
let's get Bailey home safe and sound and deal with the
consequences later. You're only going to make it worse if
she takes off and we have to look for her again."

This makes sense. I'm still furious and shake free
from Ian's grip but walk back with him to the car. The
new Bailey is sitting in the passenger seat, arms crossed
and hunched down, staring out the window, refusing to
acknowledge our presence.

Adrenaline is replaced with fatigue. I climb into the
backseat from the driver's side and silently sob in the
dark. I text Marc that Bailey is found and do not check
my phone when it pings with his replies. Bailey and Ian
exclude me from their front-seat conversation about
the evolution and history of alternative rock music, but
I don't care. It has been a very long day and night, and I
just want a hot bubble bath and a good night's sleep.

Before any such thing can happen, I have to call Marc.
When he called, I sent it to voicemail. I delete the voicemail without listening.

Once Ian and Mary Anne return to their homes and
the kids are in bed, I take Moby for a late-night walk. He
doesn't need it, but I do. On our way back up the drive, I
stop to scowl at Ian's panda. It makes me feel better.

Inside, I settle onto the couch and call Marc. I attempt

to give him a rundown of where our daughter was, but he interrupts to berate me and yell at each new turn of the story. It takes nearly an hour to get him the pertinent information. I talk for perhaps five minutes of the hour. The rest is Marc. I forget to tell him about the hair, the piercings, and the makeup.

I then call Dr. Bennett-Hill though 1) she is in Costa Rica and 2) even if she weren't she wouldn't be answering the phone right now and 3) if she were here, I would be trying to get an appointment for tomorrow, which I couldn't do in the middle of the night anyhow.

I listen to her answering message. "Hello, you have reached the office of Dr. Bennett-Hill. I am currently away from the office and will return on Monday. If you need assistance before my return, please call Dr. Jerri Subban at extension 311. If this is an emergency, hang up and dial 911 or go to your local emergency room."

I leave her three voicemails outlining the whole disaster.

I try out the bubble bath, then climb into my PJ's and bed to stare at the ceiling for two hours, contemplating my many failures as a wife and mother. I dip into Marc's failures as husband and father occasionally, but this does not produce the same bruise-poking fascination as self-flagellation.

At three a.m. I give up, start some laundry, and wipe down the main bathroom. I make myself fully caffeinated coffee and compose a text to Mathew, requesting he and whatever gas station junk food he can afford come to my house tomorrow. As I am rinsing my cup in the sink in preparation for peppermint tea, I am once again confronted with the plastic panda's inane grin, fully illuminated by two spotlights.

"Goddamn panda," I mutter, and this, like scowling at it earlier, seems to provide a kind of comfort not to be found elsewhere.

I inspect Ian's windows. All dark. He's not losing sleep over Bailey. No matter how much he might predict Caleb's eventual rebellion, Caleb was with him all day, safe and sound. No one would have predicted Bailey's. No matter how Marc might blame me for lax parenting, she's never gone missing before. She's been late, but not without good reason, not without checking in.

The panda continues his all-knowing leer. I drop the mug into the sink. Peppermint tea can wait. I walk out the kitchen door and clamber over Ian's fence, continuing through the yard until I am face to face with the smarmy little jerk.

I stare it down. It continues to smile up at me. Up close, the fingers are somehow even more improbably obscene. I snatch at him, but he doesn't budge. His feet are zip-tied to the pedestal.

I twist him from side to side, working the feet out from their bonds. The pillar rocks from side to side as I grapple. I stumble over one of the spotlights stuck into the ground. The panda falls with me, and we wrestle on the ground. With a hollow pop and some swearing I feel may have crossed a line, even if I am alone, the panda comes free.

I stand and tuck him under my arm, vaulting the fence with the easy confidence of a twenty-year-old. Unfortunately, I land on the feet of a middle-aged mother, and my knees feel like they're seventy. I limp into the kitchen and slam the panda triumphantly on the island.

This is when I realize I have done something strange and irreversible. I could go put the panda back—or leave him next to his toppled column, but I will always know that in the wee hours of the morning, I wrestled him to the ground. And every time I see his inane little face, I will live the whole thing all over again.

Also, what the hell am I going to do with him? He can't stay on my island. People will ask questions. Ian will ask questions. I have removed him from his place in my window, but now he is my panda, and I am the one that has to do something with him.

I carry him around the house putting him in various hiding places and then thinking the better of it and retrieving him—her?—it?

Eventually we are back in the kitchen together, and I am craving egg rolls. I set him on the stool next to mine and make another cup of coffee. "It's you and me," I tell the panda, though I don't really know what I mean by that. "Just you and me."

A sound. I hear a sound from upstairs. A faint thump

of feet on the ground, the creak of floorboards. The door at the top of the stairs. I move like lightning. I cram the panda under the sink on his side behind the grease trap. I busy myself righting all the cleaning supplies I have knocked over. The forest of bottles and spray nozzles obscure the panda, who is barely visible in the gloom anyway. I throw a few rags into the back. When Bailey enters the kitchen, I am wiping the door of the sink cabinet.

"Good morning," I say.

Bailey says nothing. My activity is not suspicious. She once came down to get a drink at four in the morning, and I had taken apart the faucet and was cleaning out its crevices with a toothpick. She does glare at me to let me know she's not talking to me. I wiggle my eyebrows at her à la Groucho Marx. She fills a cup with cold water, stares me in the eyes, and then downs it. She sets the cup next to the sink a little harder than necessary and then turns and goes back upstairs.

I stand, my knees aching, and yawn. The clock says four a.m. I go upstairs and climb into bed. I sleep not like a baby—babies don't sleep that well—but like the dead.

Chapter 40

The out-of-office voice mail message has not changed in two weeks. I'm praying their private clinic's phone system is not able to track the number of times I've called to check if by some small chance she has returned to work early. Why would a therapist abandon her patients for a Costa Rican vacation during the holidays anyway? I know it was reasonable to call once or twice a week, and excessively needy to do so three or four times on a daily basis, yet still choose to do so.

When Marc arrives home, I realize I still haven't remembered to mention her change of appearance. He saw it like I did—unprepared. He didn't say much to her about it, but to me he's said plenty. For weeks, Marc spins himself into a voluble cyclone. A nonstop onslaught of resentment circulates in all of his messages to make sure it is perfectly clear he is not responsible for our daughter's unwelcome transformation. I am slammed with Marc's check-ins morning, noon, and night, by phone or computer. Out of guilt, fatigue, or both, I answer each text or e-mail by letting him know Bailey is resting in her bed, going to the bathroom, or watching movies on the sofa—she is not out of my sight.

But house arrest courtesy of mono cannot last forever. After fourteen fever-free days, Dr. Butt gives Bailey permission to return to school. I'm thrilled to be relieved of prison-guard duty. Beth is back, and I get an appointment for the first day of Bailey's return to school. On the way, I get a call from an unknown number, which I ignore. By the time I reach the parking lot, the number is calling me for the fourth time. I pick up.

"Is this Bailey Hunter's mother?" asks a polite male voice. My insides go cold.

"Yes."

"Well, Ma'am, I'm the manager of the bowling alley. Your daughter tried to pay for some pop and pizza a little bit ago using a credit card with your name on it."

I rest my head on the steering wheel. "Oh really?" I say.

"I told her I could call the police or her parents. She chose you."

I grit my teeth and straighten. "Well," I say, "She's gonna wish you'd called the cops."

I am at the bowling alley before I even realize I am going to miss my appointment with Beth. A group of Bailey's so-called friends are cheering and booing a group of co-ed retirees while smoking Marlboro Lights and eating nachos. I glare at them, and a few shrink back.

I recognize some of them from the abandoned factory, and I'm sure they recognize me. One of them holds up his hands like he's surrendering to the cops and another stubs out his cigarette. It is only Bailey who seems uncowed. She sits in her chair in the manager's office and tips her chin at me carelessly. It's not even defiance. It's confidence that there is nothing I can do to rein her in.

I call Emily from my kitchen after sending Bailey up to her room. She cannot get out without going past me. There are no convenient branches, porch roofs, or drain-pipes that she might climb down. I checked. I will inform Marc eventually. When I feel ready. Emily listens to my rant about Bailey becoming a juvenile delinquent head-ing in the direction of becoming a hardened criminal and how it will be all my fault (partly Marc's) because I failed to make it clear that I won't tolerate stealing, lying, or being disrespectful to either of her parents.

"We-ell," Emily says eventually. She has that tone in her voice—that sparkle of mischief. I don't know what Marc does when he hears it. He hates mischief.

"What?" I ask. "What?"

She has an idea—an idea that makes me think I'd be friends with this woman if she weren't involved with my soon-to-be ex-husband.

* * *

"Please, Mom, don't do this," Bailey begs. the next

morning. Various degrees of being petrified, annoyed, terrified, and resigned to the fact there is probably nothing she can do about her punishment are combined into one pitiful frown.

"You have demonstrated you cannot be trusted," I say firmly. "And although I'm undecided about whether to tell your father you stole from his stash of cigarettes, I refuse to change my mind about escorting and sitting next to you for every single one of your classes today. I bet I'll finish my library book by the end of the day, don't you think? And won't it be great to have lunch together in the cafeteria?"

"Why this? Can't you just ground me for two weeks or a month like what every other parent would do to their kid?"

"Since I don't know what you're up to these days, it will give me peace of mind to become familiar with your everyday routine and get to know your new friends."

"Please, please stay here. You can take away my phone. Anything but this. Why do you have to go all crazy? Why can't you be normal?"

"Trust me, young lady, I don't want this anymore than you do. Do you think I really wanted to cancel your carpool ride so I could inconvenience myself by rearranging my entire schedule for you? If you think this is the field trip I've always dreamed about, you are sadly mistaken. The very thought of being asked a question by one of your teachers nearly sends me into a full-blown panic attack, but you have left me no other choice. Truly, you have made this a lose-lose situation for the two of us."

"Can you at least not go looking like that?" she pleads, her fists knocking against her forehead. "I'll do anything if you'll just please, please, please, please change. Please, Mom. I'm really, really, really, really begging you to not do this to me."

Pink foam rollers and as many hair ribbons and barrettes as I could find stored in a plastic basket on the girls' shelf in the hall closet are randomly rolled, tied, or clipped into my hair. My ankle-length terrycloth robe with the embroidered bunny "hopping" out of the front pocket is serving as a winter coat, and fuzzy high-top slippers function as winter boots. Underneath the robe is a pair of too short polka-dotted pajama bottoms, a black Lollapalooza 1993 vintage tour T-shirt, and green striped socks. It was perhaps taking things a bit too far, but I've also swiped a purple neon lipstick barely within the borders of my mouth and a dark coral blush along my cheekbones.

Yes, Bailey has every reason to be horrified. I am indeed a hot mess.

"You didn't consult me about your hair or piercings, so why should you get to decide what I wear to school today?"

"Mom, Mommy, Momsey, Mom, I'm begging you to not humiliate me at school in front of everyone. I'm sorry, very, very sorry for what I've done. I will do anything if you'll just stay home and trust me again. I promise. I swear I'll come home when I'm supposed to, an hour earlier if that makes you happy, and I will never ever skip school again." She is clasping her hands in the prayer position and bobbing up and down.

"No. I've heard you say sorry over and over, but your actions tell me you are not. Now get in the car, or I'll find another ribbon," I ruthlessly threaten, completely ignoring Bailey's pleas and distressed promises.

Ian's expression is priceless as he does a double take from his driveway.

"Good morning," I cheerfully fire off a greeting to the other side of the fence. "We're both off to learn something new at school today."

Ian raises his right eyebrow, but only says, "Have fun. Talk to ya later."

Bailey nervously gnaws the side of her thumbnail. A car honks, presumably saluting my crazy getup, and I give a little parade-like wave. As we approach the next stoplight, she hurriedly scrunches further into her seat and yanks her baseball cap down—the same baseball cap Kelsey loaned me when I needed to conceal a scorched face before meeting Emily for the first time. Kelsey quickly came to Bailey's defense when she learned what I had devised for her sister's punishment—big points for creativity, but major deductions for being excessively harsh.

We drive past the parking lot and into the drop-off zone.

"Next time, don't doubt for a second that I'll follow you inside. Go on, I'll pick you up after school. But don't take this to mean you've earned back my trust, understand?" Bailey looks at me with hopeful puzzlement, and I confirm her wish has been granted.

"Yes, Mommy," she squeals. "Thank you, thank you, thank you!"

"You'd better go before I change my mind."

She jumps out and blows me a kiss before running up the path to the school's front entrance. I put the pedal to the metal so I can get out of this ridiculously stupid outfit as quickly as possible. I'm getting together with my sisters and one of Christina's friends in an hour and don't want to show up dressed as a psychopathic clown on the rampage.

Chapter 41

Christina has selected a trendy vegetarian eatery for the four of us to meet at for breakfast. Flora & Fauna Café's décor matches their menu—pretty and quirky. I walk past the whimsical paintings of trees and butterflies hung in a staggered line on a moss-colored accent wall to where Amaya, who is first to arrive, is standing. After giving each other a quick hug and peck on the cheek, Amaya points out the succulent centerpieces placed in terracotta pots on each white shabby-chic table. The two of us are glad the rest of our party has not arrived so we can leisurely review the wood-framed chalkboards above the counter which list unusual menu items in a cursive font. The dishes include turmeric lattes; chia pudding with flowers, fruit, nuts, and mint leaves; white chocolate gingersnaps; and chai latte truffles. We are admiring the edible flower arrangement on a chocolate blueberry cake, almost too pretty to eat, when Christina and her friend walk through the front door.

At a first glance, Christina's friend is good looking, yet

the pretentious way her mouth moves when she speaks alters all of her facial features into an unsettling state of ugliness. You can't help but notice her petite stature, yet she dominates a wide berth of space around her in all directions. A horizontal patch of roots extending up and down the side part of her hair exposes she is not a blonde, but a brunette. Her outfit is impeccably tailored, but the cotton dress and jacket appear as if neither have ever met the flat part of an iron before. I suspect she is a Jessica or a Jane, but Christina introduces her new friend as Michal.

Michal is clearly flustered and explains, "My kids are driving me insane, so if I look like I don't know if I'm coming or going, that's the reason." She rattles off the names of her three children and their ages, her middle-management state government job title, the reason for taking four hours of personal leave, her husband's allergies, and how a to-go slice of the gluten free chocolate orange cake is a thank you gift to him for watching their kids last night while she went to a movie on her own.

Christina periodically nods in Michal's direction in response to certain key phrases or words but is really preoccupied with the phone call she has made to one of her clients while we stand in the long line.

Christina takes our collective order number that has been burnt into the backside of a wooden spoon and leads us to a table she has found near the corner window. As we figure out where to sit, Christina restates the reason for our gathering: "As you know, I love to connect people who need to meet each other for one reason or another. And when I met Michal and came to know her family's story, I knew my favorite sisters could help. It's taken a bit of time and coordination, but here we are. Michal just so happens to be looking for a seamstress." She says the last bit in a singsong voice, appearing quite pleased with herself seeing the four of us seated around the table.

"Is that sew?" I ask. I am immediately disappointed no one picks up my sad little pun.

"Absolutely," says Michal. "I need lots and lots of curtains. We're having a house built with the completion date scheduled for next spring. It can't come quick enough, this move. Melody is sharing a room with her brothers, which is okay for now, but won't be as they get older."

One of the very few things Michal doesn't mention during her endless blithering is that her two boys are black and adopted. She pulls out a pack of various pictures from the inside pocket of her purse to pass around as she shares with us the story of how her family has evolved over the years. While dating, she and her husband (Jim, the skinny Santa she points to in their family portrait from six years ago) did not want to contribute to the global overpopulation problem and were on the same page about wanting to only adopt or foster older children. According to plan, after being married for five years, they signed up and went through the training to become licensed foster parents. Denzel and Terrence (as in Washington and Howard, named for their bio mother's movie-star crushes) moved into their home when they were two and four years old. Jim affectionately assigned nicknames to the boys within an hour of their arrival. By the time Dez and T-Rex were six and eight, they were calling Michal and Jim, mom and dad.

Before reaching the legal age to drink, the brothers' mother, Diamond, had decided crack cocaine would solve all her problems, and that it was worth renting her body out to pay for the drug if it took away her innumerable fears and crushing depression. When Diamond died from an overdose in a motel room, it was a tragic turn of events that made the adoption process relatively easy. Michal knew of so many other adoptions that were held up by bio parents who resisted giving up the rights to their children out of guilt or other selfish reasons, so she felt very lucky.

Michal's laugh is interlaced with a lighthearted merriment as she tells us she and her husband were both forty-two when a home pregnancy test accurately predicated she would give birth to a baby in nine months. Michal finds more pictures in the bottom of her purse, an album dedicated to her pregnancy and the first girl in the family. We coo at the picture of Melody, now two years old, who has curly blonde hair like her father and a subtle upward slope of the tip of her nose like her mother.

"She is my angel child," the proud mama sighs happily.

"Michal is having troubles with her boys right now," Christina says so Michal doesn't have to. "They're getting into fist fights with each other and kids at their school, refusing to do their homework, swearing, stealing . . . You name it, they're doing it."

"I'm afraid they might be genetically programmed to be addicts or criminals," Michal says in all seriousness. "They are getting worse and worse every day. We've tried grounding them, taking away their privileges and all their favorite things, threatening to call the police or send them off to a military school—but nothing works. The other day Dez was suspended for punching a pencil sharpener off the wall and threatening to throw it at his teacher."

"Have you met with the school counselor?" Amaya asks.

"Yes, and the boys have seen a counselor for as long as they've been with us."

"Well, I can get you in contact with someone at the Juvenile Center, and they might be able to point you in the right direction."

"Amaya is the office manager at the Crossroads Alternative Academy out on the south side of town—you know that special school for students with behavior and mental health problems—so she knows everything about mental health services for children in our city. And Grace here, she's been having her own troubles with her oldest, which you might be able to relate to, but I also thought she might be able to talk to your boys about what it's like to be adopted since she is as well."

I bristle with annoyance when I hear what Christina has automatically assigned as my second task, but immediately feel guilty about being self-centered and manage to give a couple of affirmative nods.

"That would be so great," Michal exclaims. She breaks a generous slice of banana bread in half but quickly sets it back down on the flowers and herbs arranged prettily on her copper and blue plate. She swallows hard and tearfully confides, "They believe everyone has lied to them about what happened to Diamond. According to them, she's not dead but is out there searching for them. And we're all trying to keep her from finding them. It kills me that they think she's alive and well, and even more so that they think for a second I'd deceive them like that."

"Oh, how sad! Poor little darlings!" Amaya reacts to the thought of any child searching for comfort even in the thick of blatant lies.

"I know. It's so heartbreaking," Michal says. "And I am sympathetic, but it all goes out the window when they act out. They lash out in such unbelievably hurtful ways. We were shopping at Hy-Vee the other day, and I wouldn't let them put Froot Loops in the cart, and all hell broke out. They screamed for all to hear that I was a nigga' hatin' white cracker who was holding them hostage in the 'burbs. I could've died right there it was so embarrassing. Maybe I fooled myself into thinking race didn't matter? I was probably naïve thinking all you need is love to be a family. Maybe they should've been adopted by black parents. I knew it was complicated having a mixed-race family, but it is worse than I ever thought it would be. They keep telling me their real mother would know how to make them behave."

Chapter 42

Michal retells a gloomy account of one of the other parents in their adoption and foster care class—of what they were forced to do after adopting a twelve-year-old girl named Katya. This couple, both in their late thirties, had always wanted a girl and already had teenage twin boys. A surprise baby, another son, was born just before their daughter's adoption was official.

The two found this pre-teen female from perusing pages and pages of individual profiles of children available for adoption. Her medical history was included. Prenatal indicators foretold problems, and then a number of presenting physical symptoms when she was born confirmed the initial fetal alcohol syndrome diagnosis. Three years of abandonment added an attachment disorder to the already long list of afflictions plaguing her young mind and body. They thought they could save her, but living with the consequences of her biological mother's choices proved to be too much.

Katya was restrained by a mental and emotional

straitjacket, which she tried to escape using physical acts of violence. She punched and kicked holes into the walls. She smashed fragile household items. Her endless screaming fits were set off by the slightest offense—running out of orange juice, wearing blue instead of red, a sunny instead of a rainy day—and nothing her heartbroken family said or did could make her behave.

This tortured young lady, acting out of her own agony, got satisfaction by causing others pain. When the couple caught an indifferent Katya watching Han Solo, the blue betta fish, flop on the floor to see how long he could live without water, they were disturbed, but decided to treat it as a one-time offense. It was the girl setting fire to a pile of dried protea flowers, ironically a symbol of change and hope, in the middle of the baby's empty crib that caused the adults to move swiftly to prevent things from escalating into an irreversible tragedy. Katya was removed from the home and delivered to the care of the county.

"I love my boys," Michal preempts her next statement, "but I can't help thinking on some of the tougher days that what those people did is a viable option. I'm sure you understand more than any of us really, the difference between being adopted and having kids of your own. It's an entirely different ballgame when it comes to parenting your *real* child, if you know what I mean. You just naturally love them more. I don't why that it is—maybe biology?"

She is addressing that last sentence to me, but it's Amaya who gasps.

Michal immediately responds, "I know it sounds terrible, but I'm just being brutally honest. There's this mama-bear instinct that automatically kicks in to protect the child of your womb."

"I'm sorry, but I do think that is absolutely terrible," Amaya says firmly. "If something, God forbid, would happen to Grace, and I took in her girls, I would feel the same about them as I do about my children. Or Jacob, our brother's son—the same deal. I'd throw myself in front of a truck for any one of them. Children of your heart or of your womb, it doesn't matter as long as you love them with all your heart. That's how I think about it anyway."

"It sounds like you are maxed out with stress," I reply, taking on Amaya's role of being the peacemaker, of making excuses for people's weaknesses and errors.

"Yes, thank you, I am," Michal says appreciatively. "But, Grace, you do understand what I'm trying to say, right? Let me think of another way to put it for the others. Let's say you dated someone with a kid, who had a kid from a previous marriage, right," she hastily stumbles over her words. "Okay, so what I'm trying to say is if you had a stepchild, would you feel exactly the same about that kid as you do your own? I'm thinking not. You're not mean to the poor stepkid, of course. It's just a different kind of parenting. It's the very same kind of thing, wouldn't you agree?"

The Flora & Fauna Café advertises that matcha green tea induces calmness in the mind and body. It must be working. My breathing is evenly spaced and quiet. I'm aware of what is being said and successfully suppressing the urge to slap the woman across the face for being honest about her feelings toward her children.

"Grace isn't dating yet. She has a husband, waste of space that he is," Christina participates in her own special way in the conversation. "I'm guessing she won't be single and ready to mingle until she's done with him, which means a stepbrat won't be part of her life until then as well. That could be years and years from now the way they're handling the separation. But hey, it could be sooner if she's not having sex at the moment."

"Christina!" I screech, counteracting any positive impact the specialty tea has made.

"Hey, I'm just concerned about your sexual health. It's been almost a year since your separation from that waste-of-space cheater, so I hope you're either having passionate breakup sex, steamy affair sex, or you've got a good quality vibrator and plenty of batteries in your dresser drawer."

"Oh my God, shut up!" I squawk. Embarrassed, my skin reacts with red blotches that flare up across my neck and face.

"You've gotta try this smashed pumpkin on sourdough bread," Amaya comes to my rescue with her overenthusiastic review of the unusual dish she ordered. "I don't even like eggs, but this dish is scrumptiously sublime. I'll pass my plate around so you can all take a taste. Absolutely divine!"

"That reminds me," Christina practically shouts across the table. "I thought you could do that prayer thing you do. Michal needs whatever help she can get, however it comes and from whomever is willing to give it."

Caught off guard, Amaya laughs and then composes herself. "Of course I can do that prayer thing I do," she says. "I can and will include each of you in my daily thoughts and prayers."

I hope God forgives me. When we leave the café, I do not give Michal my contact information. I have no desire to help her out. In fact, I'm perfectly fine with never seeing her again. Ever.

Chapter 43

In therapy session, Beth listens to a twenty-minute rant about Christina's breakfast setup.

"Do you think your dislike of Michal is because of what she said about her feelings toward her adopted sons versus her biological daughter?" Beth asks before I can move on to other, more pressing subjects.

"No, it's because she's generally mean and nasty," I lie. And then I relent, "If Michal hadn't grated so much on my nerves, I would've let her in on a little secret about adopted children: we are like any other child who will use whatever they have at their disposal to get their own way, to push boundaries and buttons, to test the limits of patience and love. Her children are no different. It's just that T-Rex and Dez have a deceased drug addict for a birth mother, jealousy of a new baby sister (which is, by the way, normal for any sibling set), and their adopted parents' guilty feelings to use against anyone who opposes their will. They have learned how to leverage their adoption to justify their bad behavior and decisions."

I paused in thought for a minute and then said, "I've got to hand it to Mom. She shut down the adoption card being used against her in one single sitting when I was in the fifth grade. We were arguing in the kitchen. She was chopping parsley to sprinkle on top of a lasagna dish for a potluck luncheon to feed the cast and crew of a modern adaptation of Euripides' *Medea*. For weeks, she had been immersed in the story of a mother who murders her two children to get revenge on her husband, who abandoned her to marry another woman. Its intensity depleted any surplus of sympathy she had for me whining about being grounded.

"You see," I said, "I had been invited to a last-minute Saturday night slumber party (or slumber-less as my dad called them) by one of the most popular girls in my class. The imagined ramifications of rejecting her unexpected invitation were too much for me to handle, and I flipped out."

Realizing that the story needed more background, I explained, "The original grounding was punishment for ripping pages out of overdue books I had borrowed from the public library. I was furious because Dad refused to drop everything to drive me to the library because, as he put it, 'The lack of planning on my part did not constitute an emergency on his part,' and he had no intention of changing his plans to watch a televised baseball game because I hadn't paid attention to when my books were due.

"At first, I pretended to accept his lesson graciously and even thanked him for giving me a new way to think about responsibility. However, when he didn't budge from his chair to fetch the keys for his car, fake gratitude was replaced with my true feelings about the matter. The world revolved around me and my needs, and he should do what I demanded right then. He ignored my shouting, but immediately reacted when I started destroying the borrowed books. He grounded me on the spot, and I got my way, but not in the way I wanted. He skipped his Chicago Cubs baseball game so I could apologize and explain to the librarian why Katherine Paterson's *Jacob Have I Loved* and three other books were damaged beyond repair. He made me hand over most of my saved-up allowance to replace each of them.

"When we got back from the library, Dad ratted me out to Mom," I continued. "You would've thought I murdered a puppy the way she reacted. Mom and Dad sparred about whether a weekend isolated from the outside world was enough to get me to understand how egregious my crime was. Mom was lobbying for a two-week grounding. Dad wouldn't budge from his position that the battle was between the two of us, and therefore the punishment was up to him alone. Mom conceded, but I could tell she was mad. That was why I assumed it was out of spite that she wouldn't let me accept an invitation from *the* Becky Linder to be included in her inner circle of friends. I viewed this as a one-time chance to establish my rank among my peers for years to come. But she just wouldn't listen."

Beth's office seemed to fade as my reverie of events in that kitchen so far ago played out in exact detail:

"I hate you!" I screeched at the top of my lungs.

"Uh huh, I can understand why you might feel that way," Mom said coolly. "Can you please get the lettuce and tomatoes out of the fridge for me?" She continued looking placidly for the big wooden bowl.

"I mean it! I hate you!"

"Hate is a bottomless cup; I will pour and pour," she infuriatingly acknowledged my amplified animosity with a quote from Medea while slicing carrots into circular wedges with a sharp paring knife.

"Could I go tonight and be grounded next weekend?"

"Nope."

"What if I go for a couple of hours, but don't spend the night?"

"Again, you will not be leaving the house this weekend."

I changed tactics: "Please, please can I go? If I'm not there, it will mean I won't have any friends. Everyone will think I'm a big baby if you won't let me go."

"They can't really be your friends if that's the case. I'd find better ones if I were you," was her heartless solution.

"Do you really want your daughter to have no one to sit with at lunch or hang out with ever again? Is that what you want? Because that is exactly what is going to happen if I'm not there tonight."

"Maybe that will give you a chance to read more library books or find a new hobby to occupy your time," she suggested.

"Mom!"

"I'm sorry. You are grounded. End of story. This is the way it is, Grace. You can either make the best of it or make yourself miserable trying to change something that isn't going to change."

"You are being really, really, really mean. You're too old to understand what it takes to make new friends. If you don't let me do this, I will hate you forever. I will never ever forgive you."

"Stronger than lover's love is lover's hate. Incurable, in each, the wounds they make," she quoted, again from the play, which only intensified my raging frustration. "A lover or child," she added, sounding amused.

"I hate you so much I can't even tell you how much it is because that's how much I hate you," I shrieked.

"I'm sorry you feel that way, but the answer is still no," she said firmly. I could tell she was getting annoyed because the pace of the carrot chopping increased exponentially in a matter of seconds.

"You only want me to suffer because you always have to get your own way. You're just mad Dad told you off, and now you're taking it out on me. That's so messed up."

"That's certainly one way to think about it," she said pretending to acknowledge credibility in my assessment of the situation.

"You know what? If you think about it, I don't have to listen to you. You're not my real mother. My real mother, the one who really loved me, would let me go because she would want me to have friends. A real mother would want what's best for me. You don't." I started to hyper-ventilate. "I wish I had never been adopted. I want my real mother!"

"Careful young lady," she warned.

"No, I mean it," I interrupted. "I hate you so much! I really, really, really, really do! I wish you would drop dead and get out of my life!" I stomped my foot and opened and slammed the fridge door shut several times to make my point.

"Grace," she said wearily, worn down by my relent-less hostility, "you have no idea how much it hurts to hear these vile words come from the daughter I love so dearly. How is missing a little gathering deserving of such cruelty? But the fact that you are saying dreadful things causes me to question your real motive. Are you testing my love with your hate? Because if this is the case, you should know there is nothing you could ever do to make me stop loving you.

"I love you Grace Miju Solberg, daughter of Erik and

Evelyn, big sister to Amaya, Christina, and Mathew. You can destroy all the library books in the world, and I will still love you. You can tell me every day how much you hate me, and I will still love you. You can deny I am your real mother for all the days we are on this earth together, and I will still love you. You despise my existence? You wish me dead? It is incredibly hurtful, but I want you to know if you were to take this very knife and plunge it into my heart, I would never ever stop loving you."

She dramatically waved the knife in the air and drove it into the cutting board. *"And if the wound was fatal, and I were to collapse to the floor in a puddle of my own blood, I would make sure the very last words you ever heard from me were 'I love you, Grace. Your mama loves you always.'"*

There was nothing I could possibly say that could match the emotional punch of unconditional love. Severely reprimanded in the most brilliant way by Evelyn Jacqueline Solberg, I threw myself into my real mother's arms and gladly and gratefully accepted her embrace.

She gently rested her chin on my head and whispered, *"You will always be my little girl, no matter what."* The scent of cilantro and cucumber permeated the air, and I breathed it in as tears streamed down my cheeks.

"And besides, I know in my heart your real mother and I would wholeheartedly agree that you one hundred percent deserve to be grounded," she added as she gave my bottom a swat.

I took a moment to refocus on Beth and then said, "In that moment, all was forgiven between my mother and me. Unfortunately, Dad heard that I had wished his beloved wife dead. He grounded me for a week.

"There were two significant results of this extended grounding session—library books were returned by their due date, and I never grabbed the 'real mother' card from my bag of tricks ever again."

I summed up the session by saying, "If I had liked Michal in the least bit, I would have shared what I think is the secret to being a good parent—consistency in enforcing expectations and limitless love. I won't be the one to tell her this, but for her kids' sake, I hope Christina shares with her the legendary tale of how our mom disarmed the birth-mother weapon once and for all with a sharp paring knife."

Chapter 44

Bailey and Birch have decided to form an anarchy club with like-minded peers at their school. I find this comical. But I am not amused when I discover it means missing our family gathering to decorate Grandpa's house for Christmas.

Mom laughs when I tell her that Bailey won't be joining us to help with Operation *National Lampoon's Christmas Vacation*.

"Listen, you were quite the rebel brat at that age too," she gleefully reminds me. "I always tell my friends that Grace didn't give me stretch marks at her birth, but she certainly stretched my patience when she reached the teenage years."

"But it was different with me." I remind her that it was a gradual rebellion, a demand for more privileges and rights. "Bailey is an overnight nightmare," I complain, baffled by the transformation from sweet to sour for no apparent reason. "Is it a reaction to Marc and me separating? Emily? Is it my fault?"

"Welcome to the mystery stage of motherhood," Mom says, giving me a sympathy hug. "The adolescent years hold no answers, only questions. Next comes the guilt stage of motherhood. Wait till your grown children assign blame to you for everything that goes wrong in their life. It's a real job."

I prepare to defend myself, but then Mom gives me a playful wink and offers advice. "Just let her do her thing. She may be pulling away from the version of Bailey you've grown accustomed to, but she will always love you—that never changes. Deep down, all of us moms know we're loved even when we're told we aren't. Don't take her growing up so personally."

"Thanks, Mom."

"You bet. Glad I can help. Now let's get to work." She snaps her fingers and points at the box labelled "Dickens' Xmas Village" needing unpacked and set up on the mantle.

Phase two of the decorating party commences once our late afternoon lunch break is over. Grandpa, Christina, and I decorate three fake indoor and two large outdoor fir trees. Amaya and Mom sign and address Christmas cards for the nurses, staff, and a few of the residents at Grandma's care facility. Mathew hangs a garland on the banister and wreaths on the back and front doors. And with that, we are finished.

I am exhausted and emotionally unprepared to deal with Marc's car parked in my driveway. Kelsey alters my bad mood with a snide little snort followed up with, "Wow, those founding idiots sure took a long time writing up rules for their stupid club." I am still not in the mood to see Marc but can at least politely thank him for bringing our daughter home thanks to the snarky reminder of why he is here at this very late hour.

"Kelsey, we are going to need a private moment with your mom," Emily orders as we walk in. "Can you go to your bedroom?"

"She needs to get ready for bed anyway," is my defensive response to the ambush that is Marc and Emily hovering in my living room. "Where's Bailey?"

"She's here," Marc says in an unfamiliar tone combining compassion, concern, and fear into one terrifying sound to which I react with panic.

"Is she okay?"

"Yes, yes," Marc assures me and tells me to sit down.

"I don't want to sit down. I want to know what is going on." Each word scales up the vocal range concluding with a high-pitched, out-of-tune, unrecognizable note.

"Mom, you okay?" Kelsey peeks her head around the corner. She has her pajamas on and toothbrush in hand.

"Go to bed!" Marc shouts.

"Stop it! Don't you dare yell at her!" I catapult a growling command his way.

Kelsey's eyes widen, and she retreats to the bathroom. I can hear the faucet running.

"Maybe we should find a twenty-four-hour diner," Emily suggests. "We can talk openly then."

"I'm too tired to go anywhere. At this point what I'm imagining is way worse than it probably is, so for the love of God, stop the torture routine and just spit it out."

Emily and Marc sit in tandem on my sofa. I remain standing and give my head a swivel, a non-verbal cue that I am thoroughly annoyed and ready to receive the news that is so important that it can't wait until tomorrow.

"We caught Birch and Bailey smoking weed," Emily blurts out their wrongdoing.

"Is that all?" I release a short series of awkward laughs that seem inappropriate for the occasion, but nonetheless are unstoppable. "My goodness gracious, I thought you were going to tell me you were suing for full custody of the girls or something just as dreadful." I breathe out a deep sigh of relief. "I mean that's bad, but they are kids. So what, we ground them? Or wait, is this the first time or have there been other times? Have you been keeping their pot smoking a secret from me? Is that why you the two of you look so panicked?"

"We also caught them kissing," Emily whispers.

"Okay, a little weird, but . . ."

"Grace, there is no easy way to tell you this." Marc puts his face in his hands. "They can't ever kiss each other or anything else because they are siblings. I am Birch's father."

"What?" Although I don't want to hear the answer to

the question, I ask anyway. "What are you telling me? What . . . what does this mean?"

He clears his throat and continues with a string of facts I never suspected could ever be true:

He never lost contact with Emily.

He met her in Las Vegas for a weekend rendezvous fifteen years ago.

Emily got pregnant but didn't tell Marc after hearing about my pregnancy.

Emily cut off contact with Marc, leaving him to tend to our family.

When Birch started asking questions, Emily contacted Marc.

Marc demanded a paternity test.

They decided to keep it a secret while the two of them figured out what to do next.

As they figured it out, that is when they fell in love again.

Emily is Marc's true love. I am the loser in this love triangle.

"How long did you think that you could keep this from me?" I look at Marc for a reasonable explanation. "Why didn't you tell me? All this time you both knew and didn't say anything. Why? How could you do that to me?"

"Emily—I mean, we—didn't want to hurt you," is Marc's weak answer.

"So is this why you wanted to be my friend? So you could cushion the fall?" I shriek.

"Of course not," Emily insists. "I so wish our friendship was formed under different circumstances and, believe me, I wanted to tell you the truth, but couldn't . . ."

"Wouldn't, you mean," I counter with fury and then gasp, a chill running down the edges of my spine. "Did you make up the whole thing about Bailey having cancer as some sick, twisted way to get close to me?"

"Oh my God, no!"

"I don't believe you!" I hurl a marble paperweight through the single-pane side window. Surprised and pleased I possess the strength to create damage at that level, I throw the bigger of the two decorative paper-weights through the other window.

A frightened Kelsey defies her father's instructions. She runs into the living room, and Bailey follows suit. They stand together staring at the adults in the room.

"Maybe we should go," Emily says softly.

"Yes, good idea and don't bother coming back. You are not welcome in my home ever again."

I open the door to see them out, and a cop car pulls into my driveway.

"How did that get reported so fast?" Marc asks. "Your neighbor must be a real snoop."

My first reaction is to defend Ian, and my second is to remember that his panda is stuffed under my kitchen sink. Then I wonder if this is the true meaning of the police visit. A full squad car seems like an overreaction to a single stolen plastic statue, but I probably broke the lights on the lawn, so who knows?

Two officers get out of the car, both with grim expressions on their faces. Marc, Emily, and I stand in the open doorway and watch them come up the walk.

"Grace Hunter?"

I raise my hand. "That's me."

"Could we come in?" the second officer asks in a voice full of sympathy. If it weren't for the fact that both Bailey and Kelsey are here, I would be panicking for their safety.

I step back from the door, as do Marc and Emily.

The officers come in and follow me into the living room.

"Would you like to have a seat, Ma'am?" There is a definite "you'd better be sitting down for this" tone to the words. I sit. Grandpa? Mom? Amaya? Mathew? Christina? But if it were any of them, surely one of the others would have told me, not these officers. All of them? In one big car crash? I can't think of why they would all be in the same car, but it makes sense.

Emily makes a sound that I interpret to mean they're going to quietly slip out.

One of the officers looks at me. "This might be better if you have family or friends with you right now."

My whole family is dead for sure. And technically speaking, Marc is legally still my family, and Emily was my friend until about ten minutes ago.

Chapter 45

Emily looks at me uncertainly, though Marc is buttoning his coat and reaching for the door. Emily thins her lips into a hard, determined line and strides to me. She sits on the couch next to me and takes both my hands in hers. Her eyes are already wet. Which makes mine start to tear up as well. We've both come to the same conclusion—she and Marc and the girls are my only family now. My soon-to-be ex-husband and his mistress and my own children. With a side serving of love child. Maybe I should call Mary Anne or Ian.

Marc sighs and leans uncomfortably next to the door.

"I'm as ready as I'll ever be," I say to the officers. "Just get it over with."

"Mary Anne MacDonald died last night."

"Oh Lord!" Emily jerks in surprise.

I blink.

"It appears to have been suicide," the second officer states. "The note she left was addressed to you." The officer hands over a copy of a notecard in Mary Anne's tidy handwriting.

"But . . . she was about to get married," I mumble. "I made the wedding dress. She was so excited. Why would she do that?"

"Did she and Herbie fight?" Emily asks.

The officers exchange a glance. "Herbie?"

"Herbie Heith," I provide. "Her fiancé. He'll be devastated!"

An officer produces a notepad. "Do you have his address or phone number?"

"What?" I say. "They lived together, I think. I mean, she got groceries for him. Maybe he's still on his business trip?"

Emily shakes my arm and points to the letter in my hands. I look down at it.

"Read it," Emily says, shaking her head.

Mary Anne's final written words include a polite request to remove all of her belongings from the house before her next rent payment is due. There are three typed pages of instructions of what needs to be done to close out her business on earth. No explanation for her decision, only an apology for the inconvenience she has caused. The gravity of what is missing from her letter numbs my heart.

"Surely this isn't all," I say. "Didn't she leave anything for Herbie?"

The officers look at each other again. "This was the only thing we found."

I nod. Perhaps Herbie's note is somewhere in the house.

"There will be a short investigation to rule out foul play," an officer says. "We'll inform you when you can go to the house."

I nod. Herbie's going to have to plan a funeral, I think, instead of a wedding. No wonder she asked me to clean out the house. That's too much to ask of one man.

The officers take their leave with all possible politeness and sympathy. The minute they are out of my drive, Ian is at the door.

"I heard the window break," he says, looking at me, Marc, and Emily, "and I couldn't help but hear your . . . comments." He directs the last part at me.

"We were about to leave," Marc says. Emily puts on her coat and then grips Ian's hands as she had mine. She fills him in on Mary Anne's demise and then says something to him too quietly for me to hear. He pats her shoulder, and she goes, taking Marc with her.

I remember that Emily is not my friend, but my ex's mistress. And that my daughter had recently kissed her half-brother that none of us (except, of course, Marc and Emily) knew about. I hold Ian hostage with my weeping and whining related to the evening's updates until the early morning hours.

I am pacing the floor and reading aloud the suicide

note for what must be the hundredth time when Ian gets up and gently pries the letter from my grip.

"Grace, it isn't fair," he says. "It's not fair of her to put all this on you." I sniff. It is true. She is also dead.

"Let me help," Ian coaxes. "When the police say you can go to the house, take me with you. It's more than one person can do."

I nod. "Okay." I should refuse. Mary Anne is an acquaintance to him, at best. If anyone should help me, it should be Emily. But that is a prospect I am not yet ready to face.

Ian leaves, taking the letter with him to prevent me from continuing my obsession. I watch out the window above the sink as lights come on in his house. I regard the panda-less pedestal, neither satisfied nor guilty.

I open the cabinet and bend down. On its side behind the bottles of cleaner, it continues to smile beatifically. I reach a hand in and pat it on the head. I shut the cabinet door and make my weary way to bed.

* * *

When my cell rings at five in the morning I know, deep in my soul, that it can only be more bad news.

" 'Lo?" I croak into the phone.

"Viv? You sound like you swallowed a frog that smokes a pack a day."

"Cindy?" I sit up in bed. My college roommate? "It's six in the morning. Why are you calling?"

"It's seven here in Washington D.C.," Cindy says, "I thought it would be like, nine where you are."

I rub my forehead. "It's the other way, Cindy. Iowa is earlier, not later."

"Whoops. Well, since I've got you here anyway, I am gonna be in Indianola Saturday for a YWCA fundraiser that my mom is chairing. I have to be back in D.C. for a work meeting Monday. Anyway, I could grab some time with you Sunday.

My eyes get teary. If I ever needed a visit from Cindy, it is now. "Ya," I say. "For sure."

I suggest we eat at Flora & Fauna, hoping to write some good memories into the place. I loved their matcha, and I don't want to think about Michal every time I drop in.

As I am already awake, I give her the lowdown on Marc, Emily, Birch, Bailey, Mary Anne, and the panda. "I thought that Bailey was doing fine. But I don't know. Maybe she just needs someone other than me as an adult to look up to, you know?"

"Well," Cindy says, "I don't wanna toot my own horn, but I am pretty cool."

I snort.

"Why don't you bring her along?"

I don't think Bailey wants to hang out with her mom and her mom's old roommate. On the other hand, I still haven't told her she's related to Birch, and until Marc and Emily have told her, I want my eyes on her at every moment. This was the one thing Marc, Emily, and I agreed on. Marc and Emily have to tell the girls and Birch. Until then, Emily or Marc has to keep an eye on Birch at all times, and I have to keep an eye on Bailey. God knows none of us need accidental incest added to this family drama.

"Sure," I say. "We can give it a try."

The days following the visit from the officers sprint by in a blur of emotions and confusion. Marc repeatedly calls and leaves various versions of apologetic voicemail messages, even offering to pay for the windows I broke. Emily has two dozen yellow roses delivered to the house.

"She thinks flowers are going to fix what they did," I grumble to no one in particular while pouring water into the vase. "They surely don't think I can be bribed to forgive and forget."

Kelsey raises her right eyebrow. She must have picked up that habit from Mom, who does the exact same thing. I pretend to not see her reaction. Marc and Emily have decided on next weekend to inform the girls that they have a brother, and that one of them has kissed that brother—like Luke and Leia. But without lightsabers or wars, it seems grosser somehow.

Chapter 46

Cindy and I have maintained a snail and email friendship over the years. She was not surprised when I shared that Marc had moved out to be with another woman. She responded to my email in the blunt, uncensored way I had become accustomed to since our first encounter:

> *Well, my darling, what do you expect from a relationship that started with deceit? I take full responsibility for Vivienne Tran dating Marc Hunter, but not for Grace Solberg marrying the fool! Sending big hugs and wishes for better days ahead from your very own Cindy Crawford.*

Cindy spots us seated at the table and waves as she walks past the café window. We squeal and run towards each other as if we are long-lost friends, not dedicated daily pen pals. Bailey blushes from the horrifying decibel level emitted by her mother, but embarrassment is quickly replaced with reverential admiration after Cindy removes her coat. She is wearing a pair of faded jeans held up by a wide brown leather belt, a metallic blue fitted jacket and matching low-cut double-breasted vest, no shirt, but covering most of her bare chest is a man's tie with a skinny silver tie bar clipped slightly askew at the center. A folded white handkerchief is neatly tucked into the jacket pocket. Adorning her left wrist is an assortment of bead bracelets, and the other wrist is fitted with a bamboo watch. Bailey is clearly in awe of what is standing before her, and I can't help feeling a tad smug at having my daughter know that I am the good friend of someone so hip and cool.

Cindy gives Bailey one of her bracelets. I protest, but Cindy insists the black onyx bracelet never felt like it truly belonged to her. She says she bought it from a street vendor who must have known it would be a gift for a kindred spirit she would meet some day in the future. Bailey's grin radiates happiness and makes me realize that I needn't have worried she was no longer capable of expressing joy. I impulsively hug Cindy as a result.

Bailey has never once asked me about my brief college career, but presently she is fixated on asking questions—not to get to know me, but to make connections with Cindy. Cindy, however, kindly redirects each of her answers to include interesting tidbits of information about me.

"That's what she says about Aunt Christina." Bailey shoots a scolding scowl in my direction after Cindy tells her that back in the day, I hated being wrong about anything.

Cindy shared the genesis of my involvement with the jazz club: "Your mom joined the jazz club in spite of not being able to tolerate listening to more than two minutes of any Miles Davis song and being annoyed by the majority of the club members. She stuck with it for months because she didn't want to confess to the new guy she was chasing that she hated everything about his single greatest passion in life. That guy—I can't remember his name, something pretentious like Cole or Colby—convinced her to help him plan the club's social events, so she couldn't and wouldn't quit that stupid club until he broke up with her!"

"I liked some of the songs," I say without conviction.

"And do you know the most shocking thing about the whole deal?"

Bailey shakes her head, eagerly anticipating Cindy's take on the situation.

"Post breakup, your mom admitted she quit liking him after their second date!"

"No, uh uh," Bailey eggs Cindy on.

"Oh yes, Ma'am. She didn't want to admit that I had been right when I told her from the beginning that he was all wrong for her. She took it as a personal challenge to prove me wrong."

"But he broke up with her?" Bailey asks.

"The jerk ultimately lost interest when Grace reached

a point when she could no longer hide that she was being tortured by the distorted sounds of jazz," Cindy says, feigning sympathy. "Come to think about it, it's probably similar to how she felt about being married to Marc, a living embodiment of dissonant chords."

"Cindy! Not appropriate!" I scold her for making a disparaging observation about Bailey's father.

Bailey doesn't seem phased or offended by anything at the moment and asks Cindy, "Did you have a lot of boyfriends?"

"Not as many as your mom," Cindy snorts. "However determined she was to end up with your father, she didn't let it stop her from having fun playing the field, although she had that odd Catholic hang-up about saving herself for marriage. She had a very busy social calendar, out on a date with a different man-child almost every week. I told her she was the biggest prude-slut on campus."

"Cindy!"

"Well, it's true," she dismisses my yelp with a wave of the hand. "Do you remember that guy who accidentally dialed our number and you talked to him on the phone for hours and hours?"

"No. Well, yes." I don't want her to continue with the rest of the story and desperately attempt to change the subject by calling attention to her own scandalous behavior by tattling with, "And I seem to remember the hot guy and everyone else you flashed your boobs to at the Fieldhouse . . ."

Cindy refuses to accept my lead-in and continues on with how I got a date because of a botched attempt to order a pizza.

"That guy never asked what she looked like when he set up a time to meet your mom at the Ped Mall to grab a bite to eat. She got herself worked up into a frenzy about it and asked all of us what to do. We told her to just go! But she decided to wear a pair of sunglasses 'cause she thought that might give her some time before having to reveal she was an Asian chick." Cindy shakes her head and sums up the story: "She left at three in the afternoon and didn't get back till I think it was like midnight or maybe later. It must've been a good first date in the end."

The sunglasses incident still stings after all these years. I never told anyone he made up an excuse and ditched our date early. Humiliated, I hid out at the library till I felt enough time had passed to safely go back to the dorm without having to answer questions about the mystery caller.

"Wow, Mom, it sounds like you were pretty clueless." Bailey's critical tone adds insult to injury. "And I can't believe you never told us about pretending to be a foreign exchange student, and that's how you met Dad."

"Not my greatest moments," I mutter.

"You were a poser," Bailey piles on another insult. "For all we know, you're still faking us out."

Cindy considers. "Aren't we all posers?"

"No." Bailey rolls her eyes. "I've never lied to anyone about who I am."

Cindy puts a chin on her fist. "I don't think I knew who I was when I was your age. But I knew who I wanted people to think I was. Besides, it wasn't Grace's idea to play Vivienne. She just went along with our bad idea."

Bailey rolls her eyes again, but not quite as hard.

The last time I was at this café, I was crushed by Christina's friend's assessment of being an adoptive parent. This time, I am devastated by my child's perspective about how I behaved in the past. I think the next time I have a craving for matcha green tea and vegan dishes, I will only invite Amaya.

That night as I am cooking supper, the police call. They inform me that the house is now mine to deal with. They also ask if I would like any more details about what they have officially ruled suicide. I think on this. She's not in contact with her family, for good reason. All she has is Herbie and, apparently, me. One person is too few to mourn her death in all its morbid detail. I can't hang it all on Herbie.

"Yes," I say.

She was found in the front seat of her car, wearing the wedding dress I made. She'd closed all the doors to the garage and let the car run until she passed away from carbon monoxide poisoning. That was it. The whole thing.

"I don't know if it's allowed," I say, "but is there any way you could send me Herbie's contact info?"

The officer pauses for a moment longer than makes sense.

"Ma'am," he says, "we haven't found evidence that anyone named Herbie Heith was in contact with Mary Anne. Other than the wedding dress, we haven't found any evidence that she was engaged or dating anyone at all."

Chapter 47

I enter the keywords, "Herbert," "Heith," and "Iowa" into the Google search engine. A result comes up, but not for anyone living. One entry could have been inspirational for Mary Anne.

Herbie Heith was American magician who was born into a circus family of acrobats. In 1913, he relocated to Carroll, Iowa to open a small magic manufacturing company and magic shop. As "Mysterious Heith", he published *Magic Key* magazine from 1917 until 1918. The entry supplied question marks for both the birth and death dates. How appropriate.

Why is it that I never insisted on meeting the Snuffleupagus beau? How could I be so stupid? No one works and travels all the time. Guilt taps into the realization that I had a very limited knowledge of the person who was my client and supposedly my friend. I wonder if it is possible to piece together the reason or reasons why she wanted to end her life by sorting through her belongings.

The next day while the kids are at school, Ian and I

let ourselves into Mary Anne's 1920s bungalow. It's both contemporary and cozy inside. Her love of Bette Davis is displayed with autographed photographs, movie posters, and biographies found throughout the house.

The kitchen reflects the complicated relationship Mary Anne had with food and her body. Behind the pantry door, the shelves are filled with Weight Watchers products that are outnumbered by the packages of Twinkies, Oreo cookies, and an assortment of other junk food. Fridge magnets hold in place pictures of skinny swimsuit models, doctor appointment reminders, and inspirational quotes. One large clip magnet secures in place a *New England Journal of Medicine* article about healthy eating habits. When I turn to view the second page, the rest of the article is missing, replaced with printouts of different case studies about bulimia. With every altered version of her wedding dress, did I stitch her into an eating disorder?

The spare bedroom is a space filled by our relationship. In the bookshelf, there is a framed picture of the two of us and every card I sent thanking her for being my best client, wishing her happy birthday, sending sympathy when one of her favorite customers died, and a congratulatory card regarding her engagement which I, of course, didn't know was a fake at the time. The walk-in closet is filled with the wardrobe pieces I created under her direction. She has my patterns and drawings custom framed and hung on the walls.

Ian and I sit, our shoulders nearly touching, so we can

both read through a tattered scrapbook placed on top of a single pillow lying in the middle of the bed. It is a gloomy document of the countless foster families who never created permanency and stability for Mary Anne after her parents died in a car accident a day before her eleventh birthday. There was an accompanying journal where Mary Anne scribbled dates and cryptic but obvious notes of what had been done to her and by whom.

Ian thinks Mary Anne placed these items out in the open to explain what she didn't have the courage to tell me in person. This may be the case, however it doesn't alleviate the remorse that circulates in my heart for not asking more questions. I find a second suicide note stuck in the back of the journal that reads:

Dear Grace,

Thank you for being my one true friend. You are the only one who came close to understanding my loneliness and the constant rejection of who I am. But you are not alone, and you have not been rejected as I have, and this is why our stories are different.

We have both experienced the pain of loss, but "nothing can hurt us now. What we have can't be destroyed. That's our victory—our victory over the dark."

You have been a light in my darkness.

With gratitude and love,

Mary Anne

Numbness carries me through for the rest of the afternoon as Ian and I move furniture into the Habitat for Humanity ReStore's donation truck. The remaining household items are either boxed or tossed.

It is nearly midnight when Ian drives us home. We sit in the car in his driveway. I can't make my exit. Overcome with emotion, I am stuck sobbing in the passenger seat. Ian pulls me into an embrace that leads to a kiss. Startled, I push him away.

"What are you doing?"

"I have wanted to do that since the I watched you steal Jenny's plastic panda from my yard," Ian confesses.

"You wanted to . . . do that . . . after witnessing the theft of your dead wife's yard ornament?"

"Yep."

"That's so wrong. We can't do this."

"Why not?"

"It's not a good idea."

"Do you know why you don't think it's a good idea?" Ian asks. And even though I can feel his gaze upon me, I refuse to turn my eyes away from the dashboard.

"Because I don't like you in that way?"

"Because you are a closet racist."

"What? Are you crazy?" I gasp. "That isn't even possible."

"It is and you are. You're scared silly of being a stereotype. You don't want to be an outsider, a minority. So you pretend to be your lies."

"I have no idea what you're talking about," is the only thing I can think of saying that won't make me cry.

"Mary Anne did. She says it in her note to you."

I suck in my breath. "She did not."

"Sure, she did. Just in a nicer way, but no doubt about it, she calls you out as a liar. You think that your marriage to a cheater needs to be saved in order for you to be happy. Lie. You think that if your mom says the right things and behaves in a certain way, that means you're her real daughter. Lie. You think you are who you pretend to be. Lie. You think you're an outsider. Lie. It was Mary Anne who had no family who was truly alone. You are not."

"I think—" starts my defense which he callously interrupts.

"And what is truly sad is that you don't know what you've done. You reject—no, you hate—everything that makes you special. You pretend to hate math, and I know that isn't true." Ian makes his Grace v. South Korea closing argument. "You won't eat with chopsticks. You don't want to visit Japan, even if it's your daughter's dream trip. You make this big fuss about hating kimchi, but that day when our kids made Korean food at my house, I saw you stealing bites of kimchi when you thought no one was looking."

Ian's voice fades as he depletes his arsenal of accusations, which gives Celine Dion's upbeat "That's The Way It Is" playing on the radio an opportunity to invade our conversation.

"Well, I may like kimchi sometimes, but I absolutely honest-to-goodness hate this song and her," I affirm my position on the subject of Celine Dion.

My outburst stuns Ian into a cease-fire surrender, and he gives me a playful tap on the shoulder and laughs. "Listen Grace, I realize this isn't the time or place to explore the possibility of us. If not today, then someday. I think the reason why I moved next door is to meet you. I like what you show the world, but I love what you hide."

"I don't know. You . . . me . . . I don't know . . . well, I'm still married." Stammering, I try and collect my thoughts while smothering away the goosebumps on my arms.

"I'm not saying let's get married, Grace. I'm saying don't reject a man based solely on the way he looks. Especially a man who is absolutely crazy about you."

"Okay," I whisper in defeat.

Epilogue

Mary Anne's note is in my purse the day of her funeral. Only the first pews are filled. Most of the mourners in attendance are my guests. Ian leans over and whispers that he made a reservation at the restaurant for thirteen—a number that includes Marc and Emily. An emergency therapy session focusing on Birch's paternity has ushered in a minimal level of acceptance of their presence in my life. Civility is possible today.

As Emily sings Celine Dion's song, "Fly," I want to laugh and cry. To stop myself from doing either, I focus my attention on the crown of thorns depicted in the stained-glass window situated high above the soloist. My mind wanders to Mary Anne's note, carrying me to thoughts of loss. How life shifts based on absence and interpretation.

A pack of tissues unexpectedly lands in my lap. Bailey taps my shoulder and points to Mom so I can see her mouth the words "just in case" and blow a kiss my way. As I lift my arm to catch it, Bailey snatches my hand and firmly tells me not to embarrass her. None of her friends are at the funeral, so I'm not sure why she cares who witnesses our family codes of conduct, but I keep my hand down. I'm more embarrassed by Kelsey reading a Japanese comic book during a funeral service. Her sister's insensitivity doesn't bother her, but the capture of an air kiss does. I wonder what else Bailey will reject from how she was raised as she finds her own way in the world. My thoughts turn to what Ian said in the car that night, and I wonder if I have incorrectly categorized my own likes and dislikes to come up with a person I want to be rather than who I am.

All I know at this point is that I have been defined by an arbitrary mix of pre-selected biographical details and free will. I didn't ask to be born or to be given up by my biological mother. However, my parents chose me to be their adopted child. My father didn't choose to die. Mary Anne did. I can't force Marc to love me. Yet I chose to fight to remain married when it was obviously over. My struggle has been managing life's endless endings, interpreting them as personal rejection, and feeling as if I do not belong to anyone or anywhere.

But I do have a place in this world. I have been invited to participate, to show up, to weep, to rejoice, to grieve, to fight, to fail, to discover, to hate, to simply be. And when I look over at my children, there is no doubt I have been called to love.

And this is all that matters in the end.

About The Author

Anna Jinja was adopted from Seoul, Korea, and grew up in Iowa. Her heart is filled with love for people and their stories. She has dedicated her life to nonprofit organizations and causes as a volunteer or employee, which has led to a myriad of unexpected opportunities and adventures – including stepping into the role of a radio producer and host at KHOI 89.1 FM that has led to her hosting and producing, The Anna Jinja Show.

The Anna Jinja Show focuses on the stories, issues, and questions connected to adoption and foster care experiences. By sharing her adoption story and all that she is learning to help her navigate through personal and professional challenges, she hopes that this will lead us to believe, accept, and value the inherent worthiness of all people.

Thanks to Hope (a wise mutual friend), Anna met and fell in love with Pete while he was traveling in the Pacific Northwest during his car-top tent adventure. They were married at the Ames Public Library. Anna now lives with her husband, Pete, and their dog, Floyd, in the little blue house of happiness.

Please Write a Review

Dear Reader,
    At Midwestern Books we have worked hard to make this excellent book available for you. We truly hope you have enjoyed it. It is our mission to tell stories from a Midwestern perspective that honors its culture. Thank you for including us in your reading selections.

    Please, would you consider going to the Amazon website and write a review for this book. Reviews are crucial for helping others to know about this book and encouraging Amazon to promote it. We very much need help from readers like you to get the word out about our books and the enjoyable stories they share. Thank you for helping us.

    Midwestern Books

Other Titles From Midwestern Books

See Jane Run! Book 1 of the West River Mysteries. Amidst the scenic wonder of a quirky corner of western South Dakota, Jane Newell starts her career in a country school. She soon discovers that someone close to her is a killer, and she is determined to find out who it is.

See Jane Sing! Book 2 of the West River Mysteries. Just back from Thanksgiving break, Jane Newell stumbles over the body of a teenage boy while hunting for a Christmas tree. Jane ignores Sheriff Sternquist's warning not to investigate when she discovers a tangle of clues.

See Jane Dance! Book 3 of the West River Mysteries. What do Kindergartners and square dance lessons have to do with murder? Jane Newell is at it again, braving snowstorms and town gossip as she and the sheriff zero in on a killer dancing too close for comfort in this West River Mystery.

See Jane Dig! Book 4 of the West River Mysteries. Attempted murder during a field trip to a dinosaur excavation puts Jane's friend into a life-threatening coma. As

Jane and Sheriff Sternquist investigate the dig team, she must fight to save Beanie's life and her own before they are silenced forever.

Stay Out of that Room! Two sheltered teen aged girls spend a summer on lake Minnetonka with their wacka-doodle great aunt when a secret room lures them to break her rules, while hunky neighbor boys heighten the stakes.

Cosmic Background Radiation. Grieving his brother, Josh confronts rural life to save his family. Strange dreams take him back 2,700 years to a parallel life with his brother alive and a girl he just met as part of the household.

Your Alaskan Daughter 3rd Edition. Three months pregnant with her first child, Harriet Walker traveled to Alaska in 1953 to establish a homestead with her husband, Harold. She tells the story through the letters she sent to her family and friends, from the hair-raising trip over the Alcan to the exciting events surrounding the birth of Tommy, their first child. While camped in a small summer cottage, the intrepid couple finds a new home in tiny Hope, Alaska, where they brave the pinch of an Alaskan winter.